Transcendence

ALSO BY C. J. OMOLOLU

Dirty Little Secrets

Transcendence

C. J. OMOLOLU

Walker & Company
New York

First published in the United States of America in June 2012
by Walker Publishing Company, Inc., a division of Bloomsbury Publishing, Inc.
www.bloomsburyteens.com

For information about permission to reproduce selections from this book, write to
Permissions, Walker BFYR, 175 Fifth Avenue, New York, New York 10010

Library of Congress Cataloging-in-Publication Data
Omololu, Cynthia Jaynes.
Transcendence / by C.J. Omololu.
p.   cm.
Summary: After handsome Griffon Hall tells sixteen-year-old Cole Ryan that her strange visions are of past lives, he introduces her to the Akhet, a group of people with the same ability, one of whom seeks to love and protect her and another, vengeance.
ISBN 978-0-8027-2370-3 (hardcover)
[1. Reincarnation—Fiction.   2. Supernatural—Fiction.   3. Secret societies—Fiction.
4. Love—Fiction.   5. Revenge—Fiction.   6. Cello—Fiction.   7. Musicians—Fiction.]   I. Title.
PZ7.O54858Tr 2012   [Fic]—dc23   2011038046

Book design by Nicole Gastonguay
Typeset by Westchester Book Composition
Printed in the U.S.A. by Quad/Graphics, Fairfield, Pennsylvania
2 4 6 8 10 9 7 5 3 1

All papers used by Bloomsbury Publishing, Inc., are natural, recyclable products made from wood grown in well-managed forests. The manufacturing processes conform to the environmental regulations of the country of origin.

For Griffon
1994–2009
This time was much too short.

Transcendence

One

It's happening again.

The tingling at the back of my neck, the disconnect I feel from everything around me, the tiny beads of cold sweat on my forehead—as soon as I recognize the symptoms, I know I'm in trouble. I look down at my feet as I follow Kat from the Tower Hill tube station into the bright sunlight, trying to focus on my shoes as they keep time along the immaculate sidewalk. Except they don't feel like a part of me anymore. They seem far away, like they're someone else's size-six blue plaid Vans.

I pull the headphones from my ears, the soaring Massenet symphony becoming a distant squawk as my heart pounds and every hair stands on end. Shaking my head, I try to stop the inevitable, to pull myself back from wherever I'm going this time. I can struggle for control all I want, but I still feel myself slipping away.

I barely have time to catch my breath as the waves of images and emotions crash over me, engulfing and then obliterating everything else.

Crowds of people press in so close their warm, sour breath mingles with my own—individual faces frozen ugly with anger, hungry for blood. I cower and try to turn back, but my arms are held firm at the elbows and I am swept along, my beautiful new silk slippers barely grazing the dank, muddy ground. Even though I can no longer see the hill, I can smell the smoke from the fires and hear the pleas to God from the condemned, the metallic tang of blood infusing the very air around us. My eyes dart back and forth, trying desperately to find Connor in the crowd of prisoners as the panic mounts, but I am being dragged toward the water, away from the hill where I'd seen him last—

"Hey!" My sister snaps her fingers in front of my face, pulling me back into reality. "Cole!"

I blink hard trying to focus on her, tearing my thoughts away from what I've just seen and felt. The sharp smell of the smoke still seems to saturate the air, and I try hard to convince myself that I'm back. I'm not wearing a long velvet dress and delicate slippers, but my usual jeans and slightly scuffed shoes. Everything is normal. And I'm not losing my mind.

"What?" I say, trying to put just enough annoyance in my voice to cover my racing thoughts. I have to get a grip on these dreams or hallucinations or whatever they are. My stomach is heaving and I feel like throwing up, as if getting rid of whatever bad things are inside of me will stop the visions from coming.

"I'm starting to think that you find my company less than

stimulating," Kat says, her perfectly manicured thumbs flying over the keypad on her phone.

I pull out my water bottle and take a swig, trying not to call attention to the fact that my hands are shaking. Kat hasn't noticed anything wrong so far, but bursting into tears or throwing up into the nearest trash can is bound to get her attention. As hard as I try to come up with a logical reason for what's happening, I know deep down it's getting worse. The minute we landed in London, little things began to feel freakishly familiar—almost like coming home to a place I've never been before. Doing random tourist stuff in the city, we'll pass an old house, a shop window, or even just a small, cobblestoned street, and I'll have a déjà vu so strong that it makes me stop and stare, searching for a missing memory to go with the unexplained emotions. Now the brown walls of the Tower of London loom across the street, but no one else on the crowded sidewalk seems to feel the overwhelming sense of frenzy and desperation that hangs in the air around us. Probably because everyone else here is sane.

I take another drink, the warm, metallic-tasting water not helping all that much. "Sorry. Just distracted," I manage, the feelings of loss and longing finally falling away like sheets of water after a heavy rain. I shut the music off, the sounds of the symphony replaced by the hum of tires on the busy street. I reach for an excuse that sounds fake even to my desperate ears. "The concert and everything. It's not that far away."

"Can you lay off the child prodigy bit for once?" Kat snaps. "We're on vacation, remember?"

"Maybe *you're* on vacation," I say, knowing even as I say it that I'm going to piss her off, but my thoughts are too scattered to do more than repeat all of the things I've said so many times before. "But people are counting on me. Practice isn't optional."

Trying to slow my breathing and convince both of us that everything's fine, I open my dog-eared guidebook. Just seeing the maps and photos of famous landmarks has a calming effect as I try to shake off what's left of the weird feelings.

I glance around at the other people on the street and try as hard as I can to relax. I tell myself that nobody's staring at me. I'm just another slightly disoriented tourist with a guidebook and a backpack. I feel as invisible as I always do when I'm not up on stage with a cello in my hands. Whatever happened, it's gone now. I look down at the part of the page I'd highlighted last night. "So according to the book, we follow this road around the corner to get to the entrance."

Kat shoves her phone in her bag. "Where is it?" she asks, looking up and noticing her surroundings for the first time. "I don't see a tower."

"It's right over there," I say, pointing across the street.

"That's it?" she asks, not even trying to hide her disappointment. "Looks like every other dusty old castle in this crazy country. I thought we were going to see the Crown Jewels."

Nice. As long as the Tower of London can cough up some impressive diamonds and rubies, I know my big sister will get over whatever scraps of history she has to suffer through. "It's not like they keep the Crown Jewels on the fourth floor of Harrods," I say.

"I know *that.*" Kat wrinkles her nose and looks back at the Tower. "I just figured it would be a little fancier. Like the tower in

'Rapunzel' or something. A little gold leaf would do a world of good."

"It's just *called* the Tower of London," I say, pointing to the book. Sometimes I wonder how she managed to get all the way to senior year, although I know Kat's not stupid. Just easily distracted. "According to this, it's really a castle and a prison, with buildings that date back hundreds of years."

"Did the book happen to say why we want to deal with all of this history when we can be out shopping?" she asks, glaring across the street.

"Because it's famous, and no trip to London is complete without seeing the Tower," I say. "And because Dad already bought us the tickets, and they aren't cheap." And because part of me feels drawn here, like I need to touch the worn stone walls and feel the cobble-stones underneath my feet. Walk the same paths that the kings and queens of England did centuries ago. Back home in San Francisco, anything before 1970 is considered historical; the thought of stand-ing in a room almost a thousand years old takes my breath away. But I can't explain any of this to her, because I don't understand the attraction myself. And she'll think it's stupid.

"Dad's too busy working to have a clue what we do on this vacation," Kat complains. "He'll never know." She pulls her jacket tighter against the cold April wind. "Not like he could have a busi-ness trip in Hawaii or Cancún or someplace people might actu-ally *want* to go for spring break."

I don't have to say that, for me, spring break in London is way ahead of some hot, sweaty beach full of perfectly tanned people using as little energy as possible flipping from front to back on their striped beach towels. I don't have to say it because Kat already knows.

"What's going on over there?" Kat asks. "Another site where somebody famous got hacked to death or hit by a bus?" A group of people are staring down at a bronzed plaque a few feet off the sidewalk, and I check the book to see if it can tell us what is so fascinating.

"Close. Most of the executions at the Tower of London actually took place right over there," I read, pointing to the small square outlined in tiny cement markers just off the sidewalk. "Many innocent people were beheaded here, to the cheers of thousands," I continue reading. My mind flashes back to the scene in the vision and I shiver involuntarily.

"Thank you, geek's-guide-to-London." Kat looks at the cars speeding up the street and the tourists casually walking on the sidewalk. "Must have looked a lot different back then."

I gaze over the cars, across the grass field at the imposing walls and tall stone buildings that have been there for centuries. This must have been the last thing a lot of the prisoners saw as they knelt, waiting for the blow that would seal their fate. For a second I can almost hear the loud cries of desperate men echoing off the walls. "Not so different," I say quietly as we cross the street.

"So if we're going to do this," Kat says after we pick up the tickets, "let's go straight to the Crown Jewels. If I can't shop for jewels, at least I can look at them." She looks down to admire the insanely expensive new heels she bought just the day before. "Too bad there's not a shoe store in there." She glances at me. "There isn't, is there?"

"No," I say firmly. "There isn't."

I'm suddenly nervous as I look up at the square turret that tops the nearest tower. It doesn't take a whole lot of imagination to picture the guards in their heavy armor pacing up there, weapons trained on the murky water below. I look around for any signs the vision is coming back, but all I see is Kat's seething impatience with this whole thing. I flip the book open to the page I've marked with my finger. "It says that we should take a tour first and then go off on our own. Besides, it comes with the tickets."

"Oh, come on, Cole," Kat says, putting her hands on her hips. "Can't you just dump that stupid book for one minute and do something spontaneous? This whole vacation has been nothing but 'what the book says.' It's like that thing has become your bible. You're sixteen, not sixty."

"I didn't hear you complaining when it helped us get to Harrods, the mecca of shopping experiences," I say, irritated that we have to have this discussion again. "Or when it found that awesome Indian restaurant by the theaters."

"Give me that." Kat grabs the guidebook and turns the page. "There's a whole section on ghost tours in London; maybe we'll get lucky and see a ghost. That would at least keep this whole day from being a total waste."

I grab the book back. I don't believe in ghosts. Or vampires. Or visions of people being killed up on a smoky hill outside of the Tower of London. "There's no such thing as ghosts."

"So now you're the expert? Your precious guidebook says there are ghosts. Maybe we should bail on this whole Tower thing and do a ghost walk. Now *that* might be cool."

"Those ghost tours are just a scam." I was having enough trouble with weird visions coming to me. The last thing I wanted was to go looking for them.

"Why can't you even let yourself believe for one minute that there are things out there that you don't understand?" she asks. "Sometimes you have to forget about logic and go with your gut, and my gut says that this place has to be crawling with ghosts. Besides, it's printed right there, so someone must have checked it out."

I honestly don't have an answer for that, so I start toward the entrance, knowing she'll follow me. Kat can't stand being alone even for a minute.

Walking through the arch of the outside wall, I pause, trailing my fingers over the rough stone. The old Tudor buildings, the grass, the castle in the middle of the green—as I look from place to place in the compound, I feel a chill that has nothing to do with the wind that whips our faces.

"That tour is just about to start." I nod toward a red-uniformed guard standing on a small cement block. "Come on. We'll do the Jewels after."

Kat's shoulders fall, but she follows me over to the edge of the stone wall where people are gathering.

"Good morning, ladies and gentlemen, and welcome to the Tower of London." The guard is met with quiet muttering from the crowd, so he tries again, a little louder. "Good morning, ladies and gentlemen." He cups his ear and leans toward us so that we have no choice but to shout "good morning" like we're back in fifth grade. I sigh. I never like tours or classes where enthusiastic participation is required.

Kat nudges me. "He's kind of cute," she says, grinning.

I look back at the guard, with his largish nose and funny black hat. The wind has given his rough cheeks a pink glow, and he needs a shave. He has to be at least forty, which is old even for her. "Seriously? You just like his uniform. And his accent." Kat has fallen in love with a British accent attached to a questionable guy at least twice every day since we got here.

"It is my pleasure to be your guide today, and I hope that you will enjoy some of the nine hundred years of history that have taken place within these very walls." I look past him to the tall glass and steel buildings on the other side of the river. The modern structures seem to diminish the historical effect, reminding us that even here, all that is left of the past is made of stone and wood. The people who have experienced it are all long gone.

After blazing through several hundred years of history in under a minute, the guard directs our attention to Tower Hill, over by the tube station where we'd been just a few minutes before. "Imagine thousands of people standing and cheering as the poor—often innocent—soul gave his last address to the masses." I nudge Kat and point to the book. She glances at me out of the corner of her eye, but pretends to be absorbed in what he's saying.

"And when the prisoner was done speaking, he was obliged to tip the executioner a small fee in the hope that the deed would be done swiftly and with a painless chop of the axe. That, of course, has given rise to what we now know"—he pauses dramatically—"as severance pay." He waits for a response from the group, only to be greeted with a few quiet chuckles. He grins. "And that was my best line."

Kat laughs out loud, and he smiles at her. "After the prisoner had put his neck on the block, the axe would come down, and with a great crunching of bone and gushing of blood the deed would be done." He brings his arm down like an axe chopping off a poor guy's head while the crowd giggles nervously. "Grabbing hold of that severed head, the executioner would raise it high for all to see and declare, 'Behold the head of a traitor.'" Everyone in the group winces, and there are a few groans of disgust as he continues. "It's a pity that most of those beheaded were guilty of no other crime than displeasing the king or queen of the time." He pauses, and then motions with his arm. "Right. Follow me, then."

We walk over cobblestones worn smooth from centuries of footsteps until the guard stops in front of a few stone steps that lead down to a big iron gate. "Behind me, please admire the Traitors' Gate. Through this passage into the Tower of London came many of the poor men and women who were imprisoned between these walls, never to leave again. Both Anne Boleyn and Thomas Cromwell trod up these very steps to await their deaths."

As he speaks and gestures to the stairs, it suddenly feels like I'm watching from far away; his words grow tinny and faint. I blink to try to pull everything back, but an image pushes itself forward until the guard and the crowd fade away.

Shouts echo against stone and water laps against wood as the narrow boat maneuvers through the gate. Hands reach out to escort us up the slippery stairs, made more dangerous by the darkness that is broken only by torches flickering on the walls. I can smell the fear and panic in the air as we are hurried up the steps and through the tall, stone walls of the Tower.

"The water," I say without thinking.

Kat glares, while the guard turns his attention to me. "I'm sorry, miss?"

My heart is still racing and my palms are wet as I look around at the eager faces of the tour group. I *so* didn't mean to say that out loud. "Um, I was just saying that there was water here. People came through this gate in a boat."

"Give the young lady a prize for knowing her history," the guard says as he leans back and points to me. "I was about to say that this was originally called the Water Gate, as the moat that once surrounded the Tower provided for boats to enter the grounds at this very spot. Most of your prisoners did indeed arrive by boat."

"Guess your book came in handy for something," Kat whispers to me as the guard moves on to another building and we follow. "Way to impress the tour guide."

I nod quickly and then glance down at the book. I've been through the section on the Tower of London enough times to know that it never talks about the Water Gate.

"You okay?" Kat asks, her eyes intent on my face. "You look funny."

I run my hand over my forehead and squeeze my eyes closed. "Yeah. I'm fine," I say quickly. I feel panicky and a little sick to my stomach, but I don't want to go back to the hotel. I have to prove to myself that this is nothing. That the fact that what I saw in the vision is actually the truth doesn't mean that I'm seeing ghosts— although a more rational explanation is escaping me at the moment. "Come on, they're leaving us behind."

We stand in front of the White Tower as the guard talks about the kings and queens who lived there over the years. As we listen, it's easy to imagine people from hundreds of years ago crossing this same courtyard and peering out these same windows, a fact that I'm a little less enthusiastic about than I was just a few minutes ago. I want to get through the rest of this tour seeing old men wearing black socks and sandals with big, bulky cameras hanging around their necks, not anyone dressed in velvet hats and flowing gowns.

Perched on his little cement post, the guard is really revving up now, gesturing at each building as he describes its purpose, and I try hard to concentrate on what he's saying. "Now that you've seen where some of England's kings and queens lived, follow me and I'll show you where some of them actually died."

We follow him to a grassy area with a low iron fence. He stands on a small platform and waits for us to quiet down. "Let me draw your attention to that circular memorial," he says, pointing to what looks like a mirrored coffee table with a glass pillow on top. "That memorial is placed where the scaffold for the executions of noblemen and women was constructed. Only ten men and women were executed within the walls of the Tower itself. Who they were and why they died I'll explain to you once we're inside the Chapel Royal."

Kat nudges me as everyone else follows the guide inside the entrance to the Chapel. "I'm bored. You ready to be done yet?"

I watch the rest of the tour group file into the stone church. Swallowing hard, I nod my head, feeling a little too fragile to hear gruesome stories of the beheadings that took place on this very spot. I have to get a grip on myself, or the rest of this vacation is going to be ruined.

We slip away from the back of the crowd as Kat checks the map we'd been handed along with our tickets. "On to the Jewels," she says. I follow her past the glass memorial that looks weirdly modern and out of place among the old buildings and green lawns. People actually died right on the spot where I'm standing, and if there are wayward spirits anywhere in the Tower, they should be here. I don't feel any of the things I felt outside the tube station—no unexplained emotions, no overwhelming feelings of fear, no graphic images replaying in my head. As an experiment, I put my hand out to touch the metal railing surrounding the memorial, close my eyes, and feel . . . nothing. I open them again and look around, relieved.

"The line for the Crown Jewels still looks pretty long," I say, pointing to the snaking rows of people waiting to get into the stone building. I check the time on my phone. "It's going to be lunchtime soon—maybe we can sneak in when everyone else takes their kids to the café."

Kat eyes the line and reluctantly agrees with me. "Let's figure out which is the least boring building." She reads from the map and points to the big castle in the middle. "That's the White Tower. It's where the weapons and armor and stuff is." She rolls her eyes, and I can tell that we won't be spending a lot of time there.

I tap the map on the spot where we're standing. "Let's start with Beauchamp Tower. It's right here, and there's supposed to be some graffiti written on the walls by the prisoners as they were waiting to be executed."

Centuries-old tagging seems to appeal to her, so we walk up the stairs and into a large stone room with arched doorways and tiny windows set into the thick walls. I stop by one of the window ledges and peek out through the narrow opening to the paths and grass below, feeling my heart pound like it always does whenever I'm more than a few feet off the ground. I step back from the window and imagine sitting in this very spot, watching life pass by below, knowing that my time left on earth is almost over. It smells musty in the low-ceilinged room, as if centuries of desperation have worked their way into the walls.

Kat peers at the designs that are etched into almost every stone surface. "I wonder what they used to carve them? You think the king was stupid enough to give them knives and let them go at it?"

"I doubt it. See if it says on the display board over there." I walk slowly around the edges of the room, gazing at the carvings that were done by doomed men so long ago. Some are really elaborate, with images of lions and pleas to God for mercy. Others are just names and dates chiseled roughly into the walls. I end up standing in front of one carving, a simple square filled with words I don't recognize. I place my hand over the clear Plexiglas that protects all of the carvings and feel a subtle energy flowing from the solid stone. There are feelings of fear and loneliness, but overriding it all is a sense of peace. There's a tug of connection, and I long to put my skin on the bare stone, to touch the lines that have been carved by another hand centuries before: *For eternity. 1538.*

Kat leans over my shoulder, and I jerk my hand away. I feel guilty, but I have no idea why. "What's that one?" She looks closer. "*Ad vitam aeternam?* What is that, Latin? At least I can read the date—1538. But it doesn't say who did it or anything."

"Um, I don't know," I say, my voice shaky. *Ad vitam aeternam—* *For eternity.* I've only seen Latin in a few musical scores, but I know, deep in my heart, that this is what the carving says, as plainly as if it had been written in English. *For eternity.* The words echo through my whole body.

"There sure are a lot of carvings in here," Kat says, looking back at the map. "It says that there's a carving done by Lady Jane Grey's husband just before they were both beheaded. That is *so* romantic. Let's find that one."

Kat wanders off in search of her tragic graffiti and I follow her, glancing back at the small, square carving on the wall. It's one of the least elaborate carvings here—no names, no fancy drawings, just a few mysterious words and a date.

Somehow, it feels like the most important one in the place.

Two

The line for the Jewels is a lot shorter now. Let's go," Kat says as we stand near the exit. Walking out, I glance up at the small window that marks the prisoners' room. I have the nagging feeling that I'm leaving something important behind. *For eternity.* Goose bumps appear on my arms despite the rising temperature.

In fact, the sun is beginning to blaze as we cross the pavement toward the entrance to the Crown Jewels exhibit, and I unzip my jacket for the first time today. Spring has finally shown up—just in time for us to be heading home. The path is wider here, and there are fewer people wandering around. Apparently, hunger calls to most families a lot more strongly than the royal diamonds.

I can see the small line at the entry door, and next to that is a narrow wooden hut with a redcoated soldier standing at attention.

He has on one of those huge fur hats like at Buckingham Palace. As soon as Kat sees him, I know what's coming next.

"Ooh, take a picture of me with this guy," she says, unwinding the strap of her camera from her wrist. Most of Kat's photo collection from this trip consists of her posing with various soldiers and guards at all of the tourist sites in the city.

I back away, waiting for people to pass while she stands in front of the small iron railing near the soldier. "Can you get everything in from there?" she calls, shading her eyes with her hand. "I want the whole thing. I think you need to step back a little ways, otherwise you're going to cut stuff off."

I move back a few feet toward the White Tower, knocking hard into someone walking behind me. As he reaches out to steady me, I start to feel dizzy, and it's like sparks are racing through my body. My ears fill with a rushing noise and the blazing sun is replaced with the cold, gray fog of a winter morning.

There is a hush in the air, a feeling of dreaded expectation. In one hand I hold a small book, and in the other, a white lace hand-kerchief and the silk bag containing some coins and the silver pendant that is the last thing Connor gave me. My heart is beating so fast, it feels that at any minute it will rip out of my chest. I know that as much as I want to run and scream, I am to comport myself like a lady and to behave in a manner that is expected of my station in life. My heavy black dress is scratchy at the neck, and I rub the material between my fingers as the wooden surface above me is prepared. There are few other people in the yard, although there is a great deal of low whispering. The air is heavy with the threat of rain and the smell of the straw that is strewn about the wooden floor of the platform. The soldier standing next to me nods sharply, and I know it is time.

My feet find their way first to one step and then the next, until I am standing on the raised surface. A muffled cry comes from my lady-in-waiting, and I glance at her briefly before focusing my attention to the matter at hand. I am compelled to believe that someone will call off this insanity before it is too late. I have done nothing wrong, only loved my husband with all my heart—and for this we are both to die? I go through the motions, secure in the knowledge that a just God will never allow the deed to be carried out.

All eyes are on me as I open my little money bag and draw out the coins and Connor's pendant, the ruby in the center blazing brightly despite the somber morning. I run my finger quickly over the curve at the top of the cross. The money means nothing to me, but handing a stranger the necklace that is the symbol of my most cherished relationship is devastating. I know Connor is dead, executed in the chaos of Tower Hill, and this feels like the last connection to my beloved.

My fingers tremble, and for a moment I fear I will drop the coins and pendant before they land with a soft clink in the palm of the masked executioner. I find myself surprised that his waiting hand also trembles, and I glance up into his dark brown eyes, which are the only visible parts of his face. Rather than look into mine, he turns away and stares across the lawn, folding the payment into his palm with an air of finality.

I press my handkerchief and prayer book into the waiting hands of my lady, whose silent weeping is escalating into what I *fear will be a noisy crescendo. I give her tiny pale hand a squeeze, attempting to assure her, despite my pounding heart and short-ness of breath, that all will be well in the end. The executioner kneels at my feet, his eyes averted, and I grant the customary for-giveness with a wave of my hand. It is as if we are in a play, with each person knowing his assigned part and dispatched to complete the tasks in order.*

With forgiveness granted, he stands and indicates the small, square block positioned toward the front of the platform. I search the crowd, wondering which one of the men standing at attention will be the one to stop this. I decline to make the expected declara-tion of guilt, standing tall before the assembly and saying only, "In my life I have never so much as imagined a traitorous thought against His Majesty."

The masked headsman holds out a simple white handker-chief to cover my eyes, but I push it away. "I do not fear the axe," I say, loudly enough for those standing closest to the scaffold to hear. I stare into his eyes and can feel his indecision as he helps me onto my knees, for with a light touch, he holds my elbow, only reluctantly releasing it when I am positioned before the block.

As is my part, I put my neck on the wooden block, pulling my plait aside so that the cold wind reaches the bare white skin of my neck. My breath is coming rapidly, as if I cannot force the air into my lungs quickly enough.

The signal must have been given, for next I hear from below the scaffold, "What dost thou fear, headsman? Strike as you must!" and I am confident I will be spared. The headsman will not raise the axe to an innocent neck! Turning my head only slightly, I see

*his boots take one step back and the curved metal blade of the
axe lift from the straw. "I cannot save you, my lady," the headsman whispers hoarsely, and I glance up to see a blur of motion
and a flash of metal as the blade rips through the air—*

"Damn, Cole, what happened?" Kat is standing over me, blocking out the bright sunshine that has reappeared over her head.
"One second you're taking a picture, and the next minute you're
flat on your ass."

I shake my head to clear it, panic filling my chest. The other
visions I've had were short, like quick glimpses into another time,
but this one is different. I can still feel the emotions that were
running through the girl's mind as she stood on the scaffold. Her
pounding heart, the sense of betrayal. It all felt so real.

"Don't get up too fast," the guy I've run into says. He puts his
hand on my back to help me up, but as we touch, he pulls away
as if he's been shocked. "What are you doing here?" he whispers.
His voice holds both recognition and astonishment.

"What are you talking about?" I ask. "Visiting the Tower."
What else would I be doing here? I study him more closely. His
eyes are a distinctive shade of light brown rimmed with gold, and
his skin is just dark enough to make them startling. I'd definitely
remember if I'd seen him before.

He seems completely flustered. "Of course. Sorry. I thought you
were someone else." He puts his hand out. "Let me help you up."

"I'm okay," I say, struggling to my feet. I look around to see if
anyone else has noticed. So far it just looks like this guy and his
friend. I can feel my face heat up with embarrassment. "Thanks,
but I'm fine."

"Griffon has a habit of running into pretty girls," the friend says with a Scottish accent that makes Kat's eyes light up. "But he usually stops short of knocking them over."

Griffon looks irritated. "Owen. Seriously?"

Kat takes a step closer to Owen. Griffon is obviously American, so he's off her radar, but Owen's accent is so thick you can barely understand a word he's saying. "Oh, it's totally her fault," she says. "Not looking where she's going again."

Griffon looks embarrassed but says nothing, glancing away quickly as if the whole scene is making him uncomfortable too. His gestures are quick, like he's nervous about something. "I'm not so sure," he says quietly. "You might need a trip to the infirmary."

I brush off the back of my jeans and try to slow my racing thoughts. "No, I'm sure. It's probably just jet lag. And maybe dehydration. No big deal."

"Are these young men bothering you, ladies?" Our tour guide appears behind Kat. "I've had my eye on them all day as the troublemaking sort. I can get them tossed off the property if you wish." The guard has a smile on his face, but I can't tell if he's kidding or not.

"No, no," Kat insists. I can tell that she wants Owen to stick around. "My sister passed out a little and they were just helping."

"Oh, I'm so sorry," the guard says, with a look of concern. "Are you all right, miss?"

"Yes. Really, I'm fine," I say, the images from before flashing through my mind. I need to get out of here and clear my head. Enough communing with history—I just want to get back to the hotel. "Come on, Kat, let's go."

"If you won't go to the infirmary, at the very least allow this young man to buy you a cup of tea at the café," the guard says. He pulls out some colorful bills. "On me."

I know my face is beet red by now. This is all getting way out of control. "I couldn't do that," I say. I manage to walk a few yards toward the green and am starting to feel a little better. I find a bench and sit down hard on it. "I just need to sit down for a few minutes."

"As a Yeoman Warder of the Tower of London, I insist that you get some tea," he says, handing the bills to Griffon. "As this young man's father, I insist that he accompany you." I almost miss the look that passes between them. Griffon shakes his head slightly as if to answer an unspoken question.

"I'm leaving you in the boys' capable hands. If you need any further assistance, please do not hesitate to ask," the guard says, and with a tip of his hat, he walks toward the waiting tour group with long strides.

"Wow, is that guy really your dad?" Kat asks as she watches him resume his duties.

Griffon nods slowly. "We, ah . . . we don't look that much alike." With his curly hair and dark skin, that's the biggest understatement I've heard in a while.

"But he said on the tour that all of the guards actually live at the Tower." Kat looks at him with growing interest. "Do you live here too? Right up next to the Crown Jewels?"

"Sometimes. During school I live in the States with my mom," he says. "But during breaks and summer I come over to visit."

Kat looks around at the buildings of the Tower. "So, which one do you live in? Is it haunted? Doesn't it freak you out? Oh my gosh, what's it like around here at night?"

Griffon smiles slightly, revealing deep dimples on each side of his mouth. "That round tower by the front entrance. That's where Dad lives and where I stay when I'm here."

"Isn't that creepy?" Kat asks.

"Depends on who you ask," Owen says, smiling at her. "The door to the bedroom is the same prison door that's been there since the fifteen hundreds. Late at night you can still hear the echoes of the prisoners pounding on the heavy wood."

"Knock it off," Griffon says. He turns to Kat. "There's no pounding, no bloody heads. Just a little wind through the leaky windows on a cold night. It's really no big deal."

Kat shivers and looks toward the building, obviously enjoying Owen's story more than Griffon's.

"Now let's go get that tea," Griffon says. "Otherwise Dad'll have my hide for not being a proper host."

"I don't really think that tea will help—" I begin.

"Of course it won't." Griffon stands up. "But the English believe that tea cures everything, so humor him."

I get the sense that he's only doing his duty, and I want to let him off the hook. How many crazy tourists does he run into every day? Okay, maybe not *literally*, but I'm sure he has better things to do than play tour guide. "Kat really wants to see the Crown Jewels," I say, glancing toward the building. A quick trip to see the Jewels, and then I can go back to the hotel, lock the bathroom door, and lose it for real. I can probably keep it together that long. "Might as well get it over with."

"The last thing you need is to stand in a stifling queue," he says. He looks over at the growing line. "And it's not going to get any better than this for the rest of the day."

Owen looks at me. "Tell you what. If you really don't care"—he turns to Kat—"and you really don't mind, then why don't I give you my famous tour of the Jewels, and Griffon can take your sister to the café right on the other side of the White Tower? We'll meet them there when we're done."

Kat shifts her weight on the high heels that look so out of place, not to mention uncomfortable. "Are you sure you don't mind?" she asks me, glancing meaningfully at Owen.

I hesitate. She'd never forgive me if I took this opportunity away from her. "I don't if you don't."

"Great. We'll meet you at the café as soon as we're done." She barely gets the words out before she's wobbling across the cobblestones, walking so close to Owen that I think she's going to knock him over. He reaches out to catch her and then leaves his hand on her arm as they continue walking. I suddenly see why Kat insists on wearing totally impractical shoes all the time.

"You sure you're okay?" Griffon asks as soon as we're alone.

"I'm fine. Really." At least my stomach has finally stopped churning.

"Right. I'll stop asking. The Armouries Café is right in that building over there," he says. We walk a little way in silence, but I notice more than a few guards grinning at him as we pass. My mind is racing, but I can't seem to think of a single thing to say.

"Two truths and a lie," Griffon says suddenly, turning to look at me.

"Two what?" I have no idea what he's talking about.

"Truths. And a lie. You tell me two things that are true and one that is a lie, and I have to guess which is which."

"Sort of like Truth or Dare?"

"Right. But instead of a dare, give me a lie. But make it a good one. Something believable."

I think for a second, but my mind is a total blank. I can't think of a single thing about me, true or not. "You first," I say, trying to buy some time to come up with something that might make me sound interesting and a little mysterious.

"Okay," he says. "Um . . . I've had dinner with Oprah Winfrey."

I watch him carefully, but I don't see anything, no matter how unbelievable this sounds. There's no way I can tell him that I can pretty much always tell when people are lying. There's something in their eyes or the way they move when they're talking that always gives it away.

"My favorite food is peanut butter," he continues, and in a split second I see it. A brief twitch of his mouth that tells me this is the lie. "And I have a tattoo."

"So you're probably not going to order peanut butter and jelly for lunch."

He stares at me and breaks into a big grin. "Right! I hate peanut butter. How did you know?"

I shrug. "Lucky guess."

"If you say so," he says skeptically.

"So you really did have dinner with Oprah?"

"I really did. Do you want to see my tattoo?"

If he's offering, I'm assuming it's in a public-friendly place. "Sure."

Griffon holds up his right hand and points to a spot between his thumb and index finger. "Right there."

I don't see anything. "Where?"

He moves his finger out of the way. "Just there. See that dot?"

I look closer and see a tiny black dot a few shades darker than his skin. "Looks like a freckle."

"It's not. My friend's brother had a rig and offered to give us both tattoos. This was as far as I got before I chickened out." He smiles at me. "Now it's your turn."

I laugh a little. I usually hate games like this, but somehow it's making me feel better. I try to think of the craziest things that have ever happened to me. "Okay. I've met the queen. I was switched at birth. And I don't know how to ride a bike."

Griffon stares up at the sky and looks like he's thinking hard. "There's no way you met the queen, so that must be the lie."

"Nope. I met the Queen of Greece at the symphony last year."

"I thought you said *the* queen."

"She is *the* queen. Of Greece. Deposed, but still. You have two more guesses."

"You can't ride a bike?"

"Of course I can ride a bike. Almost everyone can ride a bike. That was the lie." I pause, not knowing how far I can push him. "You're really not very good at this, are you?"

He smiles, and I know he's not annoyed. "So you're trying to tell me you really were switched at birth?"

"My mom says it was only for an hour and then the hospital figured it out. Sometimes I wonder, though. Kat and I . . . we're not all that much alike." Understatement of the year. She's the very definition of the gorgeous blond California girl. And I'm . . . not.

Griffon nods and flashes a dimple. "Too bad for her."

His direct gaze gives me another kind of fluttering inside. I bite my lip and look down at the ground as we walk. Maybe he has a thing for short, brown-haired girls who don't wear anything that requires a trip to the dry cleaner.

"I bow to the master," he says, holding the door of the café open for me. "I think you won that round. Not even close enough for me to contest."

"Just beginner's luck."

Griffon leads me to an empty wooden table by the window. "I'm going to get some tea. Sit here, stare at the tourists, and I'll be right back."

The café is crowded with families, and the noise echoes off the walls of the big brick building. I can't help watching Griffon as he walks up to the counter. Where his dad is totally what you'd expect from a guard at the Tower of London—short bristly hair, white skin, and pink cheeks—Griffon is completely different. He has light brown skin and broad shoulders that dip down into a narrow waist, and his light brown curls have tiny blond streaks in them that I can tell come from the sun, not a bottle. A heavy black cord hangs around his neck, but it's tucked into his shirt, so I can't see what's on the end of it.

Griffon is insanely good-looking, but it's more than that. As much as I make fun of romance novels and chick flicks, I feel a tug of recognition down deep that is almost physical, and it frightens me. While my eyes are on him, he turns to lean against the counter as he waits for the tray. I look down, but probably not fast enough. I'm still examining the wooden tabletop when he comes back with the tea.

"I don't know how you take it, so I brought milk, sugar, lemon, and honey," he says, setting the tray on the table.

I look over the assortment of jars and packets. "I suppose it's wrong to say all of it?" I ask, hoping I sound more confident than I feel.

Griffon grins, and my heart races. "Well, you're allowed to do anything you want. Generally it's either milk and sugar or lemon and honey."

"I guess milk and sugar, then," I say.

"And this is clotted cream," he says, putting a jar of lumpy white stuff in front of me. "I highly recommend the cream with jam on those scones. Better than any whipped cream back in the States."

I tentatively poke the pale mass with my knife. "Maybe just some jam," I say, taking a scone from the plate.

"I insist." He grabs my scone and smears it with the white cream and jam before putting it back on my plate. His hands are strong and smooth, and I find myself staring at them as he prepares the food. "You're not one of those girls who doesn't eat, are you?"

"No," I say, offended that he would even think that. "I eat plenty. It's just that I don't usually eat things that start with the word 'clotted.'" I take a bite, and it's as good and rich as he promised, like thick whipped cream without too much sugar. So much for not being able to eat; I devour half of it before coming up for air. I try to regain some sort of dignity by sipping the tea, wondering if English people really drink it with their pinky out like they do on that PBS show Mom likes. Griffon just sits with his arms folded, watching me, so he's no help.

I put the cup down on the table after a sip of the watery tea, realizing through my swirling thoughts that neither of us has said a word in the past several minutes.

"Sorry about Kat," I say. "And all of her questions. She's not much for history, but she loves a good ghost story."

"Most people do," he says. "I get asked things like that all the time."

"But you don't, right?" I ask. "Believe in them, I mean."

"No. Not ghosts. Although other people claim to see them here. Maybe the ghosts know I don't believe in them and don't bother showing up," he says.

"What about all of the people who died such violent deaths right here in the Tower? You don't think there's some sort of leftover energy floating around? Some sort of spirit activity trying to right the wrongs that were done to them?" I can't believe I'm asking that, but there has to be some sort of rational explanation for what just happened out there. At this point, ghosts are the most rational thing I can think of.

"No," he says, looking at me strangely, stalling for just a beat too long. "I don't."

I'm a little disappointed in his finality. Restless spirits are a much friendlier explanation than the fact that I might be losing it.

Except I don't *feel* crazy. If it wasn't for unexpected Latin translations and visions of beheadings, I'd be just fine.

"I just realized," he says, sitting forward in his seat, "that we
haven't been properly introduced. I'm Griffon Hall."

"I know. Owen said."

He looks at me. "And you are?"

"Oh!" I say. Of course. What an idiot. "Cole Ryan. Nicole really,
but only my mother calls me that. It's Cole to everyone else."

"Cole," he repeats. "That's nice. I'm guessing you're not from
around here."

"No," I say. "My dad's on a business trip and brought us along.
We live in San Francisco."

Griffon nods slowly. He must meet people from all over the
world here.

"Have you ever been there?"

"San Francisco?" he asks. "A few times. Where do you live in
the city?"

"Upper Haight. Just at the panhandle before Golden Gate Park."

"Is there still a Ben & Jerry's there?"

I smile. "Right around the corner from our house."

Griffon holds my gaze for a split second, then looks around at all
of the other people in the café. "Are you enjoying your trip so far?"

I search for something interesting to say. Pretty soon he's
going to notice that I've got the conversational skills of a first-
semester foreign exchange student. "It's been great."

"What else have you done?"

I open my mouth to tell him about the master class I took with
the London Symphony Orchestra and how I got to sit backstage at

the concert earlier in the week, about meeting some of the cellists I'd been worshiping for years and having the chance to play privately with them. But Griffon doesn't know me as the cello prodigy. He only knows the awkward girl who talks about ghosts and falls into total strangers, and suddenly I wanted to keep it that way. "You know, the usual stuff," I finally say. "Buckingham Palace, the Tate Gallery, museums."

"How about the Eye?" He nods his head across the river toward the towering Ferris wheel.

Right. The only way I'd get into a small glass box suspended hundreds of feet in the air for half an hour is at gunpoint. And maybe not even then. "Um, no. Not yet."

"I usually hate tourist things like that, but it has the best view in the city."

"Maybe tomorrow," I say, knowing it'll never happen. "It feels like we don't have enough time to do it all, but it's been great so far. I've always been fascinated by this city. By all of England."

"Tell me you didn't get up in the middle of the night to watch the royal wedding."

"I didn't," I answer honestly. Kat had recorded it. "It's just that I love history, and I really wanted to see the places I've read about." I'm tempted to tell him about the vision, about the girl on the scaffold. Something about the way he looks at me makes me feel safe and grounded. Like I can say anything and he'll believe me. "In some ways, London feels like home. It's almost like everything is familiar. Except it's not."

Griffon's eyes scan my face intently. "Like déjà vu?"

"Exactly," I say. "It's weird. I'll be walking by a house and all of a sudden I'll feel homesick. Or I'll know exactly what the next street looks like even though I've never been on it."

He nods, listening to me intently. "It's weird feeling that you've been someplace before, or seen something before." Griffon looks thoughtful. "But that doesn't seem to cover it most of the time."

"It doesn't," I agree. "It's more than that. It's not like I've just seen it already. It's like I've . . ." I suddenly realize that I'm sitting here spilling my guts to a total stranger. A total stranger who feels really familiar.

"Like you've lived it before?" Griffon finishes for me.

"Right," I say. I'm surprisingly calm. "Like I'm seeing things that already happened through the eyes of the people they happened to. Things that happened a long time ago. I don't know if it's spirits, or some kind of supernatural energy." I pause, and it's as if the thread that momentarily connected us has snapped. "Or if I'm going crazy."

Griffon smiles. "You're not crazy," he says. "Far from it."

"So if I'm not slowly going insane, what is it, then?"

He hesitates, and I can see indecision play across his face. "I guess people sometimes try to bury the things that they most need to see."

"And for some reason I need to see these glimpses of other people's lives? That makes no sense."

"Maybe it will someday," he says cryptically.

I look at our hands on the wooden table. Our fingers are only inches apart, and I have a sudden urge to reach out and touch him. I want the feel of his skin on mine, a physical connection, even if it's only for a second. As if he can read my mind, Griffon pulls his hands from the table and sits back in his chair. I feel as embarrassed as if I had actually reached for him.

Griffon looks out toward the Green, where the other tourists are wandering around. "So what do you think of the new marker for the scaffold site?" he asks, nodding toward the Chapel.

I follow his gaze, thrown by the rapid change in topic. "That glass thing? It's interesting."

Griffon's face clouds over a little. His emotions seem to be just under the surface, and I can already see the dislike in his expression. "I think it's awful. Like a big glass coffee table right in the middle of the square."

I smile. "I kind of thought the same thing."

"The worst part is that they didn't even put it in the right spot," he says.

"They didn't? I thought that's where all the executions happened. That's what the guidebook says."

"No," he says. "Don't believe everything you read. Years ago some Warder just pointed to that spot when Queen Victoria came for a visit and asked where the beheadings took place. Poor old guy didn't have a clue. The Yeoman Warders just go along with it so the tourists don't get confused. It's tradition."

"So where did they really happen?" I ask, glad that we seemed to be having a normal conversation again. Living right on top of it all, he must know all the dirty little secrets.

"Well, the scaffolds were put up and taken down for every execution, so they weren't always in the same spot. Actually," he says, "most of the beheadings happened on the north side of the White Tower."

"Which side is that?" I ask.

"Near where they keep the Crown Jewels now," he says. "In fact, they say that the most famous executions happened near the Green." Griffon leans forward and studies me. "Right on the spot where you fainted."

Three

Spring break feels a million miles away as Ms. Lipke's marker squeaks across the whiteboard at the front of the room. Rayne slides into her seat, glancing up first to see if she's going to get busted for being late to class again. "So what's he like?" she whispers.

"Who?" I ask quietly, knowing exactly who she means. It's pretty impossible to keep anything from her. I'd purposely left Griffon out of my updates while we were gone, but I should have known that Kat would go telling everyone. I've spent enough time analyzing my entire conversation with him, and I don't want to have to go over it with Rayne too. Griffon is a part of the trip that I want to keep to myself. At least for now.

"Kat told Sienna that you two met some amazing guys in London. I can't believe you've been back two whole days and didn't say anything."

The minute Griffon told me about the executions, I felt sick all over again. As soon as Kat showed up I made excuses about jet lag and practically ran out of there. He didn't even ask for my number, and it's not like I was going to shove it in his hand. And now we're back home and in school as if everything is the same. Even though everything feels completely different.

"Come on," Rayne urges, facing forward so we won't get caught talking. "I can't believe you didn't tell me about something so important. Spill."

"Nothing to spill," I say. "I met a guy. He was cute. He didn't get my info, so I'll never see him again. End of story."

"That's not what Kat says. She says you, like, totally fainted right in the middle of some tower and that this guy rescued you."

Just thinking about it makes my stomach hurt. Sometimes, when I'm doing the most random thing, a scene from that vision will flash through my mind, and all of the same emotions get churned up all over again. At least nothing like that has happened since we've been back. Hopefully that was the worst—and the last—of whatever it was, and the visions stayed in England where they belong. "It was just a cup of tea," I say. "Hardly qualifies as 'rescuing.'" Ms. Lipke gives us both a look, saving me from having to explain any more for the moment.

It's ridiculous how much I think about Griffon, considering we'd probably spent all of an hour together. Even though we'd only had one more day in London, I was tempted to try to get back to the Tower, visions of beheadings or not. We passed the Tower walls in a cab the next day and I pictured him sitting at a table in the café, probably talking to some other hapless tourist girl who needed his assistance.

"Should I even ask what you're doing after school?" Rayne asks as we're finally released from language arts. "I think some people are going to hang out over at Café Roma."

"Can't," I say, leaning my cello case against the wall of lockers in the hallway. I fish around in my backpack for my phone, as much to find it as to avoid her eyes.

"Cello practice again? When are you going to take a break and get a real life?"

I sigh. I love Rayne, but she just doesn't get it. "This *is* real life. *My* real life. There was the trip, and now the concert's coming up, so I'm way behind."

I've tried to explain that you don't choose to be a musician, it chooses you. The feeling of transcendence I get when a piece is going well, the combination of contentment and exhilaration that makes it seem like I'm completely outside myself, is impossible to explain without sounding like a crazy person. It's something that pushes me from the inside, that makes me anxious if I don't get in practice every day. I like to blame it on my parents just so that I won't look like a complete music geek, but the truth is, I don't just *like* to play—I *have* to play. I doubt that people who are training for the Olympics and spend hours every day at the ice rink or in the gym have to make excuses like I do.

"Just don't call me when you're a fifty-year-old spinster with arthritic hands and thirty-two cats." She grins at me. "So are you giving a lesson or getting one?"

"Both," I say, relieved we're off the subject. "I have makeup lessons all week with Steinberg for an hour, and then I'm giving a cello lesson at five."

"Who's the student?"

"That fifth-grader from Yeshiva Day," I say. "He hates the cello, but his parents think it's good for his 'enrichment.'" Students who are forced into lessons are the hardest to teach. Adults who are really into learning how to play are the best—a little overenthusiastic sometimes, but at least they practice and don't mess around. Overindulged private-school kids with hovering parents are the worst. And the kind of students I have most often.

"Sounds fun." Rayne makes a face as we head toward the bus stop on the corner. "Talk later?"

I sit in my usual seat on the city bus with the cello case propped up beside me like a silent guardian. Mom used to pick me up and drive me home every day, but she finally let me start taking the bus a couple of years ago, and I like the few minutes of quiet that bridge the two parts of my day. As we roll toward the studio I press my forehead to the window and stare at the people swarming the sidewalks. I always like watching people from the safety of the bus, catching a few seconds of their lives before we rattle on down the street, them never realizing I was there at all. In the middle of all of this chaos are things that are like signposts in each neighborhood as we ride down Geary: the guy sitting in the folding chair on the tiny strip of sidewalk between the Chinese restaurant and the Indian market, or the people clutching their cups and staring intently at their laptops inside Peet's Coffee.

As the bus idles at the light, a woman looks up from a window table and gazes out at the street. With a start, I recognize her as one of my cello students. I wave as the bus pulls into the intersection, but Veronique has already turned back to her work.

I lift the cello out of its seat and pull the strap over my

shoulder as I get off at my stop. I use the lighter carbon-fiber cello for travel and running around, but with the case it still weighs a ton, and I'm glad there aren't any hills to climb as I head toward the studio. My good Derazey cello has to be content with practice at home and occasional orchestra visits, ever since my parents took a second mortgage on the duplex to buy it a couple of years ago. The graceful curves of a nearly two-hundred-year-old instrument don't come cheap. Whenever I think about the money they've spent over the years on instruments, gear, the conservatory, and private lessons, my chest feels so heavy I can barely breathe. If the guilt starts to settle in too heavily, I just put in a few extra hours of practice.

As I step into the studio, the familiar, safe feeling sits close around my shoulders, and I inhale the combination of rosin, antique instruments, and sweat that only exists here.

Portraits of famous musicians line the walls, and I touch Guilhermina Suggia's frame for good luck like I always do when I come through the door. She was one of the first female cellists, and whenever I feel discouraged, one look at the painting of her fiery red dress, her head tilted at an angle that's full of attitude as she attacks the cello, always makes me feel better.

In the back, I can hear the rich, mellow sounds of a cello echoing off the wood-paneled walls, and I feel my blood surge as I listen to Steinberg play. I creep down the short hallway, avoiding the squeaking boards next to the coatrack, until I can see him sitting bent over the glossy wood, both hands working in harmony to wring every ounce of feeling from the instrument, his eyes closed, everything abandoned to the music. In the years we've worked together I've learned to match him note for note. I've mastered the technical skill to play complicated pieces without a mistake, spent hours copying his fingering. My heart races as his bow glides over the strings, an unspoken communication that fills the room, replacing the air with sound and emotion.

I set the cello down gently, watching as Steinberg finishes the piece, feeling every note as it fades into the woodwork. Even more than our house in the Haight, this is home to me, and I feel a physical tug inside from being away so long.

As if he can sense me in the room, Herr Steinberg turns and gives me a welcoming smile. I take my place in the empty chair next to him, eager to get back to the one thing in my life I can always depend on.

∞

On our front porch, I shift the cello case to my other shoulder as I lean over to put my key in the lock. "Mom, I'm home!" I call out as the door swings open, taking my key with it and refusing to let go. I jiggle it in the rusty old lock until it finally surrenders, swearing at my parents for not wanting to change any of the original features of our drafty old Victorian house. Sure, the wavy glass windows are originals, but they leak like crazy, and sometimes we have to wear jackets indoors during the wintertime.

"Ma?" I call again, dropping my things by the doorway and heading into the empty kitchen. She knows I have a lesson today. Mom and Dad don't let me give lessons unless somebody's home, and if she forgot again I don't know what I'll tell Oscar's parents.

I think about just grabbing the phone, but Dad hates it when I call him from downstairs. Swiping an apple from the bowl on the island, I trudge back through our front door, cross the porch, and let myself in his front door. "Dad?" I call up the stairs. After their divorce, Mom and Dad bought this duplex so that Kat and I wouldn't have to shuttle between houses. He has the flat above ours, which means that right inside his front door are about a million stairs. Yelling is easier than climbing.

"In my office," he calls down.

"Just wanted to tell you I'm home. I have a lesson in a few minutes."

"Come up and give your old dad a hug," he says, his head appearing over the upstairs railing. "I downloaded the photos from our trip. There's some great stuff in there."

"I really don't have time," I say. "How about I come up after dinner?"

His eyes look a little sad, but he manages a smile. "Okay. I'll save dessert for you, so don't forget."

I shut his door behind me and walk back into our flat. I suppose that having him right upstairs from us is a lot better than having him in some faraway city, but I feel bad when he's up there all by himself and we're down here. Neither Mom or Dad has really dated much since the divorce—or at least I haven't seen it—and I sometimes think I wouldn't feel so guilty if Dad would at least get a steady girlfriend.

Kat isn't home yet, but that's not a surprise. She has an after-school job at a boutique on Union Street, and when she isn't selling clothes, she's out somewhere buying them. To her, our house in the Haight is slumming it, so she spends as much time as she can in the "better" neighborhoods. She's going to fashion design school in September, which is just about killing Dad, who's had visions of her going to Stanford since before she could talk.

Just as I toss the rest of my apple into the compost bin, our doorbell rings. I can see the watery shadows of Oscar and his mom through the glass in the front door.

"Hi, Mrs. Garcia," I say, opening the door wide. "Hey, Oscar."

Oscar pushes by me with barely a grunt, half dragging, half carrying his cello. This is going to be a very long lesson.

Oscar's mom shakes her head. "I don't know what I'm going to do with that boy," she says. "He doesn't appreciate all that we're doing for him. Trying to broaden his horizons." She perches on the wing chair that Mom has set up for parents, although it's a lot easier for me when the chair is empty. If it's just me and the student I can relax a little bit, maybe show them some things that might be more interesting than the classical fingerings and scales that their parents feel they're paying for.

Mrs. Garcia puts her handbag in her lap and watches Oscar unpack his cello in the living room. I glance at her bag, hoping that she'll get my telepathic message that it's the first lesson of the month. Payday. I don't mind teaching—sometimes it's even fun—but I hate chasing the money. And it's the parents with the most money that forget to pay me most often.

"Did you practice while I was gone?" I ask Oscar, getting my cello ready. These are things I have to ask while the parents are sitting within earshot. They like it that their kids are taught by an actual child prodigy, but they still expect me to act like a teacher.

He shrugs, which means he probably hasn't touched it since

he was here last. His bow bounces across the strings, making a grating sound that sets my teeth on edge. Some kids, no matter how much their parents want them to, are just never going to be into playing an instrument.

I set my cello against my shoulder and play a few bars of a song I've been trying to teach him for the past three lessons, and Oscar does his best to copy my motions. After twenty-eight excruciating minutes, I let him put the bow down and pack up the instrument. As he gathers up his things, his mom motions me over.

"I think he's sounding so much better," she gushes, making me wonder if she's actually been sitting in the same room. "That last song was crisp and clear. You really have a gift—we were so lucky to get a place with you."

I smile a tight smile and nod, because that's what they want me to do. I hesitate before opening my mouth. "Um, Mrs. Garcia? It . . . um . . . it *is* the first of the month and all. So I was wondering . . ."

She claps her hands together. "Oh, yes!" she says, and rummages through her bag. "I seem to have forgotten my checkbook." She smiles up at me. "I'm sure you don't mind if I bring a check next time."

"Of course not," I say, managing a tight smile. "No problem." I mentally cross off those two new books I'd wanted to order from Books Inc.

Mom meets them at the door just as they're leaving, causing a flurry of *hellos* and some grocery bag shuffling.

"How was the lesson?" Mom asks over her shoulder as I follow her into the kitchen. She puts the bags down on the counter and I start poking through them.

"Fine," I say. "Are there more in the car?"

"No," she says. "This is it."

I find one of my favorite protein bars at the bottom of a bag and unwrap it.

"Don't eat too much," Mom says. "I'm making dinner early because I have an online meeting." She closes the fridge and pulls a note off the front. "Did you get this?"

"No," I say, reaching for the scrap of paper. *Veronique would like to come today and Thursday because you both missed last week. I told her it's fine. Love, Mom.*

"Well, I'm sorry," she says. "I put it where I thought you would see it."

"That's so weird," I say, glancing at the paper again. "I just saw her. In Peet's."

"When were you at Peet's?"

"I wasn't," I say. "I was on the bus. Never mind. It's not important."

"Well, she's coming around six."

I look at the clock—she's due here any minute. "You should have called me."

"Sorry," Mom says. "You know I'm not crazy about you spending all this time on lessons in any case. Especially if it's going to cut into your schoolwork and your own practice time."

"You guys won't give me extra money, so what else am I supposed to do? It's better than working at McDonalds," I say. "Or at the O'Farrell Theater." Kat actually knows someone who works as a topless dancer, and she really does make good money. We both know I'd rather die than take my clothes off in front of strangers, but still, point made.

"Don't try to be funny," she says. "We get you everything you need, and there's nothing funny about you wasting your gift teaching untalented beginners how to mutilate a cello instead of taking extra classes at the conservatory like we'd planned."

"Nothing funny about increasing my allowance," I mutter, making sure I'm out of earshot first. Ever since I picked up a bow for the first time when I was four, the cello has been my destiny, and Mom hates anything that might interfere with that in the tiniest way. I sometimes wonder how different my life would be if we hadn't gone to Aunt Karen's house that day. Not really my aunt, but my mom's best friend from college, Karen had an old cello sitting in her living room, and according to family legend, I climbed up on the chair, grabbed the bow, and started playing perfect notes right from the start. I'm not sure how much of that is actually true, but what is true is that the cello comes ridiculously easy for me. It's like learning how to talk—not something I have to really concentrate on, it just happens, like I've known it forever. Within a year, I'd outgrown my first cello teacher, and my parents had me on the fast track to world cello domination.

"I'm sorry, dear?" Mom says, staring at her laptop. "What was that?"

"Nothing," I say, and finish putting the groceries away just as the doorbell rings.

"How was London?" Veronique asks before she's even through the door. "I hope you don't mind me coming twice this week, but I can't stand missing a lesson." She's holding her cello with one arm and gives me a quick hug with the other.

"London was great," I say, backing up and letting her into the hallway. "And it's totally fine to come today."

Veronique is slim and super-fashionable, with her straight

black hair cut in a severe bob—a style that my long wavy hair can only dream about. There's a tiny brown birthmark that looks like a comma over her right eye, which is good, because otherwise she'd be a little too perfect and I'd have to hate her. She's in her early twenties and is some sort of scientist over at UCSF. Whatever she does, it makes enough money for the best instrument, the latest clothes, and the freedom to be at a cello lesson on a weekday evening.

She hands me a sealed envelope and I smile, knowing it's cash. Veronique has only been my student for about six months, but I can always count on her not to forget. "Thanks," I say, shoving it in the back pocket of my jeans. "Come on in, I'm already set up."

It is actually enjoyable to teach Veronique—she isn't a natural, but what she lacks in skill she makes up for in determination. From week to week, I can tell she's been practicing, although she gets really embarrassed when I compliment her on her improving technique.

"I think I've finally decided on a name for my cello," Veronique says, lifting the instrument from its case.

"I already told you, it's not like naming is mandatory or anything. Not everybody does it." Not everybody includes pretty much only me, because everyone else I know in the orchestra has a cute or meaningful name for their instrument. I tried naming my first cello after the main character in my favorite book, but every time I called it "Harry" I felt like an idiot.

"I know, but it makes it so much more personal. Are you ready?" She gives a dramatic pause. "Bono."

"'Bono' as in U2 Bono?" I roll the name around in my head for a second. It could work.

"Yep." Veronique smiles. "If something is going to be between my knees for so many hours every week, I figure it might as well be the sexiest singer alive."

"Veronique!" I whisper, giggling. I look toward the doorway to make sure Mom isn't listening. "Won't your boyfriend get mad?"

She shrugs. "No. Giacomo thinks he's sexy too. He'll probably like it."

I hold up my hand. "Totally TMI," I say, getting so embarrassed I can barely look at her.

"Come on, Bono," she says, pulling the cello into position. "Let's get down to business."

We work on Bach's Variations for a few minutes before I suggest something new. "I just got this, and the arrangement doesn't look too hard," I say, placing the music on the stand. "It's one of the first real classical pieces I ever tried." I've barely gotten through the first bars of Chopin's *Sonata in G* before Veronique puts her hand on the page and pulls it down, the expression on her face full of pain.

"I'm sorry," she says. Her voice sounds shaky and uncontrolled, not like her at all. "But no Chopin."

I look at her out of the corner of my eye. Veronique always agrees on my choice of music. "None?" I say. "No *Polonaise?*"

"No," she says. "I don't . . . I can't stand Chopin." Veronique's face is red, and she seems flustered. I've never seen her anything but cool and calm—what is it about a little piece of music that has her almost crawling out of her skin?

"No problem," I say, picking up the pages and sliding them under my seat. "I'm not a huge fan anyway." Which is a complete lie; Chopin composed some of my favorite music, but she already looks embarrassed and I don't want it to get any worse. As I sit back in my chair, my head begins to spin, and I try to tell myself that it's just a head rush. I sat up too fast is all. The feelings of panic begin as the room feels like it's receding around me. I can see Veronique speaking, but I can't understand what she's saying.

I stand watching from the wings as Alessandra pulls the bow back and the last notes of Chopin resonate throughout the concert hall. Applause thunders through the building as she stands holding the neck of the cello, reaching with the other hand to pull her long, blond hair away from her face. Alessandra has been with the Young Masters Orchestra since she was my age, touring the world with her father as chaperone for the past four years. Now that she's almost nineteen, she is so much better than I am, and between her beauty and skill I always feel inadequate around her.

I sense him behind me well before he speaks. "Are you ready, Clarissa?" Paolo asks, his smile bright in the low lights of backstage, causing my heart to flutter like it always does whenever he's around. His dark hair shines almost black in the flicker of the footlights as I look up at him and nod quickly. Paolo touches me lightly on the elbow as he guides me onstage, where my cello and chair have been placed next to Alessandra's, and even though I should be nervous with so many people here to watch my first performance, all I can feel is the physical sensation of his skin on mine. With a slight bow, Paolo takes his position at the piano, and along with the other musicians, I put my head down, trying to concentrate on the opening notes of the next piece. Paolo belongs to Alessandra; they are so obviously in love that you often have to look away in the face of such fierce devotion. Everyone in the troupe knows that, and to even think anything different will cause an unimaginable amount of trouble.

Veronique is looking at me with concern. "Is everything okay? You look pale."

I blink and look around the room. The bright lights of the stage are gone, replaced by the colored shades of the Tiffany lamps my mom loves so much. "Sure," I say, my voice stronger than I thought it would be. "Just a little dizzy. I think it's the jet lag still."

She looks relieved. "You're probably right. Whenever I go to Italy with Giacomo it takes days to get back on the right schedule." She glances at her delicate gold watch. "It's getting late anyway. I should get going. We're still on for Thursday, right?"

"Right," I say, hoping that she doesn't notice how much my hand is shaking as I put the bow back in its case.

∞

I help Mom clear the dining room table after dinner, even though it's just the two of us. No matter how many of us are home, she insists on setting the table and sitting down to a meal every night. I wonder if she'll still do that when it's just her in a few years. The thought of her sitting down here alone while Dad sits upstairs by himself is vaguely depressing.

"I'm going up to see Dad," I say once the dishwasher is loaded. I'd almost forgotten about my promise to look at the photos.

"Okay," she calls from the laundry room. "Did you finish your homework?"

"I did some in school."

"How about your practice time? We can't have you falling behind just because you went on vacation. Herr Steinberg mentioned that the little red-headed girl is just itching to challenge you for first chair."

"I'll do another hour before bed," I call back. "I won't be long."

Dad has the classical music station blasting as I walk up the stairs. I find him at the computer, a half-eaten burrito on a plate next to him, along with some chocolate-chip cookies from my favorite bakery in the Mission.

"Hey, there's my girl," he says, turning around and giving me a kiss on the cheek. "There are some great shots from the trip. Want to see?"

"Sure," I say, grabbing a cookie. I always forget to take pictures, and Kat's camera is filled with the ones I took of her and various guards and Beefeaters. I know she took a couple of Owen in front of the Crown Jewels building, and I kick myself for not having her sneak a picture of Griffon. Despite the pang I get in my chest whenever I think of him, his image is already fading in my memory, and I'm not sure if I'd even recognize him again. Not that it matters.

Dad, on the other hand, takes pictures like he's terrified of short-term memory loss. Every moment has to be documented so that nothing is forgotten. "There's you and your sister on the plane, all sleepy," he says as the slide show starts on the computer.

I wince at the huge image of myself with my hair sticking out of a messy bun and bags under my eyes. "It was like three o'clock in the morning, our time," I say defensively. I'll have to sneak in later and delete all the unflattering shots.

"Oh, you look beautiful, as always. Look, here's one of that place we ate dinner that first night. The one in the theater district."

Dad has a comment for every photo. The doorman at our hotel, a series of big red buses, us in front of the nearest tube station. "These are from the walk we took to Piccadilly Circus that evening, remember? Here's the two of you in front of that statue."

I glance at the photo of me and Kat on the cement steps, but something in the background makes me gasp. "Wait, stop." I look closer, a chill running up my spine. "When did you take this one?"

Dad puts the slide show on pause. "Well, they're in order, so that would have made it the second day of the trip." He looks at the photo up on the screen. "That *is* a nice sunset, isn't it? See how the sky is all pink behind the buildings? It almost matches the neon of the signs on the other side."

But I'm not looking at the sunset or the signs. I'm staring at a guy about five feet behind us, casually leaning against the statue, but staring right into Dad's camera. If that was taken on the second day, then it was a full four days before I actually met him at the Tower. I'd thought I might not recognize him, but my heart races as I look at the random stranger with the curly hair and sharp brown eyes lounging in the background of the photo. Griffon.

Four

I don't know where the camera is," Kat says. "It's probably still in my carry-on bag—like most normal people, I don't unpack my suitcase the second I get home." She shoots me a look as she heads toward her room, but I don't want to get into it with her right then. I've waited up late for her to come in, alternately glad that I have a photo of Griffon and totally freaked out that he's there at all. Maybe it *is* just a coincidence. After all, lots of people go to the tourist spots in London. Happens all the time. And then we met him at the Tower because that's where he was staying. I'm just going to tell myself that over and over until I believe it.

I follow her to the back of the house, lowering my voice so as not to wake Mom. "Well, can I see it?"

"What's the hurry?" Kat kicks her shoes off and flops down on her bed.

"I . . . I just want to compare your shots with some that Dad took, that's all," I say.

She studies me for a second. "All right," she says, hauling herself back off the bed. "Let me see if it's in here." She rummages through her bag and tosses the camera case to me. "But don't delete any. I've got some good shots of Owen in there that I want to put up as a screen saver."

Owen. "Have you talked to him?"

"He's been messaging me."

"So he knows how to get ahold of you?"

She looks at me funny. "Yeah. Why? He's a totally hot guy. A totally hot Scottish guy. You never know when he'll end up on this side of the world."

Of course she'd be in touch with him. Why haven't I thought about that before? There's a glimmer of hope stirring somewhere down deep. Owen is only one step removed from Griffon. I hesitate, but I have to ask. "Does he ever talk about Griffon?"

"Sometimes. I know that they've been friends forever. I guess Griffon went home right after we did, but he gets to go back during the summer." Kat smiles. "I wish we could go back this summer. Do you think Dad can get another business trip to London? That would be so cool." I can see that she's already imagining herself with Owen in a chic London flat along with two impeccably dressed blond children sporting adorable British accents.

I turn the camera on and try to sound like I don't really care. "Do you think he ever talks about me?"

Kat puts her arm around me, but it feels more condescending than sisterly. "You really liked him, didn't you? Those curls were

amazing. Made you want to run your fingers all through them."
She looks over my shoulder at the camera display. "No. I don't think
he mentioned you. At least, Owen didn't say anything."

Something about the way she glances away from me tells me
she's lying. Maybe Griffon did mention me, but not in a way she'd
be in a rush to talk about. I shrug. "Not like I really knew him or
anything," I say. "We only hung out for a little while."

"Yeah," Kat says. "You didn't exactly meet him on your best
day."

I don't answer, just start flicking through the photos, searching
the backgrounds for any sign of Griffon. There's Kat at Buckingham Palace, Kat on the London Bridge, me at the symphony, and the
pictures of Owen at the Tower, but nobody in the background that
looks even a little bit like Griffon, at least as far as I can see. I'm
relieved. Mostly.

"Did you find what you were looking for?" Kat asks.

"No," I say, handing the camera back to her. "But that's a good
thing."

∞

"So you have no idea where he lives?" Rayne asks. "Not the city or
the state, or anything? I thought I trained you better than that."

I smile at her. Rayne is always trying to pull me back from the
edge of Loserville. I've spent so much time with the cello the past
few years that it's like I've been dating it instead of boys. Rayne's
trying her best to help me make up for the time I've lost.

"No. He could find out my info through Owen and Kat, but it
looks like he hasn't bothered. It's . . . awkward. I mean, I fainted

right into him. He was just being nice by getting me something to drink. Nothing more to it."

Rayne shakes her head and takes a sip of her extra-hot soy latte. "I don't know. If you're talking about him at all, that means you're thinking about him. A lot." She looks over at me. "You are, aren't you?"

I don't want to have this conversation, but it feels like if I don't share just a little of the feelings swirling inside I'll go crazy. I printed out the picture from Dad's camera and have it in my folder, but I'm not ready to show anyone. Not even Rayne. As much as I don't want to admit that I think about Griffon so much, I can't lie to her. "Yeah," I say. "I guess I do."

"Then you should totally tell your sister to have that other guy give Griffon your number," she says, the excitement building in her voice. "Maybe you two are destined for each other. Ooh, can you imagine how romantic it would be to tell your grandchildren how you met? The Tower of London—where he rescued you."

"Come on, Rayne," I say, looking around to make sure nobody else in the café is paying attention. "Settle down. For all I know he lives all the way out in New Jersey and is a total creep." Rayne's mom has pumped her head full of hippie ideas about destiny and auras and ridiculous things like that, and she's always making a big deal about every little coincidence. Nothing is allowed to just *happen*. Everything has a hidden meaning.

Rayne reaches up and unties her necklace, handing it to me. "Here," she says. "You need this more than I do."

I look at the light pink stone that hangs on a black cord. "Thanks, but pink isn't really my color." I never wear necklaces. The feeling of weight around my neck is always a little suffocating.

Rayne stands up and ties the cord around my neck. "Like it or not, you need it," she says. "It's rose quartz—the symbol of universal love. It attracts positive energy, and that's what you need right now, I can feel it."

I lift the stone and feel it thunk back against my chest. Despite its pinkness, it *is* pretty, and I don't want to hurt her feelings. "Thanks," I say. "Let's hope it works."

"Some people are just meant to be together," she says. "Their spirits search the world for their match, and when they find it, everything else melts away until they're united."

I nod. "Right. I'm sure that's what's going on." Even though I think she's completely nuts most of the time, she is my best friend. My phone chimes, and I reach over to read the text.

"That's weird," I say, reading it again. "Kat wants me to meet her at the shop after work." Except for vacations when she has no choice, the two of us don't exactly hang out.

Rayne downs the rest of her coffee. "That *is* weird. Maybe she needs money. Or maybe she's in some kind of trouble that she doesn't want your parents to know about. That's why she wants you to meet her out of the house."

"I doubt it," I say. But I can't think of a more logical reason.

∞

The glass door is already locked and the CLOSED sign is in the window when I get to the store, so I knock as loudly as I can. Kat has worked at the shop for over a year, but I've only been here a couple of times. It's one of those places that doesn't have much on display, but you know that the few pieces that are here cost way more than you can afford. The owner designs everything from shoes and bags to dresses and scarves, and everything is laid out and lit with tiny little ceiling lights like you're at an art exhibit. I never come into places like this if I can help it.

"Sorry," Kat says as she turns the key in the lock on her side and swings the door open. "I'm cleaning up in the back. Come on in, I'll just be a minute."

The store smells like flowers, and thumping music is playing softly in the background. A woman with long, wavy dark hair is bending over a glass jewelry case, rearranging some necklaces in a velvet-lined tray. She's thin, and has on one of the flowing, sleeveless tops that hang on a wall rack along with dark blue skinny jeans and high-heeled red shoes. Every finger holds a ring that is larger and more colorful than the last one, but she wears almost no makeup that I can see. She's one of those women who can leave the house wearing only a paper bag and make it look like the height of fashion, and because Kat talks about her incessantly, I know it's Francesca, the owner.

"How old is she?" I whisper just loud enough to be heard over the music.

"Twenty or twenty-one," Kat says. "Somewhere in there. She was still going to design school when her father gave her the money for the store." Her eyes soften, and I can tell that Kat practically worships her boss. "She'll make it to the top of the fashion world before she's thirty, guaranteed."

Francesca smiles and walks over to us. "Katherine, you should be done here," she says with an accent that is vaguely European but impossible to place. She smiles at me. "Go and have a marvelous evening with your friend."

"My sister," Kat corrects. "This is Cole."

"So glad you came to see our store," Francesca says, giving me an air kiss on both cheeks.

"Thanks," I say glancing around. "It's really nice."

Francesca puts both hands on my shoulders and looks me up and down. "She has a fantastic figure," she says to Kat, as if I'm not even in the room. "That new tunic would look amazing on her. With some leggings and that new necklace Drew just finished, the one with all of the gears. Ooh! And those gold heels we just got in."

Kat laughs. "Those aren't really Cole's style," she says. "Besides, didn't you sell the Clockwork necklace this morning?"

Francesca puts a finger to her lips and smiles. "That's right, I almost forgot. Got a great price for it, too."

As they look me over, the bell on the front door rings and a guy comes in carrying a white paper sack. It's obvious from the casual way he walks across the showroom floor that he isn't a customer, and after depositing the bag on the front counter, he approaches Francesca from behind and grabs her around the waist. He looks like he'd be right at home on one of those fifty-foot-tall Calvin Klein billboards in Union Square.

"So what are you two looking so happy about?" he says, nuzzling Francesca's neck. He has a smooth Australian accent that goes perfectly with his short blond hair and white teeth.

Francesca squeals and pretends to swat him on the arm. "Only that I sold one of your most expensive pieces," she says, turning to kiss him on the mouth.

"Oooh, nice," he says, pulling back to look at her. "Good thing I stopped at the cupcake shop after I picked up your salad. You deserve an extra commission today."

"If you two are done . . ." Kat steps in. She's smiling like she's only joking, but I can tell that there's more going on here.

Francesca kisses him hard on the mouth. "Mmm. Yes. So sorry. Drew, this is Kat's little sister. Cole, is it?"

I nod. Drew smiles at us, his bright blue eyes crinkling at the edges. "Good to meet you. Francesca would be lost without your sister."

"Not true," Kat says. She looks away and smiles, but the red that creeps up the back of her neck says volumes, and suddenly I know what's up, although it's so obvious I can't believe I didn't figure it out before. She totally has a crush on him.

"We should go," I say, apparently the only one uncomfortable in the slightly awkward silence that has descended on the room.

"Right," Kat agrees, looking around for her bag. "We should go." She grabs her things and we walk out the front door, Kat turning around and making an extra effort to wave to Francesca and Drew through the glass. They're so wrapped up in each other I don't think they even notice we're gone.

"What was that all about?" I say, once the door is shut behind us. "I was standing right there. I'm not a complete idiot, you know. I can dress myself."

"I know," Kat says, giving my clothes another look. "But I

wasn't wrong, was I? I mean, you'd never wear any of the stuff in the shop, would you?"

"Not really the point," I say. I look at the storefronts as we walk. All of the stores are closing things up for the night. "Where are we going that's so important?"

"Just here." Kat steers me into a dimly lit old café. These kinds of places have been totally off Kat's radar until recently. Now all the old things are cool again, and everyone wants a piece of the "authentic" San Francisco. This one has been here for decades, the walls lined with dusty trophies and black-and-white photos of movie stars from generations ago.

Kat pushes a plate of biscotti toward me after she orders our drinks. "I thought you might be hungry," she says, fidgeting with her bag. "My treat."

I bite into a chocolate one and realize how hungry I am. "Thanks," I say, instantly suspicious. Buying biscotti and hanging out at cafés isn't part of our usual routine. Either she's getting worse at hiding things or I'm getting better at figuring them out, because all of a sudden I know that she has a secret. And that it's a big one.

I sit up straighter. "Did you get a tattoo? Because you know Mom and Dad are going to kill you if you did."

Kat laughs, showing her perfect white teeth. "No," she says. "Not yet, anyway." She glances toward the door. "This is a different kind of something."

She's staring over my shoulder when I hear his voice. "Hey, Cole."

I turn to see Griffon standing behind me. He looks exactly as I remember him—brown curls, broad shoulders, and amber eyes that are so intense I have to look away. I don't trust myself to speak, but I manage a weak smile as he sits down in the empty chair. My heart is racing, and I can feel my cheeks getting hot. I'm starting to feel lightheaded, like I'm spinning around way too fast, and the last thing I need is to have a vision right here in front of them both.

"Check it out!" Kat says loudly, with a little squeal. "Griffon lives in Berkeley, of all places! I was *so* lying when you asked about him the other day."

I clear my throat, looking everywhere in the café but at him. "I have to . . . um . . . ," I stammer as I push the chair back and walk as quickly as I can to the safety of the bathroom in the back of the café. Locking the door behind me, I force myself to breathe normally and try to organize my racing mind into something resembling rational thought. I lean against the sink and stare into the mirror until the panic starts to recede. I'm not having a vision. I'm just freaking out.

Griffon is here. In San Francisco. He shows up unannounced in photos that were taken days before we met and thousands of miles from here. Just when I think I'll never see him again, he appears right in front of me, and my first response is to lock myself in the bathroom. Oh God. This line of thinking is not helping me calm down much.

"Cole, what the hell?" Kat says in a loud whisper from the other side of the door. "I go to all this trouble, and now you're making me look stupid."

I lean against the door. "I know. I'm sorry. I'm just . . . surprised, is all."

"So what now?" she asks. "After I brought him all the way over here, what do I tell him? That you have a weak bladder?"

"I don't know," I whisper back. I have no idea how to get out of this without looking like an idiot. "Just tell him I'll be right out."

"Well, hurry. Griffon really wants to see you, so you'd better not screw it up."

I don't answer, because we both know it's too late for that. Walking back into the room, I'm relieved to see he's still sitting there, talking to Kat.

As I get to the table, he looks up and smiles at me. "You okay?"

I grin back just a little. He must think freaking out is part of my normal everyday life. "Yes. Sorry. I just . . ." I let the sentence trail off, because there really is no good answer.

He gets up and pulls my chair back for me to sit down. I've never seen anybody my age do that before. "I should have called first. But Kat wanted to surprise you." He sits back down in his chair. "I guess it worked."

"So," Kat says, glancing at me to make sure I'm not going to run off again. "Turns out that Griffon's mom teaches at Cal." She raises her eyebrows in my direction. "Isn't that cool?"

I look at him straight on for the first time since he walked in. Griffon probably failed to mention that fact the day we met because he didn't ever intend to see me again. Which only makes this whole setup even more embarrassing. "Yeah. That's cool."

"So, um, Kat says you go to Pacific," Griffon says, in an obvious attempt to steer the conversation away from my lameness, an attempt I deeply appreciate. "I was there just a couple of weeks ago for a baseball game." He smiles. "I go to Marina. We beat you guys nine to nothing."

"Yeah, well, Pacific isn't exactly known for its sports," I say, unaware until this moment that our arts magnet school even had a baseball team. I wonder if we've crossed paths on campus. I've never been to any of the games, but maybe he passed me in the hallway or on the sidewalk while I was waiting for my bus. I went halfway around the world to meet someone who lives practically next door the whole time. Rayne is going to love this.

"Cole spends a lot of time in the music department." Kat says it almost like she's proud of that fact.

"Are you in the band?" he asks, and I can see visions of big fuzzy hats and bad polyester jackets passing through his mind.

"Not exactly," I say. I study him for any sign of impatience, wondering why he picked now to tell me the truth. He's probably only doing this as a favor to Owen.

"Cello," Kat says. "Cole's a world-class cellist. She even played with the symphony last year. The real one, not the kid one." I stare at her, not sure who this person is. She looks like my sister, but she sure doesn't sound like her. Kat is the first person to complain about the cello playing, and I've never heard her say anything positive about it in her life.

"Cello?" Griffon raises his eyebrows as if he's adjusting a mental picture.

I'm suddenly flustered and turn my face away from him, feeling overly exposed. "Yes, cello. Something wrong with that?"

"No. It's perfect," he says. *Perfect for what?* I wonder.

"You should invite him to the concert," Kat says. She turns to him. "She's been working nonstop on her solo. It's kind of a big deal."

Griffon tilts his head toward me. "Do I get an invite?"

My face must be about five shades of red as I answer. "Sure, I guess. If you really want to come. It's next weekend. At the Northern California Conservatory. Near the park." I can hear myself rambling, but am powerless to stop.

"Well," Kat says, scraping her chair back. "I've got to go." Subtlety isn't exactly her strong point.

Griffon stands up partway. "Do you have to go too?" he asks me, actually sounding like he wants me to stay.

I look up at the clock, knowing I should get home and finish the hours of homework and practice I have, but wanting desperately not to leave.

Kat jumps in. "It's Wednesday, and Mom doesn't cook on Wednesdays. Tae Kwon Do night." She glances at me. "So you miss a little practice time. Who's going to know?"

"Actually, I'm starving. Want to go and get something to eat?" he asks me. "I've got a couple of hours before I have to get back."

Despite the fact that I know he's only trying to be nice, the thought of spending a few hours alone with him makes my heart race. It's like I've been handed another chance, and I'm determined to keep my mouth shut and not go on like an idiot. "I'd like that," I say, trying not to sound too grateful.

We leave Kat at her car and continue down the street. It feels good to be walking next to Griffon—even though he's a lot taller than I am, he matches his pace to mine so I don't have to rush to catch up. I inch closer to him as we walk, barely into his personal space, but he doesn't move away, just looks over at me and grins. The sidewalks are starting to get busy with the transition from daytime shoppers to people coming home from work. Rolldown doors clatter as the shop owners secure their stores for the night.

"So, what's good around here?" he asks. "I don't get into the city very often."

"Yeah. Apparently you've only been here a few times," I say, parroting his words at the café that day. I know that sounds bitchy, but I can't help it. The mixed signals I'm getting from him are driving me crazy.

Griffon looks embarrassed, which for some reason makes me happy. "Okay, slightly more than a few," he admits. "Look, I'm sorry about that—"

I wave the comment away like I don't even care. Except I'm beginning to realize that I do care. I care a lot. "It's okay," I say. "You don't have to explain."

"I do, though. I should have told you the truth about where I live. But you took off so quickly." Griffon stops walking and stands in front of a gated flower shop, the faint smell of roses still hanging in the air. "Anyway, I knew I'd see you again."

I stop too and study his face, desperately wanting to believe him. "How? You don't even know my last name."

"These things have a way of working out," he says, like it's no big deal. "And I knew that Owen would get your sister's information."

"She might not have given it to him," I say, although that's a complete lie. Kat probably wrote her info in Sharpie across his hand before she left. "You don't know my sister."

"True. But I do know Owen. He would have never let her get away." Griffon flashes a quick smile, then looks around at the buildings on the block. "So, where should we eat?"

Slowly I look around at the street signs and try to figure out where we are. Veronique's boyfriend is Italian, and I'd overheard

Mom asking her about a restaurant in North Beach that's supposed to be nice and not too expensive. I mentally calculate how
much money I have in my wallet and kick myself for not asking
Kat for a twenty. "Do you like Italian?"

"Sure."

"I think it's just a couple of blocks this way," I say, leading us
around the busy corner.

I find the place without any trouble, amazed that for once I
actually remember the name of a restaurant. I can easily memorize all of the notes in an entire concerto, but usually mess up on
little details like book titles and restaurant names. As Griffon
reaches for the front door, his phone rings. He glances down at the
display and then back to me. "I need to get this. Can you give me just
a minute?"

"Sure," I say. "I'll go inside and check on a table."

He smiles. "Thanks. I'll be right there." Griffon walks to the
corner of the building and I hear him answer the call before I
open the door and walk inside.

As I stand waiting at the front desk, Veronique walks out of
the dining room, speaking rapid Italian to a well-dressed man
behind her. At least I think it's Italian. I'm on my second year of
Spanish II, so languages aren't really my specialty.

"Cole! What a coincidence!" she says in English.

"Hey!" I say. "I heard you tell Mom about this place. We were
just around the corner, so I thought we'd give it a try."

"Good choice. The sweetbreads are really good here." She
leans in and whispers to me. "They're actually glands, but don't
let that put you off. According to the experts, that's the sign of a

superior Italian restaurant." She indicates the man behind her. "Have you ever met my boyfriend, Giacomo?"

He gives a smile and a little bow. I don't know if it's the fact that he's Italian or what, but he seems a lot older than she is. "Very nice to meet you. I've heard wonderful things about your musical gifts. It is not often that one meets a true prodigy."

I look down at the worn burgundy carpet, glad that Griffon is outside. It's always so embarrassing whenever anyone mentions cello in real life. "Thank you. And Veronique is doing really well."

She rolls her eyes. "Nice of you to say, but I think we all know the truth." She looks around the front of the restaurant. "Are you here by yourself?"

"No," I say. "I'm with a . . . friend. He had to take a call outside."

Her eyebrows shoot up into her bangs. "Ooh! Boyfriend material? You've been holding out!"

I wish. I wonder what it would be like to say that about him. To be able to introduce him to people as my boyfriend. To walk down the street holding his hand. "No. Just a friend."

"It's always nice to start out as friends," she says, giving me a suggestive look.

I shrug, afraid that if I open my mouth I'll give too much away.

"*Dobbiamo affrettarci,*" Giacomo says, looking pointedly at his watch.

"You're right," Veronique agrees. "We're late. I'll see you tomorrow?"

"Yep. Usual time."

Griffon appears at the door just as they're leaving, and Giacomo holds it open for him. I wave as they walk out into the darkness.

"Who's that?" he asks, glancing back through the window.

"She's one of my students," I say. When he looks blank, I add, "One of my cello students. I teach private lessons at my house a couple of days a week. Veronique is my Thursday at four."

He laughs. "So the prodigy is also the teacher. Nice."

I make a face. "Not really. I just need the money."

"Maybe I can get a couple of lessons?"

"You want to play cello?" I know I sound skeptical, but I can't help it.

"How do you know I haven't always had a burning desire to learn? Maybe I've just been waiting for the right teacher."

"I might be able to figure something out," I say as we're led to our table, trying to suppress the thrill I feel at the thought of seeing him again.

Five

I think," Rayne says, "that you are in *looove*."

"I'm not in love," I say, but there's no way to stop the grin on my face. I can't help but relive moments of last night over and over again during class. The only thing that would have been better is if he'd kissed me, or even held my hand as we waited for my bus. But I keep telling myself that there's time for that. At least I hope there is. He didn't exactly make a date or anything, but he said he'd see me soon. That's almost the same thing, right?

"Don't sit there telling me you're not into him. I know exactly what that look means."

I take a bite of my apple and look around the quad to make sure nobody else is listening. We're sitting on our usual bench at lunch, which is too far from the tables to be overheard, as long as you keep your voice down. "I barely know him," I say. "Besides, nothing happened."

"Nothing?" Rayne grins. "No hands brushing as you both reach for the door? No longing glances?"

"What movies have you been watching?" I ask her. "No. We ate pasta, and then he walked me to the bus." Not that I remembered anything about the restaurant. I could have been eating cardboard for all I'd been paying attention to the food. I look around the quad. "He's not like the guys around here. Griffon's different."

"Did he at least get your number?"

"Yes," I say, not admitting that I'd been checking my phone obsessively since last night.

"Thank God." Rayne picks at her bean salad and eyes my lunch bag. "Are you going to eat that?"

I hand her my chocolate-chip cookie.

"Hello, ladies," Gabi says, sliding onto the bench next to Rayne. I haven't seen her much since we got back. "You two only look like that when you're talking about guys."

"Guy," Rayne corrects. "A gorgeous one that Cole met over break."

"Ooh, gorgeous ones are the best kind."

"Okay, can we stop now?" I ask. The more we talk about it, the more anxious I feel. I unwrap my sandwich and try to change the subject. "How was your break?"

Gabi rummages through her backpack for her lunch. "Boring," she says. "My cousins are in from Mumbai, and we spent the whole time doing tourist stuff in the city. Alcatraz, Fisherman's Wharf, Union Square. If I have to take one more picture in front of one more famous attraction, I'm going to be sick."

"Better than mine," Rayne says. "We went camping up the

coast, and I spent the entire time filthy and freezing." She shivers at the memory. "Hey Cole, what kind of sandwich is that?" Rayne's always on the prowl for something better than the sprouted-wheat and tofu creations her mother makes her.

"Tuna. You want the other half?"

"Um, no. I was reading the other day about how they're overfishing tuna," she says, looking sad.

I chew slowly, getting ready to lose another favorite food. Rayne has a way of making you feel guilty for pretty much everything you put into your mouth. "It's dolphin-safe," I say hopefully.

"Doesn't matter anymore," she says. "The tuna population is getting down so low that if nothing is done in five years, they're going to disappear forever. Like the unicorns."

Gabi and I exchange glances. "Unicorns?" she asks.

"Yeah," Rayne replies. "You know—like how the cavemen hunted the unicorns until they went completely extinct."

I love Rayne, which is good, because sometimes she's so gullible it's scary. She's an amazing artist, but totally clueless about real life.

"Rayne," I say softly. "You realize that there were no unicorns, right? They're just a fairy tale."

Rayne looks confused. "Of course there were," she says. "They became extinct thousands of years ago. Our great-great-great-great-grandchildren will talk about how there used to be big fish called 'tuna' in the oceans, just like our ancestors talked about the unicorns."

Gabi pats her on the back. "Girl, good thing you're book-smart."

"What?" Rayne asks. "Gram wouldn't lie about that." She looks so lost that despite trying desperately to keep a straight face, Gabi and I both burst out laughing.

"I'm sorry," I say, taking another bite. "No more tuna. I promise."

Gabi opens up her thermos and a strong spicy smell wafts over us.

"What is that?" Rayne asks, leaning over to get a better look. "It smells amazing."

"It's saag," she says, poking at it with a fork. "My cousins have been cooking nonstop since they got here. Want a bite?"

"Mmm-hmm," Rayne says, taking a forkful. "Oh man, that's awesome."

I lean over to get some, and the fragrant spices overwhelm me. I take a deep breath and sit back against the concrete wall, feeling dizzy and unmoored. Rayne, Gabi, and the whole school fade until all I can see is a hot, smoky kitchen, the whitewashed walls punctuated with portraits of severe-looking old men.

My mother bends before a cooking pot suspended over a fire, stirring a fragrant stew. Her long black hair is folded into a braid that hangs down the back of her neck and is covered with a loose scarf that she's gathered in one hand so that it won't drag into the flames.

I look down to see my bare feet with their stubby brown toes sticking out of my loose cotton pants. I sit on a chair, far off enough so that I don't get in the way, but close enough to feel the heat from the fire. My stomach is rumbling in anticipation of her good cooking.

With deft fingers, my mother reaches into the fire and flips a piece of flat bread, handing one to me. "For you, my son," she says to me. I smile and reach into the bubbling green stew with a torn piece of bread as the fragrance of the spices make my mouth water in anticipation—

"You okay?" Rayne says, poking me in the side. "You look a little funny."

I shake my head to clear it of the vivid images. The fragrant smell remains, and I realize that it's the same spicy scent that's coming from Gabi's thermos.

"And since when do you speak Bengali?" Gabi asks.

"What are you talking about?" I say, feeling vague and distant. I wonder what they saw while I was out of it. Obviously I didn't faint this time or they'd really be freaking out, but it was probably easy to see something happened.

"Bengali," she says, looking at me sideways. "You were just staring off into space, and you said '*ozasro dhanyabad.*' That means 'thank you very much.' The accent was a little weird, but that's definitely what you said."

The image lurks in the back of my mind, as clear as if it were a movie, except that I knew things about the scene that a person who's simply watching wouldn't. I *felt* things about it. The hunger, the anticipation, the happiness that came from being with my mother in our house. A pang of loneliness remains as I realize I miss that woman. The mother of a little boy who isn't me.

"I, um . . . must have picked it up from the Indian restaurant we go to," I say quickly, trying to cover up my confusion. I look at both of them and attempt a faint smile.

The happiness I've been feeling over Griffon evaporates, replaced by cold, hard dread. A familiar place, a strange smell—it doesn't take much to sweep me into other lives in other times. My mind races, although I know there's nowhere to go. The problem isn't anywhere I can escape from—it's all in my head.

Six

My shoulders relax and I can feel myself swaying to the rich, mellow sound that fills every open space. Flying over the strings, my fingers find the notes on their own as I fight to keep my conscious mind from interfering. My right hand holds the bow as it arcs back and forth, pulling the music from the deeply toned wooden body. As the last note resonates through the room, I hear clapping from the doorway and whirl around in alarm.

"That was amazing," Veronique says, her eyes shining with delight. She walks all the way into the room. "I can't imagine ever being able to play like that."

I pause to catch my breath, feeling wrung out as I always do from the effort. "Thanks," I say, immediately embarrassed. Mom must have let her in. I never play like that if I know anyone is standing there. I can handle playing in front of a few hundred people no problem, but one-on-one where I can see their reaction, where they almost participate in the music with me—no thanks.

"Who's the composer? I didn't recognize any of the score."

I rest the cello's neck against my collarbone and drop the bow back in the case. "It's just something I did a couple of years ago," I say. "Doesn't even have a name."

Veronique begins unpacking her cello, and I wonder if the name 'Bono' stuck. "Well, you can blow it off if you want," she says, "but that was seriously, crazy good. You shouldn't be wasting your time with students like me. You should be playing on stages around the world."

I laugh. "You must be talking to my mother," I say. "She says I was born to be a cellist."

Veronique looks serious. "Mothers have a way of knowing what's best. Maybe she knows what she's talking about." She glances toward the back of the house, where I can hear Mom watching TV. She leans in closer. "It was great to see you down-town last night," she says. "Did you enjoy the restaurant?"

"Oh," I stammer. "Um, yeah, it was great. Thanks for the sug-gestion."

"Glad it worked out." She pauses, but doesn't reach for the bow. "You're such a pretty girl. And so talented. You deserve a nice guy who treats you well."

"Thanks." I can feel my face getting hot. "I guess so. But really, we're just friends." I hope to God that Mom can't hear our conversation. Anything that gets in the way of practice time is off limits in her world, and any kind of boyfriend is at the top of that list.

We begin working on the aria from the Goldberg Variations when Veronique stops in the middle of a bar.

"This part's confusing," she says, lifting her bow from the strings. "I can't seem to get this phrase."

I point to the sheet music. "This one here?"

She shifts the bow and points to another spot on the page. "No, this one."

Our fingers touch just slightly, and I feel a shock, like the ones you get when you've been walking on carpet in your socks.

"Ow," I say, flinching and pulling my hand back. Just as I speak, the smell of the ocean seems to fill the air.

The noise and movement are overwhelming as we step off of the ferry and onto the crowded dock. It seems as if there are hundreds of horses, carriages, men, and women crisscrossing the dusty street in front of us in all directions, and I look for someone familiar to slow my beating heart. Everyone around me babbles in a language I don't understand, and the thought of being lost in an unfamiliar country is enough for panic to set in. I have always longed to see the world beyond our tiny village, but every time I'm thrust into this cacophony of sights and sounds it becomes almost too much for my eyes and heart.

"Welcome to San Francisco," Alessandra says, appearing at my side. She smiles kindly at me and brushes some dust from her good skirts.

"It's so busy," I say, my eyes darting from one scene to the next. "Have you been here before?"

She shakes her head. "No, but trips to Paris, London, and New York helped me prepare."

"Paris!" I say, not able to even imagine something so grand.

Alessandra leans toward me. "I played with Suggia there last spring."

I take in a sharp breath. "Is she as good as they say?"

"Better," Alessandra says with a grin.

She glances over the busy street before us. "You didn't get much time to acclimate before we set off on this tour—you'll get used to it. Still, San Francisco possesses its own rustic charms, I would say."

"And two of this city's most charming attractions look as if they're in need of assistance," Paolo says with a short bow, raising Alessandra's hand to his lips. Turning to me, he makes the same gesture, his brown eyes glancing up with amusement as he grazes my skin. I shiver inwardly and cough in order to cover my reaction.

I fear that Alessandra will be jealous of Paolo's attentions, but she is already turning to the matter of our trunks, which are starting to pile up beside us. As we walk toward the luggage, Signore Luisotti races up, the conductor's usual frantic nature replaced by near hysteria, his customary cigar already chewed down to a nub.

"Idiots!" he shouts, his voice shrill with the rise in volume. "This country is populated by nothing but idiots and fools."

"Relax, Antonio," his wife soothes. Out of all of the adults in our group, Signora Luisotti is always the voice of reason. "We have plenty of time."

Signore Luisotti pointedly takes his watch out of his small vest pocket to check the time. "Nonsense. Signore Sutter is expecting us in two hours, and we still have to make our way to the hotel first. We'll never make it at this rate. Where are the rest of the trunks?"

As his shouts continue, Alessandra's father appears with a flat cart loaded with the missing trunks and instruments.

"Signore Barone!" Luisotti cries, throwing his hands toward heaven. "You are a savior."

"I'm afraid I do have some bad news," Signore Barone says, his mustache drooping as his face falls. "Signorina Catalani's instrument has sustained some damage on this trip."

The rest of our troupe gathers around the cart as he lifts my damaged cello case and sets it on the ground. Even above the din of the ferry dock you can hear an audible gasp as my fellow musicians see the ragged hole in the top of the case that reveals the splintered head of the instrument my parents had spent their life savings to buy.

"Can it be fixed?" I cry against all hope. I look around the circle at the faces full of pity that are turned toward me.

Signora Luisotti reaches over and puts her arm around me. "Perhaps," she says. "But, Clarissa, it will never be the same."

"She's right," Signore Barone says, leaning over to get a better look. "Damage like this would forever affect the quality of the tone."

"What am I to do?" I ask. If I have no instrument, I'll be sent home from the tour, and my dreams of playing in a truly world-class orchestra will be forever extinguished. I can't go back to our village now that I've had just the smallest taste of success. Hot tears pull at the backs of my eyes.

Alessandra puts her arm around my shoulders, and it is all I can do not to cry into her new traveling jacket. "Hush," she says, her voice as soothing as her playing always is. "For tonight and until we can get this matter resolved, you will play your parts on my cello. We are onstage together only for the divertimento, so that is the one piece that will have to be reworked."

I look up at her. "I can't do that." Each instrument is as individual as a fingerprint, and having her make such a sacrifice is unthinkable.

"Nonsense," she insists. "I will hear of no argument. And while this isn't Genoa, there must be an instrument in this city that will serve our purposes, at least in the short term."

"But," I start, wishing that it were all as easy as it sounds, "we . . . I cannot possibly pay for another cello."

Alessandra waves the thought away as if it is a trifle. "My father will be glad to help," she says. Signore Barone looks as if he is going to protest, but she continues quickly. "And we can work out some sort of payment plan as the tour progresses. Right, Papa?"

Signore Barone's face wears an expression of resigned exhaustion. "Of course, my dear," he says. He leans over and kisses her cheek. "Whatever you wish."

She smiles broadly at him. "Then it's settled," she says. She turns to Paolo, standing between the two of us throughout the exchange, his eyes locked on her in an expression of adoration. "Now, what about the assistance I was promised?"

"I'm sorry," I say, looking around the living room.

Veronique smiles like nothing happened. "It's static. I attract it like crazy." She reaches out and puts a finger gently on the back of my hand. "See? It's gone now."

"Right," I manage. "Static." I swallow hard and try to slow my breathing. The black notes on the page look like ants, and make about as much sense right this minute. "Which phrase was it again?"

Veronique points to the music with her bow, this time keeping a careful distance between the two of us. "The transition here, to this D sharp."

It takes everything I have to concentrate on the paper in front of me. "It's like this." I show her the fingering while my mind races with images of carriages and a broken cello. Veronique doesn't seem to notice anything wrong as we finish the lesson.

I close the door behind her just as Mom calls from the kitchen. "Hey, can you go out and grab the garbage cans? I forgot to bring them in when I got home."

Still a little shaky, I call back, "Yeah. No problem."

As I walk down the steps to the street, I try to think about what I was doing when the visions happened. Something is triggering them, but it seems so random that I can't figure out what. Grabbing the can, I turn to wheel it up the curb when I see Griffon sitting on the planter box next to our stairs.

I jump back, losing my balance on the curb. "God! You scared me!"

"Sorry," he says, standing up and walking toward me. "I didn't mean to. Baseball practice was canceled today, so I thought I'd come by."

"It's okay," I say, stepping back onto the sidewalk. I glance up at his face and know I'm not going to be able to keep the grin off mine. "You could have knocked, you know. You didn't have to sit out here."

"I know," he says. "But I didn't want to interrupt your lesson. You play beautifully. Kat wasn't exaggerating."

"What do you mean?"

"The cello. Earlier. I heard you playing just before Veronique came." He points to the half-opened bay window in the living room.

I glance irritably at the window, wondering who else in the neighborhood heard me. I can't believe he spent the last half hour just sitting down here. "Thanks. But I didn't know anyone could hear me." I think for a second. "And how did you know her name?"

"Veronique? You told me. At the restaurant. You said she's your Thursday at four."

"Did I?"

He shrugs. "I have a pretty good memory. Here, let me help you." Griffon grabs the other two cans and follows me to the side of the house, where we park them up against the ivy. As we start to walk away, one can begins to roll toward the sidewalk.

"Whoa!" Griffon yells, and reaches around me to stop it. As he does, his shoulder bumps mine and my eyesight gets fuzzy just for a moment.

The window is nothing more than a narrow slit looking over the courtyard. I sit on the wide stone ledge, my forehead pressed into the small space, watching people come and go down below. Everything inside is screaming, but my outside is calm, my hands folded neatly among the folds of my gown.

I blink, and see Griffon watching me intently. "Has that been happening a lot?" he asks quietly.

"What?" I shake my head to clear it. I can feel beads of panicky sweat trickle down my back.

"That," he says, his eyes locked on mine. "You were somewhere else, weren't you? Just for a second."

"I don't know what you're talking about," I say, running my hands over my hair.

Griffon steps closer. "You said it in the Armouries Café the day we met. The feelings of déjà vu. The blackouts. Strange feelings. Experiencing things you couldn't possibly have seen." He bends down until I can feel his warm breath on the back of my neck. The sensation causes me to inhale sharply. "Look, you don't have to hide it from me," he says softly. "I get it. I understood the minute I met you in London. I've been there. I can help."

Tears fill my eyes as I look up at him. I thought things were getting better, but they aren't. I didn't leave the visions in London—they've followed me here, and are happening more and more often. The thought that Griffon might really understand is overwhelming. I wipe my eyes with the back of my hand, part of me wanting to run inside and slam the door and make it all go away. But I know it's not going away. I have to find a way to deal with what's happening.

"Can you come out for a little while?" he asks. "We need to be alone if we're going to talk."

I shake my head. "No. I . . . um . . . I'm waiting for a friend to come over." Rayne and I are supposed to go to the movies at the Red Vic, but that all seems so far away right now.

"It won't take long," he says. He indicates the house. "I think someone's worried."

I look up in time to see Dad pulling back the curtains in his office that overlooks the front of the house. I wave at him and he tentatively waves back, raising his eyebrows at the sight of Griffon.

Griffon turns back to me. "If you want help—if you want answers, then come with me. If not, then go back in the house and I won't talk to you about this again. But just know that what's happening to you isn't going to stop. It's only going to get worse."

Answers. What kind of rational answers can he possibly give me for what's been happening? Just the slightest possibility that I might find the truth makes me want to give him a chance. I'll be no worse off than I am now. "All right. But I say where we go."

"Fine," he says, with a hint of a smile.

"Wait here, I'll be right back." Trying not to look like I'm rushing, I walk quickly up the stairs and into the house.

I pick up my phone from the table in the hall and walk into the kitchen. "Mom, I'm going out for a little while."

She looks up from her laptop. "Dad called down to say that there's a strange boy out front," she says. "You should invite him in."

More and more I'm regretting their choice of living arrangements. It's like having two spies for the price of one, and the last thing I want to do right now is invite Griffon in to meet her. "Please, Mom," I beg. "Not right now. I promise I'll be careful. Kat knows him and everything." I wave my phone at her. "I have my phone. We're just going for a walk to the park." I give her a kiss on the cheek. "Okay?"

She sits thinking for a few moments before she nods. "Okay. But I want to meet him next time. What kind of a boy comes to a girl's house and doesn't meet her parents?"

"He's just . . . a friend," I say. "No big deal. I'll have him in for milk and cookies next time."

Passing my backpack, I stop and grab the photo of him out of my folder and stick it in my back pocket. As long as we're having an honest discussion, I want to hear his explanation for this, too.

It's still a little shocking to see him standing out in front of my house. "Where to?" he asks as I join him on the sidewalk.

"This way," I say, and begin walking quickly down the street toward the park. It's one of the first truly warm afternoons of spring, and there are more people than usual crowding the sidewalk. Dodging tourists, homeless people, and the guy that always stands out in front of the burrito shop handing out flyers, I soon find myself several yards ahead of Griffon.

"Are you trying to ditch me?" he asks, running to catch up. "For someone so short, you sure can walk fast."

I slow down, but my thoughts continue to race. "What did you mean when you said you'd been there too?"

Griffon swerves to the left to avoid running into a lady with one of those twin strollers that takes up the entire sidewalk. He looks around at the other people on the street. "Let's save that for when we're really alone." We walk silently for a few minutes.

"I love that record store," he says as we pass Amoeba Records. "You know, that place used to be a bowling alley."

"Rock 'n' Bowl," I say, smiling. "My parents are always talking about it. If I hear one more time about how cool the midnight bowling was, I'm going to scream."

We cross into the park and through the tunnel that always reminds me of *Alice in Wonderland*—go into the tunnel from the city and you come out into the country. Well, the park, anyway. People are scattered on every green surface, lying with their faces turned to the sun, taking advantage of the warm evening.

"Down here," I say, heading for the children's play area. It's changed so much since I was little that I hardly recognize it anymore—they took out all of the fun, rickety old wooden play equipment and put in safe, boring plastic stuff. Walking through the play area, I take a left and climb the steep steps that have been carved into the hill next to the long cement slide. This is my favorite part of the park, and the only part they haven't messed with.

"We're going on the slide?" Griffon asks, not at all out of breath after our climb.

"You can if you want," I say. "I'm heading here." I point to a large rock just behind the start of the slide. I sit down on top of it and pull my feet up. From here, you can see the entire play area and part of the meadow, and aside from a little kid or two, nobody is around to hear us.

"Perfect," Griffon says, sitting down beside me as close as he can without actually touching. I can feel the heat from his body, and smell a warm, earthy, boy scent that makes my insides flutter. He's still wearing that black cord around his neck. I can see the outline of the pendant under his shirt, and I wonder if he's maybe some kind of a religious nut with crucifix issues. At this point, an exorcism might not be completely out of the question.

"So," I say quickly before I lose my nerve. "What were you talking about?"

Griffon nods. "Ah, the lady is direct. I like it—no preliminaries." He focuses on a point in the distance, and I suspect it's to avoid looking at me. "It starts this way for all of us, I think," he says evenly. "First some odd feelings that come out of nowhere and seem completely random." He glances at me. "Like the déjà vu we were talking about at the Tower that day." He pauses. "You might feel completely at home in a place you've never been before. Then you might start getting visions of things you've never actually seen, at times in history that you didn't even know existed."

As he speaks, a shiver runs up my spine that makes every hair on my head tingle. "You try to make up rational explanations for everything," he continues. "Maybe you think you're going crazy. Or that you're just dehydrated." He looks at me, and I remember the excuses I gave for fainting that day. "Or that you're seeing ghosts."

I force myself to keep breathing as he talks, closing my eyes so that I can focus on his words. "Any of this sound familiar?" he asks.

I bite my bottom lip and nod, too scared to speak. He's describing everything I've seen and felt for the past several weeks. "So, what is it? If it's not ghosts and I'm not crazy, how can you possibly explain all this away?"

"It's the transition," he says. "Sometimes it goes quickly, and sometimes it takes an entire lifetime. You had a vision the day we met, didn't you?"

I can barely manage a whisper. "It was on the Green," I say. "Everything went dark, and then, as clearly as I can see you, there was a girl, and she was being led up the scaffold . . . there were people, but there was no one to save her . . ." My voice trails off and I can't continue as I remember the tumble of emotions that ran through me as I watched.

"And all of this happened right where the scaffolds were really located," Griffon says.

I nod. "I keep thinking there has to be a logical explanation, right? That it's all just some kind of crazy dream. Even crazy is more logical than . . ." I trail off. Than what?

"There have been other times too, haven't there?"

"Yes," I say slowly. "At first it was mostly just feelings. But the actual visions are coming more and more often. Today at lunch . . . I saw a boy who was watching his mother cook. An Indian boy. One minute I'm trying a friend's lunch, and the next minute I'm someplace else completely. And there have been others—in a concert hall and at a ferry dock."

Griffon stays silent, but shifts closer to me. It's all I can do not to reach out and touch him, but I don't. It feels like I'm on the edge of something big, and as much as I don't want to hear it, I don't want him to stop. I need to get through to the end.

"Think for a second," he says. "The visions that you're having. You didn't really *see* a boy and his mother, did you? That girl being led up to the scaffold . . . you weren't *watching* her, were you? You said it yourself."

All of a sudden I know what he means, even though everything inside pushes against the thought. None of the visions have been like me watching a movie. It's like being *in* the movie. "No," I say, barely above a whisper.

"Where were you when all of these things were happening?" he pushes.

I squeeze my eyes shut, knowing that it makes sense, but not wanting to admit it, because if I admit it, everything changes. Everything I know about life will be different.

"Come on, Cole," he says. "You already know."

"The girl on the scaffold is me," I say quickly. "They were all

me. I'm watching as these things happen to *me*, not other people."
I open my eyes and look at Griffon. He's looking at me with a sad
smile on his face.

"That's right," he says, as if I'm a child who has finally learned
to read. "They are all you." He pauses before continuing. "All of
the things you're seeing happened to you. Sometimes they're big
moments in a life, sometimes they're just small things triggered
by a smell or a place."

It feels like the truth is dangling there in front of me, just out
of reach. All the pieces of the puzzle are right there, waiting to be
put together. "Why has this been happening now? I've gone my
whole life without any of this. Why now, all of a sudden?"

A strand of hair falls in front of my face. Griffon starts to
reach up and tuck it behind my ear, but stops himself the instant
before he touches me. As he pauses, I realize I've been holding my
breath, waiting for the feeling of his fingers on my cheek. "Because,"
he says, folding his hands around his knee. "You're starting to
remember."

I sit on the rock, watching the kids slide down the hill, feeling
like my sanity is slipping away too. Griffon is studying me as I
turn all of this new information over in my mind.

"Starting to remember what?" I finally ask, partly afraid to
hear the answer.

"Other lifetimes. *Your* other lifetimes."

There's a catch in my throat as I inhale, and it feels like the
wind has been knocked out of me. *My other lifetimes.* "Like reincarnation?" I say it softly because I can barely get the words past
my lips.

"Exactly," he says. "Reincarnation. Past lives. All of that. Remembering them is what happens when you become one of us."

I look into his face, trying to find a sign that he's lying. I want to see his eye twitch, or a glance away for just a split second that will tell me that it's not true. That people don't get reincarnated and that the visions I'm having aren't glimpses into my past lives. But I don't see any of that. He's telling the truth. At least, the truth as he believes it. "What do you mean *us*?" I ask. "Who is 'us'?"

"Akhet," he says, looking me straight in the eye. "You're becoming Akhet."

Seven

I take the stairs two at a time, making it halfway down the hill before I even realize I'm moving. Everything Griffon said is so horrifying that there's no way it's the truth. There's no way the girl on the scaffold was me. That I was the one who was executed. That I was actually there that foggy morning, climbing the wooden steps to my own death. Just the thought sends shards of fear rushing through my system.

Griffon runs to catch up. He matches my stride in that familiar way he has and we walk in silence for a minute or two. Slowing his pace, he says softly, "Look, I know it's a lot to take in. And you probably have a million questions."

"Now there's an understatement," I say, walking a little faster.

Griffon continues, even though I've given no sign at all that I still want to talk. "Akhet are people who can remember who they were in the lives they've lived before. It's an Egyptian word that's been used to describe us for thousands of years. We keep our memories while everyone else has to start all over again each lifetime."

I struggle against the tide of questions that are churning through my brain. *Akhet.* I turn the word over in my mind. I know I've never heard it before, but at the same time it's almost familiar. It feels like ideas are going by too fast for me to reach out and grab just one to examine. I stop at the edge of the playground and turn to face him. I feel almost angry, like he's getting something out of making me believe his big joke. "You said 'us.' So you're . . . one too?" I can't bring myself to use the word, as if acknowledging it means that I believe what he's saying. And I can't believe him. It's crazy.

"I've been Akhet for a long time," he says simply.

I watch the kids on the swings at the other end of the playground. I look around at all of the people on the lawn, the stoners playing hacky sack by the pond. This is real life, not some fantasy story. I want him to laugh, to tell me that he's only kidding, to take my hand and squeeze it tight, and let me know that all of this is going to be okay. But he doesn't. He just stands there, waiting for me to make the next move. So I do. "Now that you've gotten the lie out of the way," I say, "do I get to hear two truths?"

"I'm not kidding, Cole," he says, his gaze steady on me. "It *is* the truth. I can help make things easier."

I reach into my back pocket and pull out the photo from Piccadilly Circus. "Were you following us, then?" I ask, holding it out to him. My hand is shaking, and I know he sees it too.

Griffon smiles like he's been caught. "No," he says. "Not really. I was wondering if you'd see me in the picture. We just happened to be crossing the street there that day. Owen and I do that sometimes—get into the background of other people's tourist shots. Kind of like a real life *Where's Waldo*. We must be in hundreds of slide shows all over the world." He touches my image in the photo. "You made an impression, though. Sometimes you can sense when a person nearby is Akhet. So when you showed up at the Tower, I wasn't all that surprised."

"That's a pretty huge coincidence," I say skeptically.

"Coincidence," he repeats, then shakes his head. "I don't think of things that way anymore. Even the word is meaningless. It's not about coincidence. It's about leaving yourself open to possibility. Not letting your conscious mind get in the way."

I rub my eyes with the palms of my hands until colors shoot through the darkness. This is nuts. Akhet? Past lives? Who believes this stuff? I shake my hands out to get rid of some of the nervous energy that's building up inside of me. "I need to get out of here," I say, and turn back toward the path. The sun has started to set over the trees while we've been in the park, and most of the kids have been called away by their parents.

Even more disturbing than thinking he's lying to me is the fact that it all makes so much sense. His explanation feels so right. Like something I've been searching for is suddenly right there in front of me. But I can't let myself believe him. His closeness, the scent of him in the warm evening air, is turning my brain to mush.

"Just take it all in slowly," he says. "It took me years to even get where you are now."

"And where exactly is that?"

"The place where you can get some answers."

"Answers? I can't even figure out the right questions." I'm not religious or anything, but let's say for a second that he's telling the truth. Where does that leave the whole God issue? What about heaven and angels and all that? Who's in charge of how you come back and when? I think about that day at the Tower and the vision I had. Of the visions I've continued to have. "So how did you know that I'm . . . remembering things?" The rough wood of the platform and the smell of the damp grass linger in the shadows of my mind. For everything that's unexplained, I still can't imagine that I'm anyone other than who I've always been. It's impossible.

"When I touched you," he says. "After you fell, I reached out to help you up, and I could feel it." He sighs. "When you touch another Akhet, it sends out a unique vibration. But I could tell from your reaction that you didn't know."

I walk, thinking about the things I'd like to know if all this were really true. How does it happen? Where are the others? Do you ever remember *everything* about your past? "When did you first find out about . . . all of this?" I finally ask, feeling ridiculous even as the words come out of my mouth. I look behind us to make sure that nobody is close enough to overhear. Maybe I can figure out what's going on if I pretend to believe him.

Griffon blows out a loud breath and runs his hand through his hair. "It's been a long time since I transitioned. I haven't thought about that for a while," he says. He goes quiet for a moment. "It happened for me pretty much like it's happening for you—in pieces. I was living in Italy at the time," he says. "I was an older man—back then, forty was considered ancient—and I began to understand what had been happening to me my whole life. I met a woman who knew about it, and she helped me. She was an Iawi Akhet even then." He glances at me. "Sorry. '*Iawi*' are Ahket who have had their memories for many lifetimes."

"When was that?" I ask, understanding that whether or not all this is true, it's at least true for Griffon.

He looks at me as if he's deciding something. "The early sixteen hundreds. Hard to say exactly."

"How old are you now?"

"Seventeen."

"So you've been seventeen for over four hundred years?" Even he must realize how ridiculous that sounds.

He smiles sadly. "No. It's not like I'm a vampire or some kind of immortal. I've been seventeen since February. I've just been seventeen many times before." He stops and looks around. "Everyone has," he says. "It's just that some of us carry the knowledge with us. We remember what other people forget. Most of the time it's a good thing." He pauses. "Most of the time."

"So what happened to her?"

He looks confused. "Who?"

"The woman. The one who helped you back then."

"She died right after we met." A shadow passes across his face, and I can tell that he's thinking about something painful. I sense there's more, so I don't say anything.

"She was killed, actually," he goes on. "For being a sorceress. Back then, you didn't speak of these things in public." He looks around as we emerge from the tunnel back onto the busy street.

"And if you want to stay out of serious therapy, it's better not to talk about it now either."

We cross the intersection and start up the street, each of us lost in our own thoughts. I hear pounding as a bus rolls by us, and looking up, I see Rayne in the window, pointing to the bus stop on the corner.

Griffon sees her too. "Your friend?"

I nod. "The one I was waiting for." We walk to the corner and wait while Rayne pushes through the standing crowd and jumps the last two steps to the sidewalk.

"Hey!" she says, giving me a big hug. "I've been texting you all afternoon."

I feel the outline of my phone in my pocket. I must have forgotten to turn it back on after Veronique's lesson. "I missed it," I say.

"Well, I'm here. I was trying to tell you that I can meet you for the movie after all." She looks pointedly at Griffon, who is standing a few feet away with his hands in his pockets.

"Oh, um, Rayne, this is Griffon. Griffon, this is my friend Rayne."

"*Best* friend," she corrects, and gives him a little wave.

After the introductions, Rayne turns her back on him for just a second to mouth the word "wow" to me, before turning back to face him with a smile. "So, are you coming with us?"

Griffon glances at me, a look of uncertainty on his face. "I don't know," he says. "Am I?"

Rayne grabs his hand in her right hand and takes mine with her left, practically bouncing as she walks. "I think you are. Is anyone hungry? I could use something serious to eat before we go in." Despite my confusion with Griffon and his games, I glance down to where their skin touches and feel a pang of jealousy. This entire afternoon, Griffon made a point of not touching me. He's been avoiding any contact like I'm contagious.

I usually love the slices at the pizza place next door to the theater, but I can barely choke down one bite as I think about everything Griffon said. As Rayne grills him about his life, he keeps glancing over at me with a worried look on his face. The movie isn't much better. I've always wanted to see *Harold and Maude*, but as much as I try to concentrate, my mind keeps wandering back to the conversation we'd had just an hour before. That, and the fact that Griffon is sitting on my right side, his eyes not moving from the flickering screen in front of us, seemingly oblivious to the fact that we're so close it's difficult to keep my hand from accidentally brushing his on the armrest. He looks like a normal seventeen-year-old guy—okay, an insanely attractive seventeen-year-old guy—sitting in a revival movie theater, which makes it even harder to believe what he's been saying.

As the lights come up, Rayne wipes the tears that have been streaming down her face. "Oh. My. God," she says. "That was the most amazing love story."

"It didn't bother you that he was our age and she was eighty?" I ask, vaguely icked out by the romantic parts of the movie.

"No," she says. "They were connected by so much more than mere age. They were destined to be together despite their ages. It was just beautiful."

We walk out of the theater and into the buzz of nighttime in the Haight.

"Did you like it?" I ask Griffon. He's been strangely silent since the movie ended.

"Yeah," he says. "I did." He leans down so that only I can hear. "I liked it the first time I saw it, too," he whispers. "Back in 1971 when it had just come out."

Feeling the warmth of his breath on my skin makes me shudder, and I have to pull away to get control of my emotions.

"Let's go see if we can get a seat at Café Roma," Rayne says. "I need to process some more."

"I can't," Griffon says. "I have to get back."

"Aw, come on," Rayne says. "It's only eight thirty. What in the world do you have to do?"

I freeze. He probably has a girlfriend. That would explain his no touching rule. The thought of him going back across the bridge to be with someone else makes me feel like I've been punched in the stomach.

"I just have to go," he says firmly. "Walk me to the corner?"

Rayne bumps me and glances at Griffon.

"I'll be right back," I say to her, and walk slowly up the street with him.

"You okay?" he asks.

"I guess," I answer, feeling suddenly depressed and over-whelmed. A bus pulls up beside us and we stand back to let people off.

"Hey, when is that concert Kat was talking about? Isn't it this week?" he asks.

"Yeah. Saturday."

"Do I still have an invite?"

"If you want," I say, trying to sound casual. Part of me is desperate to have him come, and part of me—a small part, but still—knows it would be better for both of us if he just got on the bus and didn't come back. Took all of his talk about Akhet and reincarnation and just vanished into the night. "It starts at eight. But you don't have to stay for the whole thing."

"Don't you have a solo?"

"Duet. I'm doing a Massenet piece with my friend Julie on piano."

"Which one?"

I look at him sideways. Except for my conservatory friends, nobody I know has even heard of Massenet. "*Meditation.* From *Thais.* It's no big deal. I think we're last on the program."

"Then I'll definitely be there." There's an awkward silence where a kiss good-bye might happen under different circumstances. The part in the movie of my life where he bends down and brushes his lips lightly against my cheek and I reach up and run my fingers through his hair as I draw him to me. Instead, he gives me a little wave as he gets on the bus. "See you Saturday."

Once he's out of sight, I blink hard and take a deep breath, more convinced than ever that he has a girlfriend on the other side of the Bay. He isn't interested in me that way. Why would he be? Apparently, I'm nothing more than his junior year charity project.

Rayne is buzzing with excitement when I get back to the theater. "So that is *insane,*" she says, bouncing up and down. "Amazing. Did he kiss you? What did he say? Are you going to see him this weekend?" She loops her arm through mine and steers me down the crowded sidewalk. "You have to tell me *everything!*"

I stop for a second, wishing I could. "It doesn't matter anyway—we're not going out, so don't get all worked up. Griffon has some ideas that are not exactly ... normal."

"Ideas about what?" Rayne whispers, completely alert now. Ideas that aren't exactly normal are totally her thing. "Like sex stuff?"

"No!" I say, a little too loudly. "Like ..." I trail off here, unsure about how much I should say. There's no way I'm going to tell her about everything Griffon said, but she *is* my best friend. Even sharing a tiny bit about what's going on might make me feel not quite so bad. "Weird ideas about death. Reincarnation, past lives, things like that."

Rayne looks at me like *I'm* the crazy one. "That's it? So what? So does half of Berkeley," she says. "My mom talks about that stuff all the time—indigo children, past life regression. Damn, in her eyes, that would make him even more perfect."

"Perfect for you, maybe," I say. "But not me."

Rayne shakes her head. "We'll see."

Eight

I pace backstage, more nervous now than I've ever been before a performance. Telling Griffon about the concert was the single worst idea I've had in weeks. Stupid. And distracting. Hundreds of people in the audience never bothers me. Mom and Dad I can deal with. Even having Veronique here is okay. I think about the moment when I told him it was tonight and wish to God I'd shut my mouth. I don't dare peek at the audience. Not only is it unprofessional—and Herr Steinberg would kill me if he knew I was even thinking about it—but knowing where he's sitting will make things worse. Maybe he didn't even come. It's not like he owes me anything. Maybe he just stayed home on his side of the Bay and forgot about the whole thing. That thought alone makes me feel slightly better. Slightly.

Julie appears beside me, dressed in wide-leg black pants and a sleeveless top like I'm wearing, but on her they look elegant, instead of stumpy. The heels I have on help a little, but they also give me one more thing to worry about as I try to walk around without falling. You think that I'd have the heel thing figured out because I'm so short, but heels are one of the things that are in Kat's domain, not mine.

"You ready?" Julie asks, standing up straighter and shaking out her hands.

"As I'll ever be." We step out onto the lit stage to enthusiastic applause. I say a silent prayer of thanks for the lights in the concert hall, because it's pretty impossible to see who's out there, and I can try to concentrate on not letting Julie—and everyone else—down.

As Julie's piano leads into the piece, I pick up my bow and take a deep breath. I love the feeling of this music and don't want to blow it. *Meditation* is from the part in the opera where the heroine is trying to decide whether to go with the monk who is in love with her and renounce her lustful ways or to listen to her heart and be who she is meant to be. In the tempo and the mood you can feel her conflict as the notes soar and fall on the scale, everything rising to a peak and then dropping back. At least, that's the plan.

The first few notes are strong and clear as I draw the bow across the strings, my hands loose, each segment flowing into the next one. As the music gets faster and louder, my fingers become the voice of the instrument, pulling the emotion from the cello, and then slowing down, softer and softer until the notes are almost a whisper. Just a few bars into the piece I give up consciously thinking about what I'm doing and just let the notes flow on their own, knowing that my best performances are the ones where I stop thinking and just go with it. I have to surrender everything and trust that repetition and instinct will carry me through to the end.

Too soon, the last notes fade into the ornate ceiling of the hall, and I open my eyes to the audience's applause. As the relief that always comes from a successful performance fades, I suddenly feel Griffon in the room, can almost hear his hands clapping over the sound of everyone else. Turning my head to the left, the lights aren't as bright, and I spot him right away, sitting several rows from the back, smiling as our eyes meet and applauding even harder. I can feel my face getting hot, and this time it isn't from the effort of playing *Meditation.*

The lobby is humming with people when I finally walk out of the hall. I glance through the crowd, but don't see Griffon anywhere. Not that I'm *looking* for him. I don't want to talk about reincarnation or Akhet. I don't want to have any more serious conversations. Things have been fine the past few days—no blackouts, no strange feelings—and I've almost convinced myself that the whole thing was some weird episode that has now passed. I just want to say thanks for coming all this way on a Saturday night when I'm sure he has better things to do.

"There she is!" Dad calls, waving me over to where he's standing with Mom and Veronique. He puts his arm around me, pulling me in close to him. "That was wonderful, honey," he says. "I literally had tears in my eyes at the end. Just beautiful."

Mom bends down and gives me a kiss on the cheek. "It was

lovely. Although I did sense a little hesitation during the adagio section at the end. I thought you were going to work on that."

"I did," I say quickly, glancing over at Veronique, who looks away uncomfortably. I give Dad's arm a squeeze. "Thanks, Dad."

"Your piece was better than I ever imagined," Veronique says, and I can feel her excitement. "Transcendent. Luminous." She shrugs her shoulders and grins. "I'm totally running out of descriptive words, but you know what I mean."

"Thanks," I say. "And thanks for coming."

"Wouldn't miss it." She glances downstairs. "I'm going for a drink at the café. Can I get you anything?"

"No, thanks," I say, too pumped from the performance to even think of food.

"I'll be back in a second," Veronique says, walking away.

Before I can say anything else, I hear a yell and feel arms drape around the back of my neck. "Awesome, Cole!" Rayne squeals into my ear, practically pulling me down with her. "Loved it! Much better than the usual boring classical crap they play around here."

"Glad to see you're still awake," I say, giving her a hug.

"It isn't easy, but your stuff is worth it," she says, faking a yawn and pulling me away from the group. "Did Griffon come?" she whispers.

"I saw him in the concert hall. But I don't know where he went." At that moment I feel someone watching me from behind, and turn to see Griffon standing a few feet away, a huge bunch of red tulips in his hand. I always thought he looked good in a hoodie and jeans, but seeing him in black pants and an indigo blue button-down shirt takes my breath away.

"Man, he cleans up good," Rayne says, following my gaze. "Go on," she whispers, giving me a little push. "You can't let him just stand there by himself."

"That was amazing," Griffon says as I walk over to him. His eyes are shining with excitement. "Just beautiful." He looks down, as if noticing the flowers for the first time. "Right. Um, these are for you."

"Thanks," I say, taking the bundle and trying to ignore Rayne's yelp as she watches. I've never gotten flowers from a guy before, and I run my finger over the waxy perfection of one of the petals, wondering if red tulips have any particular meaning. Red roses equal love. Do red tulips mean I'm-not-attracted-to-you-like-that-so-let's-be-friends?

Rayne walks over and puts one arm around Griffon. I only wish I could be so casual with him. "Sorry I can't stay and chat, but my mom's coming to pick me up. Nice to see you again." She grins at him and then at me.

"You too," Griffon says. Rayne gives my arm a squeeze as she walks away.

Silence surrounds the two of us as I try to think of something to say. "I'm glad you came," I finally blurt out. Okay, not so clever. But not totally cringe-worthy.

"So am I."

I glance back to see Dad, Mom, and Veronique standing in a small circle staring at us. I figure now is as good a time as any. "Do you want to meet my parents?"

He follows my glance. "Looks like I don't really have a choice." He smiles. "Yeah. That would be great."

"Mom, Dad," I say as we walk back to them. "This is Griffon."

"Nice to meet you both," he says, shaking hands first with Dad and then Mom. Mom smiles at him and raises her eyebrows at me, while Dad just glances at the flowers in my hand and looks suspicious.

"Nice to finally meet you too," Dad says, looking pointedly at me. "Do you go to school with Nicole?"

Griffon stands up straight and puts his hands behind his back. Somebody obviously trained him well in the art of parent-charming. "No, sir. I live over in Berkeley. I go to Marina."

"Berkeley," Dad repeats. "So . . . you know each other from the conservatory?"

"No," I jump in. I don't want to have to explain how we met. Not right now. "Kat knows a friend of Griffon's. By the way, where did she go?" I hope my attempt to change the subject isn't as obvious to them as it is to me.

"She left right after your piece finished," Mom says. "Some work thing she has to do." She nods toward Veronique, who is standing silently off to one side sipping a bottle of water.

"Oh!" I say, knowing I'm going to get a manners lecture later. "Sorry. Griffon, this is Veronique."

"Nice to meet you," Griffon says. As he takes Veronique's hand, a shadow seems to pass over his features, and his easy smile is replaced by a more serious expression.

"Nice to meet *you*," Veronique says, with an emphasis on "you" that is impossible to ignore. I shoot her a look and hope that she doesn't go on about it. "Cole has an amazing talent, don't you think?"

"She does," he says, with a short tone I've never heard before. He seems to be studying Veronique, and I notice his jaw muscles tighten like he's upset about something.

"I, um, have to get my stuff out of the practice room," I announce, suddenly feeling uncomfortable. I can't imagine what's wrong with him. He's usually so polite, but there's a hardness in his eyes right now that freaks me out a little.

As if he's working at it, Griffon's features seem to soften, and he smiles at me, finally taking his eyes off Veronique. "I'll help you," he says. He turns back to Mom and Dad. "If that's okay?"

Dad glances at Mom. "Fine with me. Saves me from having to carry the heavy stuff back downstairs."

Griffon and I walk up the stairs in silence. He seems to be lost in thought, staring off into space as we climb. At the top, he looks back toward the group and leads me to one side.

"How do you know her?" His voice has an edge to it that makes me nervous.

"Who? Veronique? She's one of my students, remember?"

"No, I mean, how did you meet her?" he demands.

I put my hands on my hips. In one quick second, he's gone from sensitive and funny to serious and demanding. "I don't even remember how we met. Why does it matter?"

"It *does* matter," Griffon says, his voice low and his eyes angry. He goes quiet and looks away as another couple passes us at the top of the stairs. He steers me into an empty classroom. "Try to remember."

His intensity makes me stop protesting, although I have no idea what's going on.

"I . . . I'm not sure." His eyes are riveted on my face as I search my brain, trying to remember how we met. "I think she was at one of the conservatory concerts last year. She came backstage and shook my hand, met my parents, and all that. Then a few days later she contacted me through the group saying that she'd heard I was giving lessons."

He takes a step closer, glancing toward the stairs. "I don't think you should see her anymore. Can you make up some excuse— say you've stopped giving lessons, or you need a break?"

I shake my head. "Why? That's crazy. I'm not going to drop one of my students." Forget about the fact that I'm not going to drop the only student who ever pays me on time.

"I can't explain it all now, but you have to trust me. She's not just a regular student. There's more to it. There's a reason she's in your life now."

I think back to all he said in the park. "Wait," I whisper. "You think Veronique is . . . you know . . . ?"

Griffon doesn't touch me, but I feel his urgency all the same. "She is, but not like us. Some Akhet come back only for revenge, to right the wrongs they feel have been done to them in the past. I got a sense of that from her essence. I don't think she's just another random cello student."

I can see the anger in his eyes, and a shiver runs up my spine. At this point I'm not sure if anyone is who I thought they were, especially Griffon. His face is still beautiful, so beautiful that it makes my heart ache to look at him, but everything that comes out of his mouth makes him seem more distant and paranoid. His words are having an effect, just not the one he thinks. "You're scaring me," I whisper.

"Good," he replies, not dropping his eyes from my face.

I push the door open, the air in the room suddenly thick and foreboding. I need to be around other people. As we reach the practice room, Veronique is just coming out. "Hey there," she says cheerfully. "I was just looking for the bathroom."

I glance at Griffon. His face is unreadable. "It's back downstairs," I say. "Just to the right of the main hall."

Veronique smiles warmly. "Right. I should have asked. I'll see you down there."

I duck into the room, put my sweater on, and grab my things. I rush around, pretending to be distracted by looking for stuff, because the last thing I want is to make small talk with anyone here. Griffon stands outside waiting, and by the time I get back, he's more like his regular self.

"Let me carry that for you," he says, reaching for the cello case.

"It's okay," I say. I like carrying the good cello myself. Even Dad has stopped asking to help. It's not that I don't trust people, it's just that if anything happens, I don't want the blame to be on anyone but me.

Griffon seems to read my mind. "I'll be careful," he says. "I know it's expensive."

I hesitate.

"Now you don't trust me enough to carry your cello?"

"It's not that," I say. I look up into his amber eyes. The funny thing is that I *do* trust him, despite all of the things he's said, and all my conflicted emotions. I hand him the cello case, as if to prove it to both of us. "Thanks."

He slides the shoulder strap over his arm and points to the steps. "After you."

I change places with Griffon so that I can walk near the wall.

I hate looking over the railing straight down three stories to the café on the ground floor. Even glancing down from this high up makes me feel woozy. We start down the stairs, but Griffon seems to lose his balance on the third step and lurches for the handrail just as the cello begins to fall.

"Oh my God!" As soon as I realize what's happening, I lean out and try to catch the cello, not thinking about how high up we are, not thinking about anything but stopping it from tumbling down the stairs.

"Cole!" Griffon yells. In a blur, I feel someone reaching out for me and grabbing my arm, but not before I twist and my head hits the railing with a crushing thump. Pain explodes in my right temple and my vision is filled with bright spots as I'm lowered to the floor.

"Are you okay?" Griffon stands over me as my head clears.

I try to shake it off, but that only makes the pain worse. "I think so." I start to stand up but Griffon holds me down.

"Stay there, you might have a concussion," he says, looking around for help.

I put my hand up to the pain in the side of my head and feel a lump already starting to form.

The stairs shake as people swarm around me. It looks like everyone in the place saw me fall. Just great.

"My God, honey, are you okay?" Dad asks, kneeling down.

I sit up on the edge of the step. "Yeah. I'm fine."

"You're not fine," he says, looking into my eyes. "You hit really hard."

"I'll go get some ice," Griffon says. "The café's still open."

Looking through the crowd of people, I watch Griffon take the steps two at a time. When he gets to the bottom, he rushes by the cello's case, which is shoved against the railing at an awkward angle. "My cello!" I try to get up, but the pain in my head makes my knees buckle. "Is it okay?"

Dad glances down the stairs. "I'm sure it's fine," he says. "The main thing is to make sure you're not hurt." That's sweet of him to say, but we all know the main thing is that my insanely expensive cello is currently lying at the bottom of the stairs.

Mom opens the case and lifts the cello out gently. "Looks okay," she calls up. "The case is a little banged up, but otherwise it's fine."

I relax a little, enough to accentuate the pounding in my head.

"What happened?" Veronique asks, slightly out of breath from climbing back up the stairs so quickly.

"I'm not sure." I look at Dad. "Did Griffon drop it?" I should have gone with my instincts on this one.

Dad brushes some hair off my forehead. "Griffon let it fall so that he could grab you," he says. "I saw the whole thing from downstairs. If he hadn't been there, you would have fallen down the whole flight." He leans in and kisses my forehead. "It could have been bad, Cole. Really, really bad."

Mom sets the case gently on the step next to me. "Looks like the shoulder strap broke," she says, holding up the end that should be connected to the case. "A bolt must have come loose. This was not a cheap cello case. You can bet I'll be calling the company in the morning."

Griffon rushes back up the stairs and thrusts a bag of ice in Dad's hand. I wince as Dad holds it gently up to the bump. I'm at that point where I know ice will make it better, but right now it's making my head hurt even more.

Mom leans down in front of me. "Let me see your pupils."

I glare up at her. "Now? Seriously?"

"She's okay, Sofia," Dad says, and for once, she backs down.

I glance down the stairs, and the foyer seems to be emptying. Now that my part of the show is over, I guess it's time for everyone to go home. I hope to God nobody got it on video.

"I'm going to head out," Veronique says. She puts one hand on my shoulder. "You sure you're okay?"

"I'm sure. Thanks."

Griffon is kneeling a few steps down and won't even look up as she speaks. I'm shocked that nobody else can see the waves of hatred coming off him.

"Nice meeting you, Griffon," Veronique says as she passes him on the stairs. He nods, but says nothing. She seems totally clueless. She must just think he's an ass.

After a few more minutes, it's determined that I've been immobile long enough, and they let me get back on my feet. Dad carries my cello and the slightly bruised bunch of tulips, and Griffon gets my bag so that I can keep the ice on the giant knot on my head that's getting bigger by the second. It takes everything I have to convince them not to call an ambulance, and I know that Mom's watching carefully to make sure I don't go into convulsions or anything as we head for the door. The cold night air hits us as soon as we get outside; it must have rained during the concert, because the streets are wet and give off that sharp smell that happens after a downpour.

"Why don't you sit here," Dad says, pointing to a bench just outside the doors. "I'll walk your mom to her car and then get mine so that you don't have to walk to the parking garage." Even when they're going to the same place, Mom and Dad never ride together.

"Sam—" Mom starts to protest, but Dad gives her a look.

"I'll just be a few minutes," he says. He tilts his head toward Griffon. "I'm sure Griffon won't mind staying here with Cole until I get back."

"I think I can manage that," Griffon says. "Again, I'm so sorry about the cello. If anything's wrong with it, I'll be happy to get it fixed."

Dad holds up his hand. "It's fine. I'm just glad you have your priorities straight. I'll be back in a few minutes." Dad hands the case to me, and I prop it up against the wall.

"How are you feeling?" Griffon asks, as soon as my parents are out of sight.

"I'll survive."

Griffon looks into each of my eyes carefully. "Your pupils look okay," he says.

I raise my eyebrows in surprise. "You're a medical expert too?"

He shrugs. "I was a doctor once. I know a few things about head trauma."

I have no answer for that. Reach far enough back into his fantasy and he's probably been just about everything. "I wish you could tell Mom and Dad that," I finally say. "They're going to be waking me up all night to make sure I'm not concussed." I look down at my feet. "Thanks for catching me. What a crazy accident."

Something flashes across Griffon's face. "I don't think it was an accident," he says, traces of anger returning to his voice. He reaches over and pulls out the strap to the cello case. "I think one of the bolts was loosened."

"Oh, come on," I say. He has the same look he did when he met Veronique. "It must have just worked itself loose. Why would anyone do that on purpose?"

He scowls. "Someone who's out for revenge would have no problem messing with a bolt to make it look like an accident."

I stare at him. "You seriously think Veronique had something to do with this?"

"She had the opportunity. She was in the practice room when we came up the stairs. I don't know exactly what it is, but I'm guessing she has a motive. If all goes according to plan, your cello is sent flying down the stairs or over the railing. Having you almost fall after it must have seemed like a bonus. If it wasn't Veronique, then it's a pretty big coincidence."

"I thought you didn't believe in coincidences," I say.

He looks at me out of the corner of his eye. "I don't."

We sit in silence as I replay him meeting Veronique in my head. Everything changed when Griffon shook hands with her. And he won't even touch me. "How can you tell?" I ask. "I mean, I know that you said there's some kind of vibration or something."

"Sometimes you can just get a sense of it. Other times, you actually have to touch the person to know for sure." He stops, like he's searching for an easy explanation. "Basically, once you get used to it, you can see things in someone's essence. You can see whether they're Akhet, and sometimes you can see if you've ever been connected in any way."

"Essence?" I ask. "You mean like the soul?"

Griffon shrugs. "Some people call it that. It's the part of you that you take from one lifetime to the next. Once you have a physical connection, you can get a sense of their essence, usually enough to know something about them."

"I've never felt anything," I say, then remember what happened with Veronique the other day when I had the vision of the concert. "At least, I don't think I have."

"When it's still new to you, recognizing someone's essence isn't easy. And even if you do recognize Akhet you've known before, your relationship can change from lifetime to lifetime. In one life, you might be siblings; in another, business partners. Sometimes you're a boy, sometimes you're a girl. Sometimes you're wealthy, and sometimes you die in poverty."

"What about cockroaches?"

He raises his eyebrows and looks at me. "Cockroaches?"

"Yeah. Like, I'd hate to come back as a cockroach or a snail. A bird might be okay."

Griffon laughs out loud, and it's nice to see the anger leave his face. "I don't think so. I only remember human lifetimes. I've met a lot of Akhet, and so far, they've all been human."

I feel the same stab of jealousy as I picture him holding hands with Rayne outside of the movie theater. "Is that why you always put your hand on someone when you meet them? To try to figure out if they're one?"

"Is it that obvious?" he asks, looking embarrassed. "It's mostly habit now, but yeah. It's like you get even more information through touch than you can with your eyes."

I look away, knowing that if I ask him the next question, there will be no going back. "So why won't you ever touch me?" I ask quietly.

"I've touched you," he answers, a bit defensively.

"Not really," I say. "When you helped me up at the Tower. And just now on the stairs. But never any other time." I watch his face to see if I can figure out what he's thinking, but his emotions are well hidden.

He doesn't look me in the eye as he answers, just keeps his gaze firmly on the street. "It's complicated. There's a lot that you don't understand . . ."

"Then tell me!" I say quickly. "I can take it. You want so badly for me to believe you, but then you won't be honest with me about everything. It's okay if you don't like me . . . like that." I realize too late that that it actually *isn't* okay. My eyes begin to sting, and I realize that despite all of his talk about Akhet and reincarnation, it isn't okay at all. I take a deep breath and will my voice to stay steady. "Look, I understand if you're just trying to help me. Like just a friend or whatever."

At that, Griffon raises his head and looks right into my face. The sight of his eyes intently on mine makes my heart beat faster, and I know that I sound a lot braver than I feel.

"It's not that, Cole," he says. His voice is strained. "You've got to believe me. I just don't want you to get too involved in something . . . in something that might get difficult."

Involved? A flash of annoyance rushes through my body. He tells me crazy stories of past lives, looks adorable while he's apparently saving my ass three flights up a rickety staircase, and then expects me not to get involved? I lean toward him almost imperceptibly. "Newsflash. I'm already involved."

Griffon doesn't say anything for a long moment, just nods slowly. "Do you want to feel what it's like?"

"Feel what?" I answer, confused.

"What it's like to recognize another Akhet," he says. "It might help you believe what I've been telling you."

Damn. I thought I was hiding it better. "It's not that I don't believe—"

"It's okay." Griffon holds his hand up to interrupt me. "I know this all sounds crazy." He looks around at the empty sidewalk, unbuttons the cuffs of his shirt, and pulls the sleeves up. "This is why I've avoided touching you. It can be . . . overwhelming, if you're not ready for it."

Griffon puts his bare arms across his knees and turns to face me. "You can feel it through clothes once you've learned what to look for, but it's easier without."

Trying to avoid the mental image that statement conjures up, I turn toward him on the bench, inches away from his body. His arms are smooth, with strong ropey veins pulsing just under his brown skin. I carefully inch my sleeves up so that my skin is exposed and slowly reach toward him, willing my hands to stay steady and not give me away. So many times I've thought about touching him, about what his skin would feel like. What it would feel like to have him touch me.

Griffon jumps as soon as I touch him, and I can't help smiling at the effect I'm having on him. "Your hand is freezing," he says. "From the ice pack."

So much for the laws of attraction. "Sorry," I say, rubbing my hand on my pants to try to warm it up some. I take a deep breath as I gently place my arms on his, at first feeling nothing but the warmth of his body and the steady beat of his pulse as we connect. I can sense Griffon taking deep, even breaths, almost like he's meditating. His eyes are closed, and I find myself staring at his dark lashes as they rest on his cheek. My heart is pounding so hard that I'm sure he can hear it, that the electricity racing through my blood is going to give me away.

And then I feel something different. At first, it's faint, like a humming from deep inside, but as I focus my attention, it gets stronger and steadier, like the molecules between us are vibrating. It feels like a swarm of bees sounds—alive and thick with energy.

"I can feel it," I whisper, wondering all the time if I'm just imagining things, if all this talk about Akhet and vibrations has got me wanting to find things that aren't really there.

Griffon opens his eyes. "You're really strong. Especially for such a new Akhet." His face is serious, as if he's trying hard to control something. He shifts on the bench and clears his throat. "Once you've been doing it a while, you can sense even the faintest vibrations—like the ones coming from Akhet who don't know what they are yet." He smiles at me. "Pull your hands away slowly," he says quietly. "See if you can feel when it stops."

I lift my hands the slightest bit, and the vibrations grow

fainter. As my arms rise above his, the sensation grows weaker and weaker until, just an inch away from his body, I can't feel it at all. "It's gone," I say, closing my eyes, trying to hide the emotions that are so close to the surface. I already miss the sensation of his skin on mine.

The sounds of the street seem to fade away as I feel Griffon's fingers pushing back my hair, his thumb tracing my cheek. He says nothing, but I open my eyes to see him staring intently at my face, his expression a mix of sadness and relief. Biting his lip, Griffon leans toward me, but just as I lean in to meet him, he pulls his hand away and moves a few inches backward. I sit back too, the reality of what almost happened between us still forming in my mind. My heart feels like it's fluttering in my chest, both from excitement at what might happen and disappointment because it didn't.

"I'm sorry, Cole," he says, looking away from me. "I didn't mean to do that. It's just that I—"

I wait for him to finish the sentence, but the words just hang in the air. "It's okay," I say, feeling the awkwardness fold in around us again. I put the ice pack back up to my head as my headache starts to grow.

Griffon sits back on the bench and studies the oncoming traffic. "Listen, I have baseball practice tomorrow, but it should be over around five. If you can get away, why don't you come over to my house after that? I guarantee you'll get a lot of answers to your questions. Maybe enough so that you'll finally believe what I'm telling you."

I can't help my pulse racing at the thought of seeing him again so soon. "What, do you have some kind of manual hidden away that will give me step-by-step instructions?"

"Better," he says with a mysterious smile as Dad's car swings to the curb in front of us. "I have my mother. She's Akhet too."

Nine

Griffon smiles broadly as soon as I spot him on the sidewalk outside the BART station. Just the sight of him standing there in his jeans and a leather motorcycle jacket is enough to make my heart ache, and I realize in that split second that "want" is quickly being replaced by "need."

"Glad you made it," he says, placing his hand lightly on the small of my back to guide me down the crowded sidewalk, a gesture he never would have made before last night, and one I can't help but notice. Even through several layers of clothes I can feel the steady hum of his touch, and have to concentrate on my surroundings in order not to give in to the sensation.

"It was pretty easy," I say. At first Mom didn't want to let me go out, but the bump on my head was almost gone this morning, so she relaxed a little. I just told her that I was having dinner at

Rayne's, and I feel surprisingly unguilty about the lie. As long as she knows my practice hours are logged in, she isn't likely to check up. Sixteen years of playing the good girl is starting to pay off.

A hint of concern crosses his features. "How's the head feeling?"

"Fine," I say. "Not concussed at all."

"Good. Janine's been running around all day getting supplies for dinner," he says.

"Janine?"

"My mom."

I imagine what Mom would do if I started calling her "Sofia," and it isn't pretty. "Have you always called her by her first name?"

"No," he says. "Not when I was really little. But when I started to be aware that I was Akhet, it just seemed more natural."

"Aren't . . . Akhet . . . always aware?" It's the first time I've said that word out loud, and judging from the look of surprise he gives me, Griffon notices it too. I still think all of this is insane, but I don't have any more rational explanation for what's been happening. At least, not yet.

"Not exactly," he says slowly. "A brand-new baby with the memories of all his past lives would be pretty creepy. Worse than those talking babies on TV."

I grin. I love those talking-baby commercials. "So, what? Is there an age limit? On some special birthday do you get all of your knowledge in one go?"

"No. It's not that organized. I regain my memories really early, like about three or four. I've heard for some Akhet it's later. But it's not in bits and pieces like you're getting it now—it just seems like it's all always been there, like knowing how to walk and talk."

"That must make you one weird little kid," I say.

"It used to," he agrees. "In one lifetime, early on, I started correcting my Latin tutor on his grammar. Here's this six-year-old kid who suddenly spoke perfect Latin. Considering I was Chinese at the time, it really freaked everyone out. My parents were convinced I was possessed."

I laugh. "What did they do?"

"Called in an exorcist," he says. When he sees my expression, he laughs too. "No, seriously, the Taoist version of one, anyway." He shakes his head, remembering. "The guy did the whole bit— starvation, prayer, hours and hours of meditation. After that I learned to keep my mouth shut."

"That's hilarious," I say. "Sad, but hilarious."

"It is," he says. "That's why it's been great having Janine around this time. She's still my mom and all, but it's more of a . . . partnership than anything else." He smiles. "Drives my grandmother crazy."

"She doesn't know?"

"No," he says. "Janine is the only other Akhet in the family. Nana just thinks we're crazy hippies living out in California, smoking dope and dreaming up ways to save the world. Dad knows, though."

I thought about the looks that had passed between them at the Tower that day. Griffon must have said something about me right away.

"It almost makes sense," I say, knowing that making sense is relative at this point because it all sounds crazy. "I just don't remember much. It's like flipping channels on a TV really fast. Just bits and pieces. A scene here and a scene there."

"I think that's normal," he says. "You don't remember everything at once. It can take two or three lifetimes before it all comes
back."

"Do you remember everything? From every lifetime?" Even as
I say it, I'm shocked at how normal this conversation feels. Like
he's telling me about his vacation to Hawaii or something.

He nods. "When you've been Akhet for a while, there are some
things that improve every time you come back. You remember
more things. You have more experience and can do things better.
Quicker."

"What kinds of things? Like psychic stuff?"

"That would be great. But no." Griffon smiles. "We can't read
minds or move anything without touching it. At least, no Akhet *I*
know have figured that out yet. It's more like memory, languages,
numbers, dates. They say that people only use a small percent of
their brainpower. I don't know if that's true or not, but because
of our experience, Akhet use a lot more."

"Sounds like those autistic people who can tell you what day
of the week any date is."

He shrugs. "Sort of. Because I've been alive so many times, I
remember everything I read and experience. Comes in handy
sometimes."

"Right," I say. "You're a genius." I smile just a little. "But can
you tell me what day of the week I was born on?"

"When's your birthday?" he asks, still serious.

"Come on, you can't really do that."

"Hey, you asked. What's the date?"

"August twenty-seventh."

"And you're going to be seventeen, right?" He barely pauses to see my confirmation. "A weekend baby. That was a Sunday."

I stare at him, alternately amazed and a little irritated. For once, I want him to not be able to do something. Not have all the answers. Not catch me as I'm falling. Not be so damn perfect. "Lucky guess. You had a one-in-seven chance of getting it right."

"If you say so." He breaks into a grin so wide his dimples look like parentheses on each side of his face. If there was something more than perfect, it feels like he just attained it.

We stop beside a big black motorcycle parked in the street. Griffon reaches into his pocket for a set of keys and bends down to unlock two black helmets that are strapped to the side. Turns out the motorcycle jacket isn't just a prop.

"This is yours?"

Griffon hands me a helmet. "Yep," he says. "Our house is kind of far from here. Too far to walk. You okay with that?"

I stare at the big silver pipes coming from underneath the solid black body. Mom and Dad don't want me to get my driver's license or even ride in a car with any of my friends who have one because it's too dangerous. They'd kill me if they knew I was even thinking about getting on a motorcycle. "Um . . ." I hesitate, staring at the helmet. I don't want to look like a baby, but I'm not sure what to do.

"You worried I'm going to kill us both?" he asks, tucking his helmet under his arm.

I look from him back down to the bike. "A little," I finally admit. "Or that my parents will."

Griffon takes a step closer to me. "I've been riding motorcycles . . . a long time," he says, glancing around to see that nobody on the crowded sidewalk can overhear. He looks me in the eye. "I'm an awesome driver, and I wouldn't risk hurting you for anything."

I can feel my cheeks flush as I stare into his face, trying to figure out what his words mean. "It's not you I'm worried about," I say, looking out at the cars racing down the busy street.

Griffon pulls his helmet down over his head. "It'll be fun. Are you in?"

I look at the helmet and then at the bike, willing myself to trust him. "I'm in," I say, pulling it over my head, wincing a little as it presses against what's left of the bump from last night.

Griffon pulls his heavy jacket off and hands it to me. "You're probably going to need this," he says. "It's a short ride, but it can get cold." I start to protest, but he pushes it into my hands. "I'll be fine. Just take it."

The fabric inside is still warm from his body, and as I zip the front I'm enveloped in the earthy scent that's uniquely his. I wonder if I can find an excuse to keep it, just for a little while.

Griffon straddles the bike and holds it steady for me. "Just get on the back and hold on to me," he says over his shoulder, his voice muffled by the front of the helmet.

I nod, my head feeling heavy in the helmet, and swing my leg over the seat, grateful that I don't like to wear skirts. Scooting closer to him, I feel his muscles stiffen as our bodies touch. The vibrations are barely noticeable through the leather as I wrap my arms around his waist, but either they're getting stronger or I'm getting better at finding them.

As we merge into traffic, I can feel Griffon's muscles relax as his attention focuses on the road and not on me. Stopping at the first traffic light, I realize that any nerves I was feeling have been replaced by complete confidence in his ability to get us there safely. The bike is steady underneath us, only matched by the power I feel as we gain speed on the asphalt. I wish I could stop time and make this moment go on forever, me tucked against his back as he pushes the bike faster and faster. Too soon, Griffon makes a turn off the main road and down a small side street until he comes to a long driveway beside a large brown-shingled bungalow.

I manage to slide off the bike without falling, and wait while he parks and pulls the key out of the ignition.

"That wasn't so bad, was it?" he teases as I pull off the helmet and pat down any noticeable bumps in my hair.

"No," I grin, handing the helmet back so that he can lock them up. I could get used to this.

He nods to the small red pickup truck that's parked beside the house. "Janine's home."

I realize that I've forgotten to be nervous about meeting his mother until just now. It must show on my face, because Griffon laughs.

"Don't worry, she's cool," he says. "I've already told her about you, and she's excited to meet you. You'll find she's ... different from most parents."

"Different how?"

"You'll see," he says, and leads the way through the small gate and into a courtyard that's filled with tall grasses and bushes dotted with flowers of every color. "Janine's really into naturalized gardening," he explains as we make our way up the path to the front porch. "Her way of relaxing."

As we cross the yard, a small gray cat runs up to us and rubs its head against Griffon's leg.

"Hiya, Spike," Griffon says, bending down and giving him a scratch on the neck.

"He's so cute," I say, listening to him purr. "Is he yours?"

"No. He thinks he is, though. He really belongs to the neighbors." He gives Spike a last pat on the head. "Okay, buddy, we have to go now."

Our footsteps echo on the wide wooden porch as Griffon opens the front door. "Hey," he calls. "We're here."

"Be right there," a voice calls from somewhere in the depths of the house.

I look around at what I can see from the front door. Just ahead is a wide staircase that leads up to a small landing between the floors, where it turns and disappears into the second story. One large wall in the living room is dominated by a moody and incredibly realistic painting of an English street at sunset. Every vertical surface is covered with big African fabric pieces and intricately carved masks. A big woven trunk sits in front of a bright yellow couch covered with mud-cloth pillows.

"Crazy, isn't it?" Griffon says, grinning as he watches me look around the room. "Looks a little bit like a Pier 1 threw up in here."

"I like it," I say, nervously wondering about the woman who matches the décor. I don't have long to wait.

A small African-American woman appears from a back hallway, wiping her hands on a towel that's stuck into the waistband of her jeans. She has on the standard Berkeley black fleece jacket, but her hair is a mass of tiny braids, each with a bead or shell on the end that makes a faint clacking sound as she walks.

"Come on in," she says as she approaches us. "Put your stuff down anywhere. You must be Cole—so glad you could come! I'm Janine."

Her energy is so warm and welcoming that I can't help but relax a little. "Thanks," I say.

Janine grabs my right hand in both of hers, as much to feel the vibrations as a greeting, I suspect. As she touches me, I get a strong sense of excitement and confidence from her.

"Janine!" Griffon's voice has a touch of irritation in it. "Leave her alone. She just got here."

She unclasps my hand, and the feelings immediately vanish. "Settle down, Grif. No harm in trying." A look of concern crosses her face. "How's your head? Griffon told me about last night."

I glance at him, wondering what else he told her. "It's better, thanks."

"Are you hungry?" she asks, leading the way back to the kitchen. "It's going to take me awhile to get it all together, but I've got some snacks laid out on the island."

We follow her back into a brightly lit kitchen dominated by a huge, stainless-steel stove that's covered with steaming pots. Loud hip-hop music is coming from a small iPod in the corner. "I picked up some samosas at Vic's," she says, indicating the fried dumplings laid out on the wooden island top. "We're not having Indian, but I'll use any excuse to get samosas from there. Grif, why don't you grab the plate and go into the front room? I'll call you when it's time to set the table."

Griffon leads me to the living room, which is almost dwarfed by a shiny black baby grand piano. He sets the plate on the coffee table, while I sit on the piano bench and let my fingers wander gently over some of the keys. I don't know much about piano, but even I can tell that this is an expensive instrument.

"Do you play piano too?" he asks, sitting down beside me.

I poke a key so that one lonely note hangs in the air. "No," I say. "Kat did for a while. It's funny; other than the cello, I'm not all that musical. Mom tried to get me to take piano lessons when I was little, but I wasn't that into it."

"Hmm. Guess that rules out you being a concert pianist in another life."

"What, like if I played piano before, then I probably could now?"

"Sure. That's the way it usually works."

I stare at him, wondering why I hadn't thought of it on my own. "You mean, the reason I just 'know' how to play the cello is because I learned in another lifetime?"

Griffon gets up off the bench and walks toward the food. "Probably," he says. "You learn something in one lifetime and you carry it over into the next, sometimes subconsciously. You probably played cello before, and there is enough of a break in your memories that allowed that knowledge to slip through. Bam—instant prodigy."

A feeling of dread starts to grow in my stomach. It makes so much sense. As far back as I can remember, it felt like I just knew how to play, and all I had to do was train my body to match the ability I had inside. "So it doesn't have anything to do with talent or hard work? It's just memory?" It suddenly feels like my whole life has been a lie. The fact that I could play always seemed like magic. I don't understand it, and in a lot of ways I don't really want to, because somehow understanding it might make it suddenly vanish. But now it's like the curtain has been pulled back, and there's an angry little man at the controls. It's not magic at all.

Griffon sees the look on my face. "Memory isn't everything," he says. "You still have to have the passion and the discipline to bring that memory forward in this lifetime."

"But it's not real," I say. "It's like I've been cheating this whole time."

Griffon smiles. "Is it any more cheating than when you didn't know the truth? When you just knew that you could pick up a bow and the notes flew like magic from your hands into the cello?" He looks at my hands and frowns. "Using what you've learned in each lifetime isn't cheating. It's what makes you special."

Except I don't feel special. I feel like a fake.

Ten

So tell me what you know about this Akhet cellist," Janine says as she passes me a bowl full of rosemary-scented potatoes. It's a little disconcerting the way she says it as casually as other people ask about your day at school. How was English? Did you do okay on your test? Do you really think that you wronged Veronique in a past life and she's out to get you?

"I don't know all that much," I admit. I spoon some potatoes onto my already loaded plate and pass the bowl to Griffon. I've never had such amazing vegetarian food before—it's so good that I don't miss the slab of meat that would have gone along with it at my house. I carefully pick the tomatoes out of my salad and put them on the side of my plate, hoping she won't notice. If it was the last food on earth, I wouldn't eat a tomato, but I don't want to insult Janine. "She's just one of my cello students."

Janine doesn't look surprised about Griffon being involved in my life. The way they interact reminds me more of roommates than mother and son—like there aren't all that many secrets between them. "But you've never felt anything from her? No signs of danger, no uneasy feelings?"

"There have been some memories when I'm with her," I say, not really wanting to admit to anyone, even myself, that Alessandra and Veronique might be connected. It makes Griffon's theory that much more possible.

Griffon puts his fork down. "There have been? Why didn't you tell me?"

"I didn't really connect the two of them before. I've had visions of being a cellist. I think I'm from Italy, but we're in San Francisco. There's another girl there, a little older than me. Her name is Alessandra. But this is where it doesn't make any sense: in everything I've seen, she's really nice to me. We're friends. If Veronique really is Alessandra, I'm not seeing anything dangerous at all." I picture Alessandra onstage with her cello. "But if Alessandra could play cello so well in that lifetime, why can't Veronique play it in this one? Wouldn't she carry that with her like you said?"

"Maybe she can," he says. "Maybe she really can play, and is just pretending she can't to stay close to you."

"I think I'd be able to tell," I say. Veronique is getting better, but I don't think anyone can fake it that well.

"Not everything comes through every time," he says. "Especially if you're still a young Akhet. If she's not Iawi, it's possible that she didn't bring that ability with her in this lifetime. Not likely, but possible."

Janine chews thoughtfully and then glances at Griffon. "So you think she's Shewi?"

Griffon shrugs his shoulders. "Not Shewi. She didn't feel like a new Akhet. Rogue, maybe. She's definitely hiding something. Something to do with Cole."

"What do you mean, 'rogue'?" I ask, trying to keep up with the conversation.

"Rogue Akhet aren't part of the Sekhem, the organization most older, Iawi Akhet belong to."

"What's that? Some sort of Akhet secret society?" This was sounding more and more like an Indiana Jones movie.

"Sort of. It's . . . it's more like a way to organize what we're all here to do," Griffon says. "The ways we give back. Fix things."

"Like what things?" I ask. Janine and Griffon exchange glances across the table.

"Everything," Janine finally says. "Everything that humans have helped screw up over the millennia—hunger, poverty, disease, climate change. Anything that threatens our continued existence. Each Akhet becomes specialized over time, using the skills they have to keep improving and working on a specific issue through each lifetime. As your abilities increase, your responsibility to the Sekhem increases." She spears another potato with her fork. "In any case, Griffon isn't usually wrong about these things."

"But how do I find out what Veronique wants?" I say, growing uneasy with the conversation. "And more importantly, what can I do about it?"

"It's hard to say," she says. "Sometimes rogue Akhet just want to disrupt your life. Throw some trouble into it to make up for whatever they feel was done to them." She pauses. "Although Griffon thinks that she wants more than that."

"Her essence feels dark," he says. "I don't think she's been Akhet for all that long—a hundred years maybe, but sometimes newer Akhet are the most dangerous. Like baby rattlesnakes that don't know how to control their poison. Whatever happened between you in the past, I don't think she'll be satisfied with a bump on the head."

Janine frowns. "It's just so unusual for a rogue to be after an Akhet who's so young."

"But it happens," Griffon insists. "Remember that girl who was kidnapped—?"

"No need to scare her," Janine interrupts, smiling at me. "Cole has enough going on without you piling horror stories on top of it."

I look back and forth between the two of them. "So what do I do now?"

"I think you should confront her on your terms," Janine says. "See if you can get some information yourself. That might give you an idea of how dangerous she really is, and what your connection might be."

I think about the vision of the concert. "You mean, like, physical contact?"

"It doesn't take much," Janine says. "Shake her hand. Let your knee brush hers when you're practicing. Let the physical connection open up the possibilities of your psychic connection. Haven't you ever heard the saying 'Keep your friends close and your enemies closer'?" she says, taking another bite. "Makes a lot of sense."

"But won't she block her essence?" I ask, the words feeling

awkward in my mouth. I realize as I say them that I've been acting like I believe everything they're telling me. Like talking about
Akhet and reincarnation is the most natural thing in the world.

"Not if she thinks you don't know what you are," she answers.
"And for much of your relationship, you didn't. Blocking your history and your essence takes a lot of work. Few can keep it up for
very long, and most won't if they don't think there's a compelling
reason for it." She tilts her head toward me. "I can tell that you
have strong abilities, even if your awareness is new."

"Really? Like what?"

"I don't know exactly, but it's all based on advanced physiol-
ogy. When I touched you, I felt that your ability to connect with
others is exceptionally strong. It will grow and refine with time,
until you can control these connections at will."

Griffon smirks. Even that looks good on him. "Janine's working on her emotional intelligence. Some Akhet think that empathic
skills can be learned. Stuff like reading people's emotions and
information, knowing whether they're telling the truth. Sounds
good, but I doubt it."

I remember the sensations when Janine grabbed my hand.
"That's weird, because I felt something when you touched my arm
at the door."

"Like Akhet vibrations?" Griffon asks.

"No," I say. "It was different. More like some kind of energy.
Like emotions that were coming from Janine."

"You did?" Janine looks pleased. "Hmm. I must be getting
better at it, then."

"In any case, it's not safe for you to see Veronique by yourself,"
Griffon grumbles. He catches my eye.

"Won't she think it's weird if you start sitting in on her lessons?"

"I don't care what she thinks," he says.

"Cole may be right," Janine says. "Veronique doesn't suspect anything right now. Seems like she's just biding her time. No need to raise her suspicions unnecessarily."

"Almost causing Cole to fall down an entire flight of stairs isn't exactly biding her time," Griffon says.

"You don't know that she had anything to do with that," I say. "It could have just been me."

"So you don't think that Veronique was involved in the fall?" Janine asks, her dark eyes intent on mine.

"I don't know," I say. "She had the opportunity I guess, but the case could just be defective. It might have been an accident. No one's fault."

"Right," Griffon says. "You keep thinking that." He stands up and begins gathering plates. "I'll do the dishes. You two go relax in the other room."

"Coffee?" Janine asks. I nod. "I'll be right in," she says. "Go through and I'll bring your cup."

"Thanks," I say, and walk into the living room. One whole wall is a floor-to-ceiling bookcase with family photos resting on stacks of books and crowding many of the shelves. Wandering over to take a closer look, I realize that I recognize some of the faces in the pictures. Next to the normal family photos— Griffon at the Grand Canyon, Griffon playing soccer, Griffon on the baseball team—are pictures of people I recognize from the news and the Internet. There's one of Janine shaking hands with Nelson Mandela, and another with Al Gore. An adorable young

Griffon in a suit and tie hugging a woman who looks a lot like
Oprah Winfrey. Guess that really was one of his two truths.

There's one of Griffon surrounded by a smiling Janine and his
dad, still recognizable even without his Warder's uniform. They
made a funny couple—he's all buttoned-up and English and she's
borderline hippie, and I wonder what drew them together. I pick it
up to get a better look.

"Perusing the wall of fame?" Janine asks, setting a steaming
mug on the coffee table.

I quickly put the photo back, feeling guilty for snooping. She
comes over to join me at the bookcase and glances at the family picture. "You wouldn't exactly put the two of us together, would you?"
she says, making me feel a little bad for thinking the same thing.

"I don't know," I say, looking at it again. "Don't they say that
opposites attract?"

Janine laughs out loud. "Lord, I hope so. I think the two of us
will be under the official Wikipedia definition of opposites." She
nods and looks a little more serious. "I still feel bad about how
things worked out. Goes to show that you can't always use your
memories of past lives to make things work out in this one."

"But Griffon said that his dad isn't Akhet," I say.

"He's not," she says. "But I could still see our connection. We
met at a party when I was an exchange student in Scotland, and I
recognized him immediately."

"So you'd been together in the past?" That is *so* romantic. The
kind of thing that inspires thick novels and country songs and
those long, wordy Hallmark cards that Mom loves because they
always make her cry.

She nods. "We'd been lovers a long time ago. I tried to reconnect that thread, but there were too many things separating us in the end." She pauses. "He's been a wonderful father for Griffon, though. And he understands and accepts things in a way that a lot of people wouldn't." Janine shakes her head, as if to get rid of the memory.

A framed drawing to the right of the bookcase catches my eye. It looks like a map of New York City, but it's drawn as a sphere, as if the whole thing is actually a 3-D globe. Hundreds, maybe thousands of buildings, bridges, water, and parks all drawn with detail so sharp I can practically see the trash on the streets. "This is amazing," I say, stepping closer. At first it looks black and white, but as I study it, I see the tiny green squares that are the neighborhood parks and the blue of the river that surrounds the whole thing.

"Isn't that cool? Completely accurate, too," she says. "You could give this to a new cabbie and they could use it to get around the city." She looks closely at it again. "Griffon was only ten when he did this."

"Griffon drew this?" I'm speechless. It's like something that should be hanging in a museum, not as a piece of kid art in a family room.

"He drew it from memory," she says. "We took a helicopter tour of Manhattan one time, and he came up with this a few weeks later."

"That's amazing," I say, but even as the word comes out, I know it's not totally correct. "Amazing" is what you say when someone does a backflip or sings "The Star-Spangled Banner" all the way to the high note in the second-to-last verse without their voice cracking. This is something else entirely.

"That," she says, "is part of being Akhet."

We stand in silence, looking at the photos, until she reaches up to pull a silver frame off a high shelf. "And this is one of my favorite people." She hands it to me—a picture of Janine with her arm around a tall white guy with glasses.

"Who is he?"

Janine brushes some dust off the glass. "Only the man who's going to save us from ourselves," she says, placing it carefully back on the shelf.

"Save us?" For a split second, I'm hoping she doesn't mean that in a Hail-Mary, Praise-Jesus kind of way.

She glances up at his photo with an adoration that scares me a little. "Yes. Save us. If we don't do something soon, it won't matter who is Akhet and who isn't, because there won't be a planet to come back to."

I look at the face of the man in the photo and feel a flicker of recognition. "Didn't he make a ton of money in computers?"

She nods. "Software. But that's not the reason that he's so important."

I wait, but she doesn't continue. "It's not? I heard he owns his own island somewhere."

"The important part isn't how he earned his money, it's what he does with it. World health care, AIDS, poverty, climate change. All of these things are being helped by the money from his foundations." Janine turns to me, her face more serious than I've seen it all evening. "Most of us take the knowledge and abilities we possess to research issues that affect the world. Others use them to make money to support those issues. You can't choose how you are born, just who you become. It's part of our journey as Akhet."

All of a sudden I understand what she's saying. "So, wait. Is he one too?" I look back over the photos in the case. "Are all of these people Akhet?"

She looks back over the gallery and smiles. "Most of them are Sekhem. And the ones who aren't Akhet probably will be in another lifetime or two." Janine reaches up to straighten out one of the photos, and as she turns, I can see an intricate tattoo on the back of her neck—a cross with a loop on the end filled with curling ivy and flowers. As unusual as it is, it also looks familiar. Before I can get another look at it, she moves and her hair covers it back up.

I turn back to all of the photos lining the bookcase. "So you've actually met all of these people?"

Janine nods. "Some are colleagues. Many have become friends over the years."

"But I thought you were only a professor," I say, realizing how bad it sounds the minute it leaves my mouth.

Janine laughs. "I get around," she says. Her smile fades, and she looks serious for a moment. "There's a lot of responsibility that comes with being Akhet. I don't know how much you've talked about it with Griffon . . ."

"Not much," I say. Talking to Janine has made all of the ideas about Akhet and Sekhem seem more real—as long as I don't think about it too hard. Sometimes rational thought can be a liability.

She frowns. "I forget what it's like the first time," she says. "Forgive me if I assume too much."

We sit on the couch, and I pick up the coffee. Cream and sugar, just the way I like it. Janine smiles at me but doesn't say anything as I take a sip and try to absorb everything she's been saying. I can hear Griffon banging pots around as he does the dishes. I try to pick up the thread of our conversation. "So Akhet like Veronique don't join the Sekhem?"

"Not usually. But then again, not everyone does—some Akhet choose a different route. It usually takes new Akhet a lifetime or two to get hooked up with the Sekhem to see if they can serve. But rogues are different. Rogue Akhet usually do what they can to sabotage the good things others are trying to accomplish. Some of them end up the worst of the worst."

"Like who? Serial killers?"

She pauses a minute before continuing, and I can feel her measuring how much information she's going to give me. "Sometimes. Sometimes worse. If they're not stopped, some are capable of widespread destruction." Janine leans forward and sips her coffee. "Pol Pot. Stalin. Bin Laden."

"Like Hitler?" I ask, unbelieving.

"Well, he is your most obvious candidate," she answers.

"All rogue Akhet?" I ask, unbelieving.

"All very old rogue Iawi Akhet," she says. "Every time rogues like these come back, they get stronger and smarter. It may take decades for an essence like Hitler's to come back again, but they always do."

"So the essence that made Hitler who he was back in the thirties might be alive today?"

"Exactly. It might be in the body of an adorable two-year-old girl at this very moment, just waiting to get older. And stronger."

I shiver at the thought. There is one question that has been looming all week, but asking it feels like it would be tearing at the fabric of humanity's most basic beliefs. I take a deep breath.

"Who decides?" I finally manage, not sure if my meaning is clear at all.

Janine tilts her head to the side. "Decides?" she repeats. "About what?"

"About when you'll come back. Who you'll be. How many times." I look around the room. "All of it."

"You're asking if there's a God? Someone who directs our actions? Judges us on what we do in each life, like some sort of final exam?"

I nod, knowing that the next few moments could reveal the mysteries of life that hang over everyone's basic existence.

Janine sips her coffee slowly. "I don't know."

I stare at her. After everything she's told me, it's not the answer I'm expecting. The answer I feel like I deserve. "You don't know? You guys have lived all of these lives before, come back as other people, but you don't know how it works?"

"That's the hardest thing to ultimately understand," she says. "That our knowledge is limited by our experiences. We don't have any sort of direct line to God or Allah or Buddha or whatever deity you care to worship. What happens in the time between lives is the greatest unknown, even to the oldest Iawi Akhet. All I do know is what I've experienced over my lifetimes, and that it's up to me to put that experience to work in this one. It might take a year or it might take a hundred to come back, but so far, I always have."

A feeling of despair settles into my chest. Janine doesn't have any more answers than I do right now. For all of her lifetimes of experience, she hasn't found out any more than I have in sixteen years. It feels a little like a rip-off. Or maybe a cop-out. I sit forward on the edge of the couch. "So where does the . . . essence . . . go if it's not going right into another body? I always figured that for reincarnation to work, you had to go from one body right to the next, like lighting one candle with another."

Janine shrugs. "Hindus believe that the spirit takes time to rest between lifetimes, in some sort of limbo between this world and the next. The Buddhists don't really believe in transmigration at all."

"But what do you believe?"

"I'm still working that out," she says.

Griffon comes in right then, and I suspect that he's been listening at the door. "So, are you clear on everything?" he asks. "All the rules and regulations?"

"Not exactly," I say, trying not to give in to the tired feeling that's setting in. I've come here hoping for some clear answers, but all I'm getting are more questions.

He sits down on the couch, right next to me at first so that I can feel the faint vibrations in the tiny space that separates us. After a second, he glances down and slides over so that there's about a foot between us on the couch. For everything that says about how he feels about me, about us, it might as well be a mile.

"Don't try to get all the answers right away," Janine says. "Just leave yourself open to new information." That's the most Berkeley thing she's said all night. "But be careful."

She leans over and puts her arm around my shoulders. Her vibrations are even stronger than Griffon's, but seem to have a different rhythm—one that's softer, more controlled. "You're welcome here any time," she says. She nods at Griffon. "Despite appearances, you should listen to what Griffon has to say. You'd be wise to trust him."

"I do," I say, without glancing in his direction, the physical distance between us feeling larger than ever.

"Good," Janine says, standing up. "I've got a *Glee* marathon lined up on my laptop, and I want to catch some of it before I go to bed. Lovely to meet you, and I hope we see you again soon."

"Thanks for everything," I say as she retreats to another room.

Griffon sits on the chair next to me and drinks from his own coffee mug. "Do you need to go soon?"

I glance up at the old clock over the fireplace. "Soonish," I say, not really wanting to leave. Despite the gaping chasm that is the space between us, I still hold out hope that I'm not completely wrong—that there was meaning in his gesture last night as I felt us coming together, that I'm not completely delusional. Mom and Dad haven't called yet, but they'll start checking up on me soon. "My parents are still pretty strict about pretty much everything. I wish they could be cooler. More like Janine."

Griffon glances toward the open door. "She *is* pretty cool," he says. "I got lucky this time—I've never had an Akhet in the family before now. Makes things a lot easier."

"She doesn't even seem that much older than we are."

He nods. "I've been Akhet a lot longer than she has, even though she's physically older in this life. Evens things out some."

Griffon stands up and grabs two leather jackets from hooks by the door. "As long as you don't have to be home right away, how about we go for a ride before I take you back to the station?"

I can't hide my smile. Somewhere deep inside of me, hope stirs and stretches. "Sounds good."

Eleven

We wind our way through Berkeley, no longer as congested now that rush hour is over. After passing the University campus, we begin to climb the dark streets higher and higher until we're in parts of Berkeley that I've never seen before. The wind is weak but cold, and I hide as much of myself behind Griffon as I can, sinking into his jacket and letting his shoulders block the breeze. Leaving the houses behind, we enter Tilden Park, driving slowly along the winding roads as the moon throws shadows from the tall trees surrounding us on either side. I don't care where we're going, as long as I can sit quietly behind him, feeling his muscles shift and tense as he eases the bike in and out of turns.

At the top of a ridge, he pulls over into a dirt turnout flanked by giant boulders. Coasting to a stop, he holds the bike steady so

I can slide off the back. As he turns the engine off, the silence surrounds us, punctuated only by the chirping of unseen frogs and the occasional hoot of an owl.

"Have you ever been up here?" he asks, pulling his helmet off.

"I think we used to come up here to ride the train," I say, looking around. "But it's been a long time."

"The steam train is just down there," he says, pointing away from the ridge. "There's a carousel and a little farm too."

"And pony rides." I suddenly remember crying and being taken off a small white pony when I was little. Luckily, this memory is only a few years old, not a few hundred.

I can see his smile in the darkness. "I used to go there too," he says. "I think every kid in the Bay Area had to have their sixth birthday at the Little Farm. I loved those ponies, even though all they did was go around and around in a circle."

"It's amazing how many of the same places we've both been over the years. We might have passed each other a million times at the park or on the street," I say, watching a set of car headlights round the bend below us. "But we didn't meet until we were both in London."

Griffon walks to the edge and looks out at the lights that dot the city below us, then across the dark span of water to San Francisco. For once, the fog has retreated back under the Golden Gate Bridge, and it seems like you can see forever. "Maybe we did meet before," he says. "But the timing wasn't right. Your essence sometimes crosses paths with others through many lifetimes."

I walk a few steps toward the edge and feel my heart start to pound.

Griffon turns to look back at me. "Come here and check out all the lights."

Looking past him to where the solid ground drops out of sight, I know that this is as far as I can go. "I can't."

"Afraid of heights?"

I nod. "Totally." I swallow hard to keep the rising panic down.

"You know I won't let you fall, right?" he says, walking a few steps back to me.

"I know," I say. "It's almost like I don't trust myself. Like I might lose control and jump. I've always been this way." I stand on my tiptoes to look over the edge. "I can see fine from here."

Griffon laughs and moves back beside me. "You're right," he says, looking around. "It's fine from here."

We stand looking at the view from the safety of our spot. "So," I begin, wanting to get back to our other conversation, "do you think we've had a relationship before?"

"No," he says quickly. "I've searched my memories, but I haven't found anything." He looks at the smile on my face. "What?"

"It's stupid."

"Oh, now you *have* to tell me."

"It's just that I don't think I'll be able to get over it if we were like mother and son another time. Or worse."

"Well, don't worry about it. We've never had a relationship before. The fact that you're starting to get some of your memories is probably the reason that we know each other now. Like I said, Akhet are often drawn to other Akhet, even if they don't know the reasons why. Figuring it out is all part of the fun."

I zip the jacket up tighter and set my backpack down at my

feet. It's even colder up here on the ridge, but I'm not ready to go back home. I don't know if I'll *ever* be ready to go back home.

"Have you ever seen so many lights?" Griffon says, scanning the scene below.

"It makes me think of all of the people who are down there," I say. "Hundreds of thousands of them." I shiver involuntarily. "Makes me feel small. Unimportant."

"I know what you mean," Griffon says a little sadly. "You try to do big things, you know? Things that might change the world. But then you come up here and realize that you're just one tiny person in the middle of it all." He turns to look at me. "You're cold. We should go."

"No, not just yet." I glance up at him, feeling the sharp wind but not wanting this night to end. "I want to stay for just a little while longer. It's beautiful."

"Come here," he says, pulling me closer. "I'll keep you warm."

I stand in front of him, leaning my head back almost imperceptibly until it rests on his chest. Even through our jackets, I can feel the hum of his vibrations, and I inhale, trying to keep his scent so that I can remember it when I'm at home alone. I don't care what he can do—if he can name every date on the calendar or have a one-man show at the biggest art gallery in the city. I just know that I want to be with him more than anything I've ever wanted in the world.

After a few moments, Griffon relaxes and slowly puts one arm around me. I can feel his warm breath on the back of my neck as he bends his head down toward mine, and the sensation causes me to visibly tense. Despite the shivers traveling up my spine, I try to stay still, not knowing if he's just trying to warm me up, but not wanting to break the energy that's forming between us.

I try to keep my focus on the tiny lights of the cars as they cross the bridge, but Griffon's fingertips pull my hair aside and his lips brush the back of my neck so gently it seems like I'm imagining it. Barely breathing, I close my eyes as his lips trace my neck and then plant small kisses just below my ear. Unable to stand still any longer, I turn to face him, threading my hands under his jacket until I can feel the warm cotton of the back of his shirt.

Griffon pulls back and looks at me. Even in the darkness I can see the indecision on his face, and I will it to be just a few seconds earlier when his lips were still on my skin.

"I shouldn't be doing this," he says, and reaches behind his back to unclasp my hands. He steps back toward the bike, and I can feel a lump forming in my throat. The moment was perfect, and now it's gone.

"It's okay. You can tell me if you've got a girlfriend."

"It's not that," he says loudly. Griffon rakes his fingers through his hair. "I only wish it were that easy." He paces in the dirt for a few seconds, kicking up little puffs of dust that disappear over the ridge. "I've tried so hard to stay away from you," he finally says, standing several feet away from me. He starts pacing again. "I really shouldn't be doing this—"

I hold my hands up, afraid of what he might say next. "It's okay," I say. "I don't want to do anything to come between you and anyone else—"

"There *is* no one else," he says quickly. "I don't have a girl-friend. Not like you mean it. I haven't had one in this lifetime. Intentionally."

I stand still, waiting for more of an explanation. I find it hard to believe that he's telling the truth, but the look on his face is almost painful.

Griffon sighs and moves closer to me. "Remember when you asked me if I was hundreds of years old? In the park that day?"

I nod. "But you said that you're only seventeen."

"I wasn't lying, I am only seventeen," he says. "But I have memories of being twenty and thirty-five. More than once. Damn, Cole—I've been married before. Been a parent before." It looks like the memories cause him pain. "When I do get involved with someone, I wait until I'm older, until I can meet people whose life experiences match mine."

"It doesn't matter," I say, trying not to picture him with an older woman. "I don't care how old you are."

"It *does* matter," he insists. "It's like a creepy older guy going out with a hot young teenager."

I look down at the ground as he speaks, trying hard to keep the smile off my lips at those last words. "Have you ever told anyone your secret like this?" I ask. He shakes his head quickly. "It's only unfair if you keep the truth hidden. I'm not some poor inno-cent girl who doesn't know anything about you. I know about your past. All of them. Besides, you said it yourself—I'm becom-ing one of you. Soon enough, things will be equal."

I watch him consider this, happy that for once I can tell him something that he didn't already realize. Just as my resolve begins to waver, he walks toward me, his footsteps no longer kicking up dust, but decisive and strong. I say nothing as he bends down and presses his lips against mine in a kiss that feels like it's hundreds of years overdue.

Twelve

A whole week." I flop onto Rayne's bed and grab a pillow, hugging it to my chest like I need something to fill the space that feels so empty. I've been trying so hard not to cry, but every time I think back to last Sunday night, hot tears prick the backs of my eyelids. Everything was perfect. Griffon was there, really there, with me that night, and now he's gone. "It's been a whole week, and nothing from him."

Rayne flops down beside me and strokes my hair. From anyone else, I'd resent the gesture, would hate feeling like a pathetic baby. But from her, it's okay. "Not true," she says. "He texted you on Monday."

I roll over and look up at her. "Okay. Five days. Like that's any better."

"Maybe they had to go somewhere in an emergency," she says.

"Maybe his dad is getting knighted by the queen and they had to fly all the way to England to see it."

"Phones work in England," I say into the pillow. "Face it, he's not into me."

"How can someone kiss you for the first time looking over the whole city and not really like you?"

"I don't know." I can hear my voice straining at the thought and take a deep breath to try to calm down. I've played the whole night over in my head a hundred times. What had I said wrong? Had I done anything stupid? Stupider than usual? "He says all this stuff, kisses me up on the hill, and then it's like he just dropped off the face of the earth."

"Did you call him?"

"No," I say. "I don't want to look needy."

Rayne stares at me. "Mmm-hmm. You're looking like a pillar of strength right now."

I sit up and brush the stray hair off my face. "I just have to deal with it. Griffon doesn't really like me. I'm okay single. God knows I've had enough practice."

"Oh, Cole, I can tell even you don't believe that. There has to be an explanation. I saw you two together."

"Come on," I say, pushing off the bed and sounding a lot more casual than I feel. All of this wondering has built up nervous energy that I have to do something about. "Are we going out or what? I didn't come over here to talk about Griffon all day. Mom gave me money to buy some clothes, and I'm not planning on wasting it." I also don't want to sit around all day staring at my cell wondering if Griffon is ever going to call.

"Fine," Rayne says. "Downtown or the Mission?"

"Downtown," I say, suddenly in the mood for big crowds and chain stores.

Rayne slings her big suede hobo bag over her shoulder. "Let's go."

Even though summer is still over a month away, the cable car turnaround at Powell Street is nearly invisible through the crowds as we get off the bus.

Rayne looks back at me. "You really want to do this?" She's more of a Haight Street shopper than a Union Square one.

"Absolutely," I say, my fake cheerful mood starting to push the heavy weight off my chest. "Let's go this way down Market Street. I've been dying for a cream puff from the guy at City Center. Be nice to me and I'll buy you one, too."

Rayne grumbles but follows me down the crowded sidewalk, bumping shoulders with people as they hurry past. I've always liked this part of Market Street—even though the contents of the buildings have changed, the outsides look the same as they have for the past hundred years.

After a quick stop in the food hall of the City Center, we push through the crowds back outside, licking the remains of the cream puffs off our fingers. "Now what?" Rayne asks, looking up and down the busy street.

As we stand surrounded by tall buildings, I start to feel a tug inside. Not as strong as the visions that I've been having, but a feeling that I'm close to something important. The feeling like I have to go and find something. I've had these feelings before, but have always shrugged them off. Maybe all along I've been getting clues to who I've been—and maybe who I'm going to be. "Feel like walking?" I ask Rayne, both excited and horrified by what we might find. At least if I pass out again, she'll be there to help.

"Depends," she says, watching me carefully. "Where to?"

"Not sure yet." As an experiment, I try to shut down all of my logical thought and let my emotions guide me. I stop on the corner before turning left and heading up Mason Street. Apparently my emotions are guiding me toward Nob Hill.

Rayne rushes to catch up. "Not sure yet, but you're in a hurry to get there?"

"I know it sounds crazy, but I have to go find something," I say, consciously slowing my pace. "Only I don't know what it is."

"Okay, now you're starting to weird me out," she says.

"Welcome to the club." I don't say anything more, just try to focus on the feelings I'm having and the pull that I sense as I walk. I know that if I think about it too much, I'll wreck it. The only sound is our breathing as we make our way to the top of the steep hill. As we get to the top, I see it, almost as if it has a big neon sign on it. I had no idea what I was looking for, but I'm sure I've found it.

"The Fairmont Hotel?" Rayne asks, looking at the international flags flapping above the awning of the huge old hotel. "My mom's friend stayed here once."

"No," I say, looking across the street to the left. "That one."

"What is it?" We join the crowd of people in the crosswalk as the little neon man counts down how much time we have to get across.

"No idea," I reply. I feel calm and excited at the same time.

This is definitely the place. Excitement gives way to familiarity as I stare at the steps that lead up to the big columns supporting the front of the large brown mansion.

"Fancy," Rayne says, looking around. "You planning a wedding here or something?"

I shoot her a look. "Listen, if something weird happens, don't freak out, okay? I'm fine . . . I'll explain it later." Before I can change my mind, I put my foot on the bottom step and slowly make my way to the top. Images of men in top hats and ladies in sweeping gowns flash through my head. And music—cello music. I remember carriages pulling up to these very steps, and well-dressed people greeting each other as they approach the mansion.

I stand at the top of the steps, nervously watching the fine ladies embrace each other as if they haven't met in years. The men stand slightly behind the women, nodding to each other and tipping their hats, the smoke from their obscenely fat cigars circling above their heads in the late afternoon light.

Staring at the finery, I look down at my own borrowed clothing—the unfamiliar dress is itchy on my legs, and the new heels hurt my feet already. I told Signore Luisotti that these aren't clothes for playing cello, but he insisted that it is important to look the part if we are going to impress the best of the best in San Francisco. We've gone over the details a hundred times.

I watch from the side as Signore Barone greets the partygoers as if this is his house, the ice cubes clinking in his drink as he gestures wildly. It seems as though his role in the troupe has expanded from just chaperone to business partner, setting up concerts and rubbing elbows with the rich and famous of whatever city we land in. Smiles flash on the guests' faces, and once again I wish I could understand what is being said. Every now and then someone glances at me and I try to smile back, but I know that it might lead to a conversation, and I'm embarrassed that I only know enough English to order water and ask for the bathroom.

I wander down the main hall, back to where it is quieter. Signore Luisotti wants us to mingle with the guests, but while playing the cello is a pleasure, talking to strangers is not. One of the heavy wooden doors is open a crack, and I slow as I hear familiar voices on the other side.

". . . soon," says Signore Luisotti. "Look at the girl, she is practically a woman. Already tonight one of the hosts asked me how old she is. How much longer can we dress Alessandra in full petticoats and long bows in order to have her pass as fifteen? She is every inch of nineteen, and it is starting to show."

"With all due respect, Antonio," says Signora Luisotti in even tones. "What are we supposed to do? Just turn the girl out of the troupe?"

I hear ice clink in a glass. "And why not? We can hardly call it the Young Masters Orchestra when one of the Young Masters must get her breasts bound before every concert in order to keep up appearances."

I feel someone behind me and turn to see Alessandra standing in the hallway. One look at her face tells me that she's heard them too. She turns to walk away, her shoulders rounded and her head down. I rush to catch up.

"They didn't mean any of that!" I say. I place a hand on her

shoulder, but she doesn't turn to face me. "You are the best musician in the entire troupe. They would never be able to tour without you."

Alessandra finally turns to face me, the remains of tears shining in her eyes. "You're kind. But we both know the truth." She runs a finger over the bow in her hair, an accessory that I've never thought about before, but does make her seem absurdly young. "I can't continue here much longer. All of us have a limited lifespan as a Young Master, and mine is almost up."

"Nonsense!" I cry, pushing the Luisottis's words out of my head. "Besides, Paolo would never stay without you." I see her eyes lift at the mention of his name. "And neither would I. If you leave, you take half the troupe with you. Signore would be left with a few viola players and a second-rate bassist."

Alessandra smiles at that. She puts her hand on my cheek. "So nice of you to say," she says, sadness still lingering in her eyes. "And so untrue. I've had my turn, and it's almost time for me to move on. It's the natural order of things."

I fall forward and embrace her, the clean smell of soap washing over me as I bury my head into her shoulder and she tightens her arms around me. I haven't been held like this since I said goodbye to my mother at the train station so long ago, and the sensation of her touch brings tears to my eyes.

I can feel my cheeks redden as I think over the past few months, the rehearsals, the choice of pieces to play, and the reality of her words begins to ring true. They haven't brought me into the troupe to play with Alessandra. They've brought me here to replace her.

"May I help you?" A slightly angry man appears at the front door to the mansion.

"Oh, I, um, was just wondering what this building is," I say, trying to pull myself out of the vision as quickly as possible. Strong feelings of dread and guilt have settled into my stomach.

"This is the Pacific Coast Club," he says, his tone not inviting any more questions. He pulls himself up to his full height. "Members only."

The Pacific Coast Club. Doesn't seem familiar. I know I'm taking my chances by asking, but at this point I don't have a lot to lose. "Was it ever anything else? Was it called something different?"

"Before the great quake, it was one of the grandest private residences in all of San Francisco. The Sutter Mansion."

I feel a sense of familiarity and know that's it. In the memory I had of the ferry dock, Signore Luisotti mentioned a Signore Sutter. "Thanks."

He pulls his head in the door and closes it with enough force that the sound is solid and final. The carriages and finely dressed people on the steps are gone, replaced by speeding cars and a homeless guy pushing a loaded shopping cart slowly down the sidewalk. I turn and start down the steps, putting my hand on the rough stone railing for balance.

The wind is blowing hard this high above the city. All around us, the sky glows orange from the setting sun, but my eyes are riveted to a tiny figure sprawled on the ground several stories below. Her arms and legs are bent at unnatural angles, and even from here I can see the dark pool spreading out underneath her across the hard stone walkway.

The rushing in my ears seems to block the sound of my own voice. I know I am screaming, but it feels as if nothing is coming out. I lean over the side as far as I dare, hoping against hope that

she will move or twitch—that she will just get up and tell us that
this is all a terrible mistake. The wind seems to steal the sound as
I scream her name over and over.

"Alessandra!"

I feel Rayne shaking my shoulder as I pull myself back into reality. I'm sitting on the steps about halfway to the sidewalk. My eyes are wet with tears, and my throat feels raw as I remember the last thing I saw in that memory. Alessandra died that day, right here at the mansion. Did I have something to do with it?

"Cole! What's wrong?" Rayne's face is full of confusion and concern.

"I'm fine," I say, standing up and brushing imaginary dirt off my jeans. I wonder what this must look like to her, and I hope to God I wasn't actually screaming out loud. "Just slipped." I push past her and walk down the rest of the steps to the relative safety of the sidewalk.

Rayne walks beside me in silence until we reach the corner, but all I can focus on is the image of Alessandra lying dead on the pavement. The air between us feels thick with everything she wants to say, and knowing Rayne, she's not going to keep quiet for long.

"What the hell was that all about?" she finally asks. "And don't tell me 'nothing,' because I'm not stupid. Mom says that I have a gift for reading people, and what I just read over there was definitely something."

I walk just ahead of her so she can't see my face. My mind is whirling with thoughts of Alessandra. "Promise you won't tell anyone," I say, not sure I'm actually going to tell her any of it.

There's no way I would give anyone else even a glimpse of the insanity I've been sucked into, but this is Rayne, after all—the girl who believes in spirit stones and destiny.

"Promise," she says, her mood suddenly solemn.

"I think I'm remembering things," I say. "Things from..." I stop here, not able to say the next part.

"Things like what?" she prompts. "Come on, Cole, spill."

"This is going to sound nuts," I say. I exhale. "Things from other lifetimes."

Rayne whistles. "You mean like spirits? Were you guided there by some kind of spirit? Is that why you look like you saw a ghost when you were talking to that guy?"

"Not like spirits," I say. "More like my own past lives." The words hang between us as I look up to meet her eyes.

She stares at me for a moment before leaning in to give me a huge hug. "Whoo hoo!" she says. "I cannot believe the words I just heard come out of your mouth!" She takes a step back. "This has something to do with Griffon, doesn't it? I remember you saying he's into reincarnation." She pokes me in the arm. "But you said you thought he was crazy."

"I know what I said. And it does sound crazy. But even crazier things have been happening lately, and I . . . I think I believe him. I remember being at a party at that mansion," I say. "Sometime like a hundred years ago. Back when they had horses and carriages."

"Wow," Rayne says. She shakes her head in a sort of grudging admiration. "For years I've heard you laugh at all of my 'stupid hippie' ideas. Who's laughing now?"

It's a relief to share even a little part of the burden I've been carrying around for weeks. Even if I don't tell her about Griffon and the Akhet, it's almost like I'm not alone anymore.

"What time is it?" Rayne asks suddenly.

I check my cell. "About three forty-five. Why?"

"Great. She's probably still there." Rayne grabs my hand and heads for the bus stop. "Come on."

"Who? Where are we going?" I yell as we run to catch the bus that's just about to pull away from the curb.

"You'll see," Rayne says as we find places in the bus's crowded aisle. "It's a surprise."

"I hate surprises."

"You'll like this one."

"Doubtful." I duck down to watch Market Street go by out the window. A few minutes after we turn onto Mission, Rayne presses the stop button.

"This is us," she says, and pushes her way toward the back door.

We land in the middle of the Mission District. I look around at the deserted bars and cheap furniture stores. "And?" I ask.

"This way. It's just down here." Rayne heads off quickly, so I have no choice but to follow her. She stops in front of a pawn broker and rings the bell in a doorway to the right.

"Okay, now I'm totally confused," I say.

"Shhh!" she says as the speaker on the wall crackles. "Hi, Whitney! It's Rayne," she shouts into the metal box.

I hear a muffled reply and the door buzzes open. Rayne holds the door for me, and then leads me up the steep staircase that's just inside the hall. There's soft music playing in the building that sounds like chanting and bells. Hippie stuff. The smell of incense strikes me as we're halfway up the stairs, and I sneeze.

"Bless you." A small woman with curly blond hair and insanely high fuschia heels stands at the top of the stairs in front of what looks like a small apartment. Beside her sits a medium-size black dog.

"Thanks," I say, sniffing slightly. This place is allergy central.

Rayne reaches over to hug her, and then pulls back to introduce me. "Whitney, this is Cole, a former skeptic who is now in total need of your services."

"Services? What services?" I ask, still clueless about why we're here.

Whitney gives a little nod in my direction and smiles. "Former skeptic," she says. "That sounds like an interesting story. Come on into my office." The dog follows quietly as she and Rayne disappear into the next room. Not wanting to be left alone in a strange apartment, I follow.

The small room is bare except for some floor pillows and a low table. A fountain in the corner adds the sound of falling water to the music, and the windows are covered with a sheer, gauzy material. The whole effect makes me want to take a nap. And pee.

"Please. Sit." Whitney indicates one of the cushions.

As we settle onto the floor, I turn to Rayne. "Will you finally tell me what we're doing here?"

"We're going to find out what's really going on," Rayne says.

Whitney looks at me and then Rayne as she absently strokes the dog's head. "So, Cole doesn't even know why she's here?"

Rayne shrugs. "It was a spur-of-the-moment decision. But the minute I thought of you, I knew it was the right thing to do." She turns to me. "Whitney's a psychic. My mom's been coming here for years. I thought she could help you out."

I shake my head. I should have known this would be Rayne's idea of a solution. "A psychic? Seriously?"

"You stand there in the middle of the sidewalk telling me you're remembering things from past lives and *you're* asking me if *I'm* serious?"

I suppose she has a point. I think I'm a little higher up on the unbelievability scale at the moment.

Whitney's impeccable eyebrows shoot up, and she gives me a slightly more engaging smile. Apparently I've sparked a little bit of interest somewhere. "Hmm. Past lives? Intriguing. But you have to let down your barriers in order for me to assist you. That is, if you want to stay at all."

I glance around the room, which looks a lot more like a spa than a psychic's lair. I wouldn't be surprised if she offers bikini waxes along with crystal ball readings. Either one sounds excruciating. "Aren't you supposed to have scary animal heads all over the walls and heavy velvet curtains?"

"And maybe a big turban and a sputtering neon sign in the window?" Whitney adds. She waves her hand. "Strictly tourist trade."

"Don't judge," Rayne says. "The least you can do is give it a try." She nods to Whitney. "Put it on Mom's bill. She won't mind."

"So, what are we going to do?" I ask. "Auras? Tarot cards? Tea leaves?"

Whitney's expression doesn't change. "May I see your hand?"

"Palm reading!" I say. "Perfect." I hold my hand out to her just as Rayne punches me in the arm. The two of them are so serious it makes me want to laugh.

Whitney places her hand under mine, but immediately I can feel her stiffen. I watch as her eyes fly open wide and she gasps, pulling her hand away. "Rayne," she says, "do you mind if I do Cole's reading in private?"

Rayne looks at the two of us, but shrugs it off. "No, that's cool."

"There's some tea in the kitchen. Why don't you start a pot for all of us?"

"Fine. Put me to work and don't share," she says, but she's smiling as she closes the door behind her.

Whitney turns the full intensity of her blue eyes on me. "How long have you known?"

I decide to let her take the lead. "Known what?"

She places her folded hands on the table. "If you're going to mess with me, you might as well go. I can sense that you're aware of what you are, although you seem undeveloped. You're someone who can remember who they've been through the millennia. Someone who has the potential to transcend ordinary human limitations. You're young, but still undeniably Akhet."

I flinch when she says the word out loud. It seems to hang in the air like an accusation.

"What did you just say? What did you just call me?"

"Akhet," she says, her gaze direct.

It feels like all of the air has been sucked out of the room. "So it's true? Griffon wasn't lying?"

"Who?"

"I met a guy, and he's been . . . helping me." At least, he *was*.

"But I didn't believe him. I mean, it sounds crazy—past lives, reincarnation, secret societies."

Whitney searches my eyes intently. "So this boy is Sekhem?" She seems to calm some, and her face grows concerned.

I nod.

"Are you . . . Akhet too?" I didn't sense the same vibrations when she touched me, but she could just be really good at hiding it.

"No," she says. "But I've met several Akhet in my lifetime. Befriended a few. It's a very special calling, and an important responsibility."

There's that word again. Responsibility. I feel a pang of apprehension. "I didn't ask for this. I'm not sure that I even want it."

"It would be nice if you could just hand it all back and say 'no thanks.' But it doesn't work that way. You don't get to choose. You just need to accept what is and try to fulfill your destiny."

Destiny. Responsibility. First I'm destined to be a cellist, now I'm destined to be Akhet. "And how do I do that? How do I even know what it is?"

She smiles. "You have time to find your place in the world. You're still young in this life." Whitney pauses and takes my hand back in hers. She's silent, but her body isn't quiet—it feels like some unseen movement is racing through her still form. "I can sense some of what you're going through. When I touch you, I feel the confusion of many lives churning together."

"Can you tell anything about the lives? Who I was? What I was doing?" The memory of the Pacific Coast Club is still fresh, and I wonder how it all ties into Veronique. *If* it ties into Veronique.

"No. Nothing specific. That's something you're going to have to figure out for yourself as time goes on." She shakes her head as if to clear it. "I also feel abilities growing. Great abilities. I can't tell exactly what, but I feel an empathic spirit."

For a few minutes, neither of us says a word. For all I know, Whitney's thinking about what she's going to have for dinner, but my mind is racing. Images from the Pacific Coast Club rush through my brain, and I think back to what Griffon said in the park. If I had believed him sooner, would it have made a difference? Would it have stopped him from disappearing on me?

"Is there something special about the Akhet you came here to find?" Whitney asks softly.

It's so strange to hear these words coming from someone else, someone who has no connection to Griffon or Janine, who has no way of knowing that she's confirming their story. It makes it seem possible. Real, even.

I raise my eyes to hers, feeling fear and relief flood through my body in equal measure. "No. I think I've already found it."

Thirteen

The crowd at the game is noisy, but I sit a little apart on the bleachers and zip my jacket up tighter. The baseball field faces the Bay, and the wind whips across the water like it's the middle of winter. Griffon's up to bat again, and despite the fact that I'm still mad at him for his disappearing act, I can't help but feel a charge of excitement as I watch him take a few practice swings. I'm not huge into sports, but I could easily learn to be a fan of the tight gray pants they're all wearing. Griffon looks at home in his uniform, and holds the bat like it's an extension of his arm. There's an ease to the way he plays, like he's born to it, and I wonder if this is the first lifetime he's ever played baseball. I'm pretty sure I know what the answer will be.

Despite the cold wind, the sun is shining, and as I wait for Griffon to take his place at the plate, I'm increasingly glad I decided to come after all. When he finally called me last night and asked me to come to his game, I tried to say no, I really did. He can't just kiss me and then disappear for a week and expect things to be okay. I want to be the strong person who doesn't cave the second she hears his voice. I want to be the person who doesn't come running whenever he whistles. Those are all the people I want to be, but I'm failing miserably. Who I am is the person who came all the way out here to sit at a freezing, windblown ballfield because of one phone call.

"Come on, Hall!" "Kill it!" People all around me are shouting his name, and I feel almost proudly possessive watching him play. I look at the other girls scattered on the bleachers and wonder if he knows any of them. If he's ever asked any of them to come to one of his games.

Griffon taps the bat on home plate and then holds it over his shoulder, his eyes riveted on the pitcher. The first pitch goes by him and he doesn't even flinch, just waves the bat in the air waiting for the next one. The ball barely leaves the pitcher's hand before I hear the crack of the bat and the screams of the crowd. Griffon speeds down the baseline as the ball soars through the air, and I can hear excited shouts of "it's going!" all around me. One guy in the outfield races back toward the little fence, and just as it looks like the ball has dropped into home run territory, he knocks it down with his glove.

"He dropped it!" the man behind me screams so loud I can almost hear the veins bulging out of his neck. Never stopping or taking his eyes off the coach, Griffon speeds around the bases, finally sliding into third in a big cloud of dust at the same time the baseman leans out to catch the ball. Griffon jumps up grinning, and brushes the dirt off his pants as the umpire swings his arms wide and calls him safe.

It takes two more batters before the ball becomes airborne again, and Griffon easily makes it from third to home, stepping hard on the plate as he crosses, giving his team the lead that lasts for the rest of the game. They're like little boys as they try to compose themselves for the ritual lining up and shaking of hands with the losing team, breaking into high-fives and chest bumps as soon as it's over. Of all the guys on the team, Griffon is the one who draws your attention, and I know from the way the rest of the team gathers around him that I'm not the only one who thinks so.

The team is barely off the field when Griffon pulls himself away from the group to walk toward me. His curls are sticking out from under his baseball cap, and I can see a line of sweat coursing under his jaw. There are other people still standing near the field, and I wonder if he's going to kiss me out in public like this. If that's still where we are.

I don't have long to wonder. Griffon drops his bag in the dust as he reaches the bleachers, then leans down and kisses me hard, the excitement of the game still shimmering around him. His usual scent is even stronger, and I can feel my heart beating right into my core as his hand brushes mine.

He pulls away, his cheeks red from exertion and a smile playing on his lips. "I'm so glad you came out here," he says.

I look at him in his gray pants and dark blue uniform shirt. It's going to be hard to stay mad at him. "I almost didn't."

A slight look of panic crosses his face. "Really? Why?"

"Oh, I don't know. Maybe because you say these amazing things, kiss me, and then disappear for a week."

"Listen, I'm sorry about that," he says. His eyes lock onto mine. "I couldn't help it. There was something I had to take care of. An emergency."

I search his face, wanting to believe him. It would be so much better to have a crisis—okay, maybe not a *bad* crisis, but still—than to think he just doesn't care enough to call me. "What kind of an emergency?"

Griffon breaks his gaze and looks down. "I can't talk about it right now. There's some stuff I'm involved in, and I couldn't have anyone know where I was. Or be able to trace me."

"What kind of stuff? You're in high school."

"True," he says. "But I also have other responsibilities." Griffon looks around at the crowd that is slowly disappearing. "I can explain it more later." He leans over and takes my face into his hands. Leaning in, he kisses me, gently this time. "Forgive me?"

Looking into his eyes, I know there is no other choice. "For now," I say.

After a long, lingering moment, he pulls back and takes my hand in his. "Good. Are you hungry?"

I've been too nervous about seeing him to eat much so far today. "Definitely."

"I know just the place," he says, and pulls me off the bleachers. He leads me to a familiar red truck.

"No bike today?" I ask.

"No. Janine let me use this." He swings his baseball bag behind the seat. "It's easier with all of my gear."

As he starts it up, I notice the unmistakable aroma of fried rice. My heart starts racing as I recognize the first signs of one of my visions. I *so* don't want to have one now.

Griffon glances at me. "Are you okay?"

I swallow hard. "I'm not sure. All of a sudden I got a really strong smell." I know I look panicky, but I can't help myself.

"Like Chinese food?"

"Yeah. Combination fried rice."

Griffon laughs. "It's the car," he says. "Biodiesel. Janine had it converted a few years ago so that it runs on used cooking oil. She gets it free from a Chinese restaurant on Shattuck, so the car always smells like Chinese food. Sorry. I should have said something."

I laugh too, more out of relief than anything else. I'm not going to pass out and have some crazy vision in front of him again. At least, for the moment. "I'd gain twenty pounds driving this car," I say, my stomach rumbling so loud I'm sure he can hear it.

Even though it's late on a Wednesday afternoon, the streets are packed with college kids shopping or just hanging out. Every corner is filled with vendors selling necklaces or tie-dyed shirts, with ratty cardboard signs advertising their prices. As we pass the head shops and clothing stores, snippets of music blast out onto the sidewalk like an ever-changing radio station.

After a few blocks, Griffon stops in front of a restaurant with big windows that gives diners nonstop street-side entertainment as they eat their meal. "This is the place," he says, holding the door open for me.

The inside of the café is even louder than it is on the sidewalk. I stare at the chalkboard menu by the counter, trying to decide what's the right thing to eat on our semi-official first date.

"You first," Griffon says. "Their wood-fired pizzas are amazing here."

"That sounds good," I say. "I'll have the prosciutto," I tell the girl behind the counter.

"Mushroom and artichoke hearts," Griffon orders. "I've got this," he says, reaching into his pocket.

"No way," I say, not wanting him to think I'm someone who needs to be taken care of. "We'll split it."

"I asked you," he says. He smiles at me and puts a twenty on the counter before I can say a word. "You can get it next time."

The idea that he's planning on a next time makes me almost giddy, but I try not to look it. The restaurant is crowded, and we have to pick our way toward an empty table by the window. Just as we pass a table where two old guys are playing chess, I hear a crash as the board and all of the plastic pieces fall to the floor.

"Crap," Griffon says, looking at the mess. "I'm so sorry." His cheeks are red, but he stands motionless for several seconds, staring at the chess pieces on the ground.

"Just great," the old guy in the plaid cap starts to get up. "There goes the game."

Griffon puts his hand out. "No, wait, I've got this. Just give me a second." He puts the board back on their table, centering it between them, and then picks up the black and white pieces from the floor, positioning each on the board in a different spot, starting off slow but getting faster, until he finishes by leaving a few white pieces on one side and four blacks on the other.

"There," he says, relief in his voice. "That should be right." Griffon studies the board while the old guys stare at him. "Hang on!" he says, and swaps a pawn and a rook. He smiles at them. "Now it's right. Sorry again." He takes my hand and leads me to our table.

I lean toward him as we sit down, watching the old men whisper about him. "Seriously? You put every piece back where it was?"

Griffon shrugs and puts his napkin in his lap. "Yeah. It's the least I could do."

"You know that people are going to think that's weird, right?"

He grins at me. Of course he knows it. "I just saw the board right before I knocked it over, so I remembered where everything went. It's not that hard once you learn how to do it—anybody can."

I stare at him. "Anybody can learn how to memorize an entire chessboard in one second?"

Griffon shrugs. "Well, eventually anybody can."

I shake my head. "If you say so." I glance over to the old guys' table, where they've resumed their game, turning every now and then to look at him.

"Did Veronique come for her lesson on Thursday?"

"Yeah," I say. "It was fine. Uneventful."

"No more memories?"

I hesitate. Telling him that Alessandra died that night at the mansion isn't going to do either of us any good. It won't change anything with Veronique, and it will only make him worry more. "No. Nothing."

"Good." Griffon smiles at me and reaches for my hand across the small wooden table. His fingers gently brush the top of mine, and I feel a surge of electricity run through my entire body. "You have beautiful hands. I'm so glad you let me come to the concert last week."

"It was open to the public," I say with a smile. "I couldn't have stopped you."

"Well, you did an amazing job."

"Julie did," I say. "She works so hard." Practice this week had been difficult, as I listened to every piece carefully, wondering if I'd already played it before in a past life. It makes me feel guilty, like I'm nothing but a big fake. It takes some of the joy out of the whole thing. "Now it just feels like I'm cheating."

"I already told you, it's not cheating. What if some of the people at the conservatory are using memory breaks to become world-class musicians? There aren't that many Akhet in the world, but a lot of the ones who are about to transition show abilities in some way—sports, art, music. A lot of those musical geniuses are just Akhet who haven't realized their potential yet. The only difference is that you're aware of where your abilities come from and they aren't. If you're cheating, then every prodigy who comes along shouldn't be able to do what they were born to do, because they're cheating too."

"It's only cheating if you know you're cheating."

Griffon leans forward and puts his elbows on the table. "Somehow I don't think that's the dictionary definition."

"So what do you do with your abilities?" I ask. "I mean, besides drawing and putting chessboards back together."

"Like I said, I have my responsibilities," he says, tracing an imaginary line on the tabletop. "Things I need to work on from before." He sits back and stops talking as the server comes and places our steaming pizzas on the table. She pauses long enough to give him a smile as she turns to walk back to the kitchen, but Griffon doesn't seem to notice.

"Anyway," he says, continuing our conversation. "You shouldn't feel guilty for being good at something. You should feel comfortable sharing it with the world. Using what you have in each lifetime isn't cheating; it's what makes us valuable. Human beings take thousands of years to evolve, but we get to cram thousands of years of knowledge and experience into every lifetime."

"Maybe." I try to pull a piece of the pizza off the plate, but strings of cheese hang down from all sides.

Griffon laughs. "Need some help?"

I blush, embarrassed that I'm making such a mess. "No. I think I can handle this." The smell of garlic is so strong as I pull the piece free that it makes my stomach rumble. I'm glad that we're both eating the same thing, because I have a feeling I'm going to be reeking of the stuff for the rest of the day—and if there's going to be more kissing involved, which I sincerely hope there will be, I don't want to be the only one with garlic breath.

Griffon cuts a piece of his pizza and holds it out to me. "Want a bite?" he asks, in an obvious attempt to change the subject. He looks at our plates. "Wait a minute, I thought you hated tomatoes."

I think back to the dinner at his house. I thought I'd been so sly about pushing the tomatoes off to one side of the plate. "You noticed?" I ask, immediately embarrassed.

"Just a little. Don't worry. Janine didn't mind."

"I only hate regular tomatoes. Mashed up in sauce is fine."

Griffon looks thoughtful. "Maybe you had a bad tomato experience in a past life. Could be that you choked on one once, and that's why you don't like them now."

I love the thought that everything has a meaning, a purpose. Whatever you're experiencing in this lifetime somehow, some way, has ties to another past. "Really? You think so?"

"No." Griffon laughs. "I'm kidding. Not everything has a hidden meaning. Sometimes hating tomatoes in this lifetime just means that you really don't like tomatoes."

I make a face at him as I slide the piece from his fork and pop it into my mouth. "Like Freud said, sometimes a cigar is just a cigar."

"Exactly. Sometimes a tomato is just a tomato. Speaking of, how is it?"

"It's good. Want some of mine?"

"No, thanks," he says, and in that second I remember the vegetarian meal that Janine made.

"Oh, God! You're a vegetarian aren't you? I'm so stupid."

"You're not stupid," he says. "I'm not that good at it anyway."

I laugh at his attempt to make me feel better. "Not good at it?"

"Nope." He shakes his head. "I get all of Janine's reasons, and she's right. Bad for the environment, bad for animals, not part of what we're doing to make the world a better place, all of that. But sometimes I just need to sneak down to the diner down on Fourth Street and get a big fat BLT."

"So you're a vegetarian with a weakness for bacon?"

Griffon shrugs. "I try."

We finish our pizzas and emerge back into the hustle of the late afternoon sidewalk. Wandering up the street, we stop in a few shops, although I have a hard time concentrating on anything that's for sale whenever Griffon is close to me. As we walk, our shoulders brush, but he makes no move to hold my hand again, so I try to keep my mind on other things.

"Can we go in here a second?" I ask as we pass a huge record shop. "My dad's birthday is in a couple of weeks, and he collects vintage records. He'll be shocked if I get him something he might actually like."

The amount of stuff crammed into the store is visually overwhelming, and it takes a second to be able to focus on any individual thing.

"What kind of music does your dad like?" Griffon asks, scanning the rows and rows of album covers.

"Mostly classic rock," I say, wishing I'd paid more attention to his collection upstairs. "You know, Pink Floyd, Led Zeppelin. Seventies stuff."

"Got it." He walks over to a table and starts flipping through the covers. "This one's good," he says, handing me a cover. "Or this one. God, I haven't seen that one in ages."

I flip the two records over. "MC5? The Stooges? I haven't heard of either one of these."

"They're awesome," he says. "Trust me. Does he have them?"

"I don't think so," I say. I look at both covers. "Which one do you think is best?"

"Well, if he likes Zeppelin, then I'd go for MC5," he says. "A little faster pre-punk style, but still cool." He leans over toward me so that nobody can hear. Griffon taps the album. "I had this very same record back then." He laughs. "It'd be funny if it really is mine, wouldn't it? Somehow it landed at this record store and here I am, holding it all over again. You never know."

I watch him as he turns to walk down another aisle, wondering how I'd feel with so much of my past life set out in front of me. I look down at the unfamiliar record in my hands and wonder if I'd been alive in the seventies. And if I'll ever remember if I was.

"Janine said that sometimes people don't come back for years," I say quietly, catching up. "But it sounds like you were just here."

"I was," he says. "My last life finished in 1986 when I was forty-two." He glanced at me. "Heart attack. When or where we return is one of those things we can't explain. Sometimes it takes decades, and sometimes just a few years. Pretty random."

I wonder if I'll get used to the ever-growing list of questions that don't seem to have any answers as Griffon stops in front of a stack of singles, staring at the one in front.

"'Strange Fruit'?" I ask, reading the label.

"Billie Holiday," he says, with an edge of sadness in his voice. He makes no move to pick it up, just stares at the small black record with the white label.

"You want to get it?" I ask quietly.

He shakes his head. "Too many memories," he says, and from the way he says it I assume they aren't all good ones. Griffon looks around like he's forgotten where we are. "Places like this are hard sometimes." He takes a deep breath and smiles at me. "MC5, then?"

"I think he'll like it," I answer, trying to lighten the mood. "It comes highly recommended."

We stand in line in front of an older guy with long white hair.

He smiles at us, then points at the record I'm holding. "MC5," he says, his eyebrows raised. "I thought kids your age only liked that hip-hop rap crap that comes blasting out of the cars around here."

"I think that's what people said about the MC5 back in '68," Griffon answers.

The man laughs from deep within his rather large belly. "True," he says, nodding. "I imagine you're right." His smile causes the wrinkles around his eyes to deepen. "They were good, though. That's the best live album ever recorded—Detroit, 1968."

"They had an awesome show at the Fillmore East in '69," Griffon says. He glances at me with a tiny smile on his face.

"At the Fillmore, huh?" the old guy says. "I don't remember any live recordings in New York."

"I don't think they made any," Griffon says. He nudges me with his elbow and points to the cashier. "Our turn."

We walk up to the counter, leaving the old guy with a confused smile on his face. It's fun, but strange to be in on Griffon's little joke. "That wasn't very nice," I whisper. "Were you really at that show?"

"Yeah," he whispers back. "I wasn't lying. It *was* awesome."

I hand over the album and the cashier rings it up. On the counter are some silver pendants hanging on black cords. I pick one up and look at it. It's a cross with a loop on the top, but it seems really familiar.

"Here you go," the cashier says, handing me my bag and some change. She sees me looking at the necklace. "You want to add one in?"

Just holding it makes me inexplicably sad, like I've just lost something important. "No thanks," I say, putting it back. I don't like necklaces in the first place, but my reaction to this one is doubly strange. All I get is a feeling—no visions or memories that might explain it. "I was just looking."

"That's an ankh," she says. "The Egyptian symbol of eternal life. Very mystical."

Eternal life. A few weeks ago, that wouldn't have meant anything to me, but now everything is so different. Griffon is watching me closely as I murmur, "Maybe next time."

We walk out into the blazing sunlight and stand on the sidewalk, trying to decide where to go next. Instead of thinning, the crowds seem to be getting heavier and louder. Griffon squints up the street. "You know what I'd really like?" he asks.

"What?"

He turns and focuses his sharp amber eyes on me. "To be alone with you."

I smile, releasing the tiny thread of anxiety I'd felt since I arrived. "That sounds perfect."

Fourteen

As we pull up to his house, the lights are off, even though it's starting to get dark. "Is Janine gone?" I wonder how she'll feel about coming home and finding me alone with Griffon in their house. Most mothers wouldn't deal with that very well, but then, Janine isn't most mothers, and Griffon isn't most sons.

"She'll probably be back later," he says, not seeming to give it a lot of thought. He walks ahead of me to unlock the heavy front door. "Janine doesn't sit still for very long."

We hang our jackets on hooks by the door, and I follow him across the hallway. The house is quiet, and I feel how acutely alone we are in it. Griffon doesn't say anything, but I know we're headed up to his room. As we approach the stairs, I hesitate just a tiny bit, but it's enough for him to notice. "Everything okay?"

"Fine," I say. More than anything, I want to follow him up the stairs—it's all I've wanted since that day in the café, but a small part of me is afraid of what might come next. I glance up at his broad shoulders and strong jaw, and see something in him that's older than he appears. More experienced. I wonder how many times he's been in this situation, how many first times he's had. He's right, it isn't exactly a level playing field, but the pull I feel when he's near me obscures most of my rational thoughts, and I know that once I climb those stairs, everything might change.

Griffon walks back down two steps until he stands right next to me. Reaching over, he brushes my cheek with his hand and runs his fingers through my hair. He bends down and kisses me softly on the mouth, then traces a line up my cheek, planting gentle kisses on my eyelids. I can feel his hand tremble slightly as he holds the back of my neck, and I force my breathing to stay even as he presses closer to me.

Taking one small step back, he holds my chin in his hand and runs his thumb over my lips. "Never do anything you don't want to, understand?"

I nod. "I do want to," I say quietly. "I've wanted to be alone with you since the first time I saw you."

A smile flickers across his face, full of emotion yet unreadable at the same time. "Don't forget, I saw you first," he says. He holds out his hand and I take it, letting him lead me slowly up the creaking wooden staircase and through the door to his room.

I'm not sure what I expected, but the room looks like a seventeen-year-old boy lives there. Clothes spill out of his closet and papers lie across a large desk, practically burying a small laptop. Against one wall, a dark comforter has been hurriedly pulled

over a queen-size bed. "Nice to see you cleaned up for company," I
say, kicking at an abandoned red T-shirt on the floor.

"Glad you noticed." Griffon bends down to pick up the shirt
and tosses it in the general direction of the closet. "I was hoping
there'd be someone up here this afternoon to appreciate all of my
hard work."

The unmistakable meaning of his words makes my stomach
flip, and just for a second the thought that I'm in over my head
flashes through my mind. "So, pretty much anyone would do?" I
ask, trying to make my voice light enough so he won't guess how
much I want something to happen between us, and how terrified
I am at the thought that it will.

Griffon stands in front of me, his expression serious. "No," he
says. "Not just anyone."

I smile what I hope is a mysterious smile and wander over to
his desk, looking at the things he keeps, trying to find out what
they say about him. I see a spiral pad open to a page covered in
pencil drawings. They're all different views of the same girl. She
has long, straight hair that's tied in a braid over her shoulder and
is wearing a Renaissance Faire–type gown. More arresting than
what she's wearing is the fact that her face looks incredibly realistic, her eyes intent on the viewer, as if these are all photos instead
of a drawings.

Griffon comes over and pulls the notebook out of my hands.
"Damn. I should have put that away. It's just something I was
working on awhile ago." He closes the book and slides it into a
drawer.

"They're amazing," I say, trying not to give in to the jealousy I feel for the girl who is nothing more than lines on a page. Except that Janine said that Griffon draws things from memory. Buildings, streets, parks. And beautiful girls who aren't me.

"It's nothing," he says, obviously embarrassed.

On the bookcase above his desk is a photo of girl who looks a little older than me. I look closely, but she's not the girl from the drawing. This one has blond hair and green eyes, and that natural kind of beauty that looks at home in the outdoors. She's sitting on a sailboat, her arm draped protectively over the wheel. I feel another stab of jealousy, and wonder if he put all of these here to torture me. Or to let me know how things are going to be. And I guess I shouldn't be surprised; there's no reason why I should be the only girl in his life.

I turn to see Griffon watching me. He wanders over and picks up the picture. "She's pretty, isn't she?" he asks.

I shrug, not having a clue what he expects me to say to that.

"This was taken a few years ago. Even back then she was a champion racer. Has her own boat and everything." He puts the photo back on the desk. "Relax," he says, a slow grin crossing his lips. "She's my granddaughter."

"I'm sorry," I say, knowing I didn't hear him right. "Your *what*?"

"Granddaughter. She lives in Rhode Island. I've never met her; this photo is from an article about her sailing. I keep track of her online." He nods. "Some things have gotten a lot easier."

Relief floods through me. He's allowed to have pictures of pretty girls all he wants, as long as they're related to him on some level, in some lifetime. "So, you can find relatives . . . from before?" I ask, thinking about how strange that would be.

Griffon nods. "My daughter was born in 1964, my grand-daughter in 1991. Not that hard to trace people these days. It's not like I'm going to meet them in person. Can you imagine that conversation?" He sighs. "But it's nice to know how they're doing. I've never been able to before."

"Is it hard?" I ask. "I mean, they're off living their lives without you, and you're just watching from way back here."

Griffon shakes his head. "Not really. That's the way it's supposed to be." He pauses. "Is this getting too weird for you?"

"A little," I admit. "It's just another thing that's going to take getting used to." If he has a daughter and a granddaughter, there had to be a wife somewhere. I wonder if he still loves her. If he thinks about her late at night. The only thing that makes this thought remotely better is realizing that if she is still alive, she'll be old by now.

The wall by the door holds a giant whiteboard covered in complicated math problems. "Calculus?" I ask, pointing at the numbers.

Griffon glances over at the board and then quickly looks away. "Physics."

"You're taking advanced physics this year?"

"No," he says. "It's just something I do . . . on the side."

"I'm sorry. You're way too cute to do advanced physics for fun."

He laughs. "Glad you think so. It's for the Sekhem."

"Really? You're working for the government?"

"Not the government," he says, frowning a little. "Governments and countries are only temporary. The Sekhem doesn't see any nationalities or races—these are just the things that cover our essence each time we come back. We work for the world." His eyes light up from inside, like he really believes in what he's doing. "Which is why some governments have a problem with us. You'd be surprised how many people want to see the Sekhem working exclusively for them instead of for the global good," he says. "And what they're willing to do when we refuse."

"Like espionage? A little James Bond or Jason Bourne?"

"Not exactly hanging-from-ropes-over-lasers exciting all the time, but yeah, we have to be careful. Let's just say it's not a good idea to advertise your Akhet status to just anyone."

"So what do you do?" I ask, glancing at the whiteboard.

"What's my specialty?"

"Yeah. What are you working on?" I wave my hand at the indecipherable figures. "All this."

Griffon hesitates a split second. "Climate change. Alternative energy." He shrugs. "I know they're not as sexy as curing AIDS or dismantling bombs, but they're things that affect absolutely everything else." Griffon paces a little in front of the board, and he seems to get more excited as he speaks. "If we don't fix climate change and emissions, the rest of it won't matter. Hunger, disease, poverty—it'll all be gone, because this planet will be uninhabit-able." He's quiet for a minute. "In the early nineteenth century I worked to develop one type of combustion engine. So, basically, I helped cause this problem, so now I have to help solve it."

"Are you working for the Sekhem now?"

"Service to the Sekhem doesn't officially start until you turn eighteen," Griffon says slowly. "But yeah, I've started a little early. That's why I had to go away for a few days." He looks up at the equations on the board. "I'm helping to develop a special biofuel cell, and there was a break-in at our facility. I had to go and verify what they took. And how much it's going to set us back."

I look from the equations back to him, trying to understand how the two go together. Griffon isn't just a regular high-school junior, I know that, but having it all in front of me is something deeper than just knowing. Scarier. More real. "Someone stole the stuff you're working on? It's that important?"

Griffon nods. "It'll change the world. To some people with oil interests, that's not such a good thing." He hesitates. "It's not the first time it's happened."

I feel a little knot of anxiety at his words. Changing the world. Griffon has a life that's totally separate from everything familiar to me, and responsibilities that have nothing to do with me. No wonder he didn't call for a whole week. The thought of him rushing off to do things that will ultimately affect millions of people suddenly puts our relationship into perspective. A perspective I don't necessarily want. "Do you have to go away a lot?"

"Sometimes," he admits. "Although most of it I can do from here. Especially right now. Sekhem are everywhere—universities, private companies, foundations."

"Does Janine work for them too?" Somehow the thought of her watching out for him makes me feel a little better.

"Yep. She travels a little, but does most of her work here. Working for the Sekhem doesn't necessarily mean you have to go someplace special. A lot of what I do happens here in California and Washington, but there's some development in Europe." He grabs my hand. "Paris would be cool if you came with me."

I like that he's thinking ahead. And that it includes me. "Screw the bomb people," I say. "I think saving the world is pretty sexy." I lace my fingers through his, feeling suddenly vulnerable and a little afraid. I glance around at the unfamiliar territory of his room. There are so many parts to his life I know nothing about. What can I possibly give him or show him that he hasn't seen a million times before? I'm an average-looking junior in high school who knows what to do with a bow and a cello, and . . . what else? I can't speak a dozen languages or draw a city from memory or even play chess very well—forget about putting all of the pieces back where they belong. I'm just me, and for the first time since we met, I'm wondering if that's going to be enough.

"And here I was afraid you'd think I was some sort of physics geek," Griffon says.

"Maybe I've been looking for just the right physics geek." I look up at him, once again startled by the clarity of his eyes as he watches me. "So now that you've dragged me up here, aren't you even going to kiss me?" I try to sound light and uncaring, but I've never meant anything more in my life.

The vibrations in the air between us grow stronger, almost visible, as he bends down and kisses me hard, all of the gentleness from before drowned out by the intensity of his body pressing against mine. My heart races being so close to him, and all at once I understand what people mean by desire. The idea that having this person pressed up against you isn't enough, that you want more, want to be inside them so that there is no separation between your bodies. I bury my face in his neck, wishing that I could stay in this one moment, in this one lifetime, forever. I reach under his shirt, desperate to feel as much of him as I can.

Griffon pulls away slightly. "Let me go take a quick shower," he says. "I'm still all sweaty from the game."

"No. Don't," I say quickly. "I like it."

He looks surprised, but doesn't move away. Instead, he takes my hand and leads me to the big wide bed, pulling me down with him. He kisses my neck and traces my collarbone with his lips before pausing to brush my hair back from my face. "God, do you know how beautiful you are?" His voice trembles as he speaks, and I can feel the restraint he's exercising in the vibrations that are charging every inch of him.

He props his head up on his left hand as he positions himself next to me, his right hand tracing the outline of my face. Griffon's top lip curves so perfectly, so invitingly, that I can't help but reach up and touch it, running my fingers over his face, knowing that I now have permission to do these things that I've only thought about over the past several weeks. I can see his muscles move under the thin fabric of his shirt; the veins that run down his neck and disappear into his collar make me long to see more, even in the dim light that drifts in through the curtains.

I push him back against the pillows, pulling the baseball jersey over his head, once again marveling at his smooth, honeyed skin. Griffon's look is questioning, but he follows my lead and doesn't protest as I ease his shirt off and toss it aside. I inhale sharply at the sight of his outlined muscles tapering into the slight dip of his baseball pants.

As I start to explore his warm skin, he gently grabs my hand and raises it to his lips, kissing my palm and moving toward me so that there is no visible distance between us, just a tangle of arms and legs, as close as we can get for now. A dull gold pendant hangs from the black cord around his neck. I reach for it with tentative fingers and watch as goose bumps form on his torso and an audible gasp rises from his throat. It's an ankh, just like the ones we saw in the record store. And the tattoo on Janine's neck.

My mind suddenly flashes to that cold, gray day on the scaffold and the pendant I placed into the hand of my executioner. Unlike Griffon's, mine had been shiny and silver, with a dark red stone in the center, but the symbol is the same. A shiver runs up my spine as I remember what the girl in the store said about the meaning of an ankh. *Eternal life.*

Centuries ago, I'd had one too.

Fifteen

I hold my breath as I turn the corner toward my house. We'd texted all week, but Griffon hadn't said anything about coming over, and I didn't want to push it. Which is why I can't help smiling when I see him sitting outside of my house on Thursday afternoon.

"You might as well come in," I say, walking up close enough so that I'm inching into his personal space, but not close enough so that we're actually touching.

"No," he says. "I'm okay out here. I don't want to distract you from the lesson."

"Afternoon, Cole," my neighbor says as he walks out of the house next door. He's a Unitarian minister, and even though he's always been cool to me, I step away from Griffon just a tiny bit. His dog Koda comes up and sniffs the retaining wall before lifting his leg and peeing on the corner, just like he does pretty much every day.

"Hi, Mr. Proctor," I say.

"And you are?" he asks as he holds his hand out to Griffon.

"Griffon," he answers, shaking his hand and smiling broadly. "Nice to meet you, sir."

Mr. Proctor winks at him and nods to me. "You be good to our girl here," he says, while I cringe inwardly. "She's special. An actual prodigy."

Griffon smiles at me. "That's what I hear."

As soon as Mr. Proctor is out of sight, Griffon leans in and presses his lips quickly to mine. I lace my fingers through his and he gives them a tight squeeze. His eyes seem to grow darker. "I'm not going to come in, but I do want Veronique to see me as she walks up the street."

"I can deal with it," I say, trying to convince myself as well as him. "It's just a cello lesson. And Mom's home."

"Okay," Griffon says. "As long as you can deal with it, you'll be able to go out with me tonight." He says it lightly, but without his customary smile. "Just for an hour or so."

"What makes you think I don't have other plans?" I hadn't made any on purpose, hoping I'd see him, but I don't want him to think I'm waiting around for him. Which I am.

"Do you?"

I grinned. "I do now."

"Good. I'll come up and get you after Veronique leaves."

I glance up at our window, already trying to figure out how I'm going to get out of the house on a school night. "I'd better go and set up. Veronique's going to be here any minute. Are you sure you don't want to come up?"

"I'm sure. I feel better keeping an eye on things from down here."

It's me who leans in this time, kissing him harder on the mouth, not caring if anyone sees us. It's so difficult to untangle my fingers from his and walk up the stairs alone, and I hope the lesson goes quickly.

Veronique is uncharacteristically late, so when she finally does arrive, we go straight to work, with no mention of Griffon sitting outside. I try to keep my mind on the notes, but I keep glancing at Veronique, hoping to find a flicker of recognition.

We play together for a while, me taking the more difficult melody parts and Veronique working on the easier harmonies. I feel myself starting to relax a little bit.

At the end of the last bar, we both reach up at the same time to turn the page, but as our hands brush, a sense of doom and anger flashes through the room for just a second, and I sit back hard in my chair.

"You okay?" Veronique asks, watching me with concern. "You look like you've just seen a ghost."

I blink and shake my head. The panic is gone now, as if the wave has curled over, saturating everything around me and then retreating. I inch away from her, the echoes of what Griffon has said about her racing through my mind, and suddenly I know that the visions aren't random. Touching Veronique is what has caused them the past two times, and Alessandra in that life must be how I'm connected to Veronique now. "I'm fine," I say. "Just a little dizzy."

"Are you still getting headaches?" Concern flashes across her face. "From the accident last week?"

I realize I don't want her to know what I've been feeling and seeing. Janine's right—as long as she thinks I don't have a clue, it's probably safer. "Sometimes," I say. "The bump only just went away." Knowing Griffon is outside calms my nerves a little. Suddenly I want him closer without alarming her. "It's kind of stuffy in here. Let me open a window." Setting the cello down gently, I walk to the bay window that looks out over the street and unlock it. I peer through the glass down to the planter below, but I can't see Griffon from this angle.

Grabbing the window pulls, I yank the bottom pane up, but it only tilts about half an inch before it sticks tight. *Thanks, Mom, and your stupid antique houses.* It would be so nice to live in a place where opening a window doesn't take an enormous feat of strength. I pound on the frame a couple of times to try to shake it loose.

"Here, let me help you," Veronique says, walking over to the window.

I glance down again, but Griffon is still nowhere in sight, and that makes me feel panicky all over again. I don't want to look at Veronique in case she can tell what I know, that I'm starting to put the pieces of the puzzle together, and sometime soon I'll know where she fits. "You grab that side and I'll grab this side," I say, pulling on the brass handle. "On three. One, two, *three.*"

In T.V. shows, when something bad happens they slow it way down so that you can see every detail with excruciating clarity. In *CSI,* when someone gets sliced by shards of glass, they show the stop-motion trajectory of the sharp edges as they slice through skin, muscle, and bone, the drops of blood falling like one of those splatter psychology tests onto the victim's shirt. This isn't like that at all. Everything happens so fast I barely realize what's going on. The sounds of shattering glass fill the room, and there's a flash of fear as my left hand crashes through the broken window. Without thinking, I quickly pull my arm back inside, not noticing the long piece of glass that's sticking out through the bottom of the sill.

At first, I don't feel anything.

"Oh my God," Veronique says, grabbing my arm just above the wrist and holding it tight. "We need some help!" she shouts, without moving from where we stand frozen in place.

"It's okay," I say, trying to pull my arm away from her.

"We have to keep the pressure on it," Veronique says to me calmly, her grip surprisingly strong.

"Nicole!" Mom says, appearing in the doorway. She rushes over to the window. "Oh my God! What happened?"

"The window broke," I say, feeling hazy and confused. I watch as rivulets of blood appear from under Veronique's hands and drop onto the floor. This is all going to make a big mess, not to mention the shattered window pane. "I'm sorry, Mom," I say, my tongue feeling thick in my mouth.

"We need some towels," Veronique says. Her voice is beginning to sound distant, like she's at the end of a long tunnel.

"Let me see," Mom says, trying to pull her hand away.

"Not a good idea," Veronique says in harsh, clipped tones, as if I can't hear her. "I think she may have severed an artery. You need to call 911. Now."

Mom races out and Veronique and I are alone in the silent room. My skin feels warm and sticky, but when I look down, it seems like someone else's hand that's covered in shiny red blood. My eyelids feel heavy, and my ears are ringing. Before Mom can get back, I know my legs won't hold me up any longer.

"I think I need to sit down," I say, and slide against the wall, only partially aware of the red pool that's forming beneath me. I can smell Mom's perfume nearby, and that makes me feel better— like everything is going to be fine.

Dimly, I hear pounding at the front door and Griffon's voice shouting through the glass. I know the door is locked, it's always locked, but just lifting my head takes more energy than I have left, and all I can do is whisper his name. The wail of sirens sounds in the distance and I want to tell him that the ambulance is coming, that my mom is here, but I can't open my eyes or make my mouth form the words.

∞

The ocean air is tangy with salt as we sit on the stone stoop of the cottage, my arm wrapped in muslin and tied tight to my body. Looking up, I can see bits of blue sky through the long, brown grass on the roof

"My poor bairn," Mam says. "We'll get this changed quick as a wink and have you on your way again." She smiles at me, her blue eyes the same color as the sea that roils on the cliffs below us. The fiery red plait hangs down her back and looks like the setting sun against the whitewashed walls.

"'Tis paining me," I cry, tears filling my eyes as she deftly

pulls the bandage off the wound. Angry red skin punctuated by
yellow blisters covers most of my arm, and the sight of it is almost
worse than the pain.

"Dear, sweet Allison. Just a wee bit of salve and a clean ban-
dage will have this right as rain in no time," Mam says. A thick
covering of ointment blocks out the air, and the relief makes me
smile at her for a second, knowing that she is right.

The relentless beeping is driving me crazy. I wave my hand
around my head, trying to find somewhere to turn off the repeti-
tive noise that is piercing my brain.

"Cole?" My father's voice is soft and full of concern. "Are you
awake?"

"Hmm," I say, trying to find the words I need. I run my tongue
over my lips and try again. "Yeah." My throat is drier than I've
ever felt before. "Water," I manage.

"The nurse is coming," Dad says, patting my right hand.

Nurse? Where am I? I try to open my eyes, but the fluorescent
lights make me shut them again. "Too bright," I say.

I hear a click above my head and then Dad's voice again. "Try
it now."

I open my eyes just enough to see the top of a curtain that
hangs on a metal track from the ceiling. My head is throbbing, and
without moving it I can see a bank of machines on my right, one of
which is making the irritating beeping sound. "It hurts," I say.

"The doctor says that once the pain medication wears off, your
arm is going to hurt a bit," Dad says. I tilt my head to the right just
enough to see him. His face has more wrinkles than I remember.

"Not arm," I say, barely able to form the words I need.
"Headache."

"I'll ask about that just as soon as they come in," Dad says.

I look around, remembering the pounding on the door and feeling frustration that I wasn't able to let him in. "Griffon," I say. "Where . . . ?"

"He'll be back," Dad says. "Close your eyes and get some rest."

The effort of speaking is too much, and relief overwhelms me as I let myself slip into a dark stream of unconsciousness.

Sixteen

Griffon's curls are the first things I see when I open my eyes. His arms are folded in front of him and his head is leaning heavily against the bed railing. I can't see his eyes, but his deep, even breathing tells me that he's asleep. I watch him for a few minutes, his fingers twitching, acting out whatever vivid dream is streaming across his unconscious. He seems younger while he sleeps, as if the daily effort of keeping up some sort of barrier slips away in unguarded moments. I think about what it would be like to wake up one morning with him next to me, his curls resting on a pillow near my head, his fingers wrapped around mine.

With my free hand I reach up and gently touch his hair, then more boldly twist one of the curls around my finger, its silky curves hugging my skin. With a jolt, Griffon inhales and sits upright, looking around as if he doesn't know where he is.

"Hey," I say to him. My lips feel dry and cracked, and I'm sure that I look like a disaster. I'm still glad that he's sitting next to me.

His eyes soften as soon as he sees me, the deep indentation in his cheek giving away the fact that he's probably been in that position for a long time. "Cole," he says. The corners of his eyes look raw, as if he's been crying. "You okay?"

I nod, looking around the bed. My left arm is suspended from a pulley, white gauze bandages wrapping the entire length from fingertips to elbow. There are several bags hanging from hooks on a pole, leaking various fluids into my arm. The pain feels like it's far away, tucked in a distant corner of my brain along with the fragmented memories of the accident. I lick my lips, my mouth feeling so dry I'm not sure I can speak again.

Griffon reaches over and pours some water from a pink plastic pitcher into a matching cup. "Here," he says, handing it to me. "Can you get this, or do you want me to hold it?"

I reach for it with my right hand, the cup trembling as I bring it to my lips, but I don't spill too much on the woven hospital blanket. As I drink, my body comes back to life, and I can almost feel the blood surging in my veins. "Thanks," I manage, handing the cup back to him.

"God, I was so scared," he whispers, sitting back down in the padded chair next to the bed. "By the time I got in there, I thought it was too late. *She* was sitting there in a pool of your blood, and you were so white..." Griffon runs his other hand through his hair, tugging at the curls, and I can feel the effort he's using to control his anger.

"But I'm okay," I say, feeling stronger already. I shift in the bed, my muscles stiff. "It was an accident—"

"That's two 'accidents' in two weeks, Cole." His whisper grows harsh, and he squeezes my hand for emphasis. His beautiful eyes are dull and desperate as he looks at me. "When are you going to realize she's out to hurt you? When I think of what could have happened—of what did happen when I was standing just a few feet away . . ." He raises my right hand to his lips and kisses my fingers.

I can feel my heart rate rising and glance over at the monitors, hoping that they won't give me away. I remember the flash of danger when my hand brushed Veronique's that afternoon, but I don't really remember the details of the accident. As glad as I am that she'd tried to help, it was a pretty huge coincidence that she was there when it happened. "Then why did she save my life?"

Griffon presses his lips together. "I don't know," he finally admits. "I've been thinking about it nonstop, and I can't come up with anything that makes sense. She must have wanted it to look like an accident. Maybe she thought you wouldn't survive, and helping you would throw off any suspicion."

I stare at him, surprised at the passion in his voice. I've never had anyone worry about me so much.

"I'm supposed to protect you this time," he says quietly. "And I'm screwing it up already."

At first I love hearing those words. He wants to keep me safe. Who wouldn't love that? And then I look at them a little more carefully. "What do you mean 'this time'?"

He glances at me like he doesn't know what I'm talking

about. "I just mean now. In this lifetime. I need to protect you from Veronique."

I wonder again, despite all of the things he's said, if that's all I am to him. He's already out to save the world; why not save me on the side? "I've already told you, I don't need protecting."

Griffon glances at the machines behind me and the I.V. hanging from the pole next to the bed. "Yeah, you're doing a great job at the moment."

A door opens and Dad appears through the curtain, two cups of coffee in his hands. His tired eyes lift as he sees me, and Griffon has to reach out and grab the cups before they fall.

"Cole!" Dad says, his voice wavering. He clears his throat. "About time you decided to join us. It was getting pretty boring just sitting here watching you sleep."

I manage a small smile. Dad is famous for handling difficult situations with stupid jokes, and for once I'm glad for the distraction. "Sorry I missed all the excitement."

"Thanks for the coffee," Griffon says. He grabs his jacket off the back of the chair. "I should get going."

"You don't have to," I say. "It's okay." Just because I don't want to be the helpless female in his hero movie doesn't mean I want him to go.

"Your dad's back. I just wanted to check in and see how you were doing. I'll call you later." The door thunks behind him as Griffon practically sprints out of the room, and I know that I'm going to spend the next several hours repeating his last sentence to myself. He's going to call me later.

Dad leans over to kiss my cheek. He smoothes the hair out of my face like he used to when I was little and he was putting me to bed. In that one gesture, I realize how much I miss sitting and reading with him at bedtime every night. I used to make him read the same books over and over again, every night for weeks at a time. With a sudden rush of sadness I realize that he won't be my dad next time. Someday I'll be a little kid again and someone else will read me stories and put me to bed. And I'll remember this Dad and this lifetime, but he'll be someone else too and won't have any memory of the little girl who was me. I wonder how Griffon does it, starting over with new people every lifetime, like a new cast of characters in familiar roles. It must be lonely.

"You gave us all quite a scare," Dad says. He nods toward the door. "I've barely been able to get Griffon to leave your room since you got here."

I can feel my face getting warm, ridiculously happy at the thought that he sat here the whole time. Dad smiles at me. "We can talk about that later," he says.

There is a twinge of pain in my left arm, like you get when you bump your funny bone. I look up at where it's hanging over my head and try to bend my fingers. They twitch in response, and the feeling isn't so much of pain as it is like my whole arm's asleep. I notice Dad watching me.

"Do you want me to get more pain meds?"

"No," I say. "It's okay right now." I pause, needing to ask the question, but not sure I want the answer. "Is it bad?"

"Honest?"

"No, Dad. I want you to lie to me. Yes, honest."

A look of pain crosses his face. "It's not good. The glass severed everything right down to the bone. They did surgery to repair as much of the damage as they could."

I think about the complicated fingerings in *Meditation*. In any piece worth playing. The strength you need for the fortissimo and the control you need for the pianissimo sections. "Can I . . . ," I begin, but have to breathe out quickly and start over at the thought. "Will I be able to play again soon?"

"I'm sure it will all work out." Dad's words say one thing, but the fact that he won't look at me when he talks says something else. He looks me in the eye and grabs my other hand. "The important thing is that you're going to be okay."

It's almost cute that he thinks that this is most important thing. I know better.

Dad stands up and pulls out his phone. "Right now, I've got to call your mother. I finally sent her home to get some rest, but I promised to call the second you woke up."

I look out the window and realize it's dark outside. Veronique's lesson was at four o'clock, which means I've been out of it for hours. The last thing I remember is the sound of pounding at the door and the ambulance in the distance. I try to sit up more and am rewarded with woozy spins for my efforts. "What time is it?" I ask.

Dad looks up from his phone and glances at the clock. "It's almost midnight."

I let my head flop back on the pillow. Just the effort required to hold a simple conversation is exhausting. I yawn. "I'm so tired. How long have I been asleep?"

He puts the phone up to his ear, and I can hear a distant

ringing. Dad puts one hand on my good arm and gives it a squeeze. "Honey, it's almost midnight on *Saturday*," he says as he waits for Mom to pick up. "You've been asleep for two days."

∞

"Well, if you're okay, I have to get to work," Kat says, folding the magazine closed and stretching as Mom comes into the room. Between all of them, I haven't been alone since I got here, and it's starting to irritate me just a little bit. That, and the fact that I haven't seen Griffon since he ran out of here two days before.

"Call me if you get out today," she says, gathering up her bag. "If not, I'll come by tonight." She bends down and gives me a peck on the cheek. The accident seems to have brought out the big sister in her, and I don't completely hate it.

"Thanks," I say, watching Mom start her shift in the still-warm chair. "Can I have another drink?" I ask, flicking through the TV channels, trying to find something decent to watch. My left arm is still suspended in midair; it looks like it's frozen in a permanent wave. I can't move very far without being detached, so going to the bathroom involves moves that are similar to untying a very tangled marionette.

"Sure, baby," Mom says, bringing me the milk that's sitting on the bedside table.

"Thanks," I say, wishing it was Pepsi. I take a sip and glance at the still-full lunch tray that's next to the bed. The view out the window isn't so bad—I can even see the top of the Golden Gate Bridge if I crane my neck just right—but the food is inedible. Two days of picking mysterious things off my tray has been enough.

Mom sees my glance. "Are you sure you don't want something more to eat?"

"No. Besides, they said I might be able to get out of here today." I smile sweetly at her. "And if I don't, will you please, *please* get me some calamari and plantains from Cha Cha Cha again?" My favorite Cuban restaurant always goes a long way toward making anything better.

"That would be awfully nice of me," she says, coming around to my back to fluff up my pillow. "We'll see." Apparently now that my death is no longer imminent, I don't get everything I want.

On the other side of the curtain, I can hear the hallway door open and the squeak of Dr. Shapiro's shoes on the polished floor. He knocks on the side of the door before pulling the curtain back.

"How are things today, Miss Ryan?" he asks, glancing at the computer screen next to the bed.

"Better," Mom jumps in. "She seems to be getting some feeling back in the tips of her fingers," she adds. "And the color seems to be better too. We've been keeping a careful eye on that for the past twenty-four hours."

"Thank you," he says brusquely to Mom, and then turns pointedly toward me. "May I have a look?"

I nod and take a deep breath. When it's wrapped up tight in white bandages, I don't have to think too much about what's going on underneath, but whenever he wants to have a look, the reality of what happened sets in. Dr. Shapiro tries hard to be gentle, but just a bump sends a shooting pain straight up to my shoulder.

"Let's see what we're working with here," he says, unhooking my arm from the sling that keeps it upright and unwrapping the bandage. My arm looks small and bright yellow, which he said is from the antiseptic they use during surgery. Running straight down the inside of my arm from wrist almost to elbow is an angry red line covered in shiny black stitches. I can hear Mom sharply inhale.

Dr. Shapiro doesn't say anything, just looks at the scar from several angles. He gently pinches the ends of my fingers. "Can you feel that?"

"Some," I say.

"Still feel a little numb?"

"Kind of. Mostly from my middle finger to my pinky."

"Hmm," he says. "Let me see you move them."

The fear that it is going to hurt is worse than the actual pain as I carefully bend my fingers down as far as they'll go.

"Well," he says, opening up some new gauze to put over the stitches, "the wound is healing nicely, and I don't see any signs of infection. Which is great."

"What about the nerve damage?" Mom asks anxiously. "Will she have the same range of motion as before? You know that Nicole is an exceptionally gifted cellist, and I can't imagine what it would do to her career if—"

"We'll have to wait and see, Mrs. Ryan," Dr. Shapiro says sharply, cutting her off mid-sentence. It's so embarrassing that she doesn't see how much she annoys him. "Right now I'm more concerned with infection and saving her life than I am with some of the fine motor skills she may lose," he continues. "The ulnar nerve was completely severed, along with extensive tissue damage. At this point, she's lucky she gets to keep her hand." He smiles apologetically at me. "The scar shouldn't be too bad," he says. "I'm good with a stitch, if I do say so myself."

I look at my arm, all packaged up tight, as he hooks me back up to the pulley system. From the outside, it's all going to look completely normal, but I know with stone-cold certainty that it will never be the same. The thought that I won't be able to play again feels like a big empty space inside, as if more than just some nerves and tendons have been severed. I've been feeling guilty about making the cello my career since I found out the truth about my "gift." Maybe now, I'll have no choice.

"I think we can let you go later today, if you promise to keep it elevated as much as possible." Dr. Shapiro turns to Mom. "I'll give you some information about physical therapy and rehabilitation before she's released."

"I want the best therapists in the city," Mom says as I cringe from embarrassment. "Nicole has a promising career ahead of her, and to have something like this end it would just be so . . . tragic."

Dr. Shapiro smiles a tight smile. "I've done everything I can do. Now it's just a waiting game to see how well the nerves react." He squeezes my foot through the covers. "I'll check back in before you go."

I wait until the door shuts behind him to say anything. "Do you even hear yourself?"

"What? It's true! In order to become a truly world-class musician, you need to have quick reflexes and strong fingers. If you don't get all of the feeling back, I just . . ." She puts her head in her hands. "I just don't know what we'll do."

"Who's 'we'?" I demand. "Didn't you hear him? I could have

bled to death, and all you care about is whether I can play the cello again! Sometimes I think you don't even care about me. Just what I can do."

Mom stands up and takes a step toward the bed. "How can you say that? After everything we've done? You know we love you."

"I know you love the fact that I can play the cello. And that you get to be the mother of a child prodigy," I say, anger and frustration spilling over into my words. "But guess what, Mom—you can't be a child prodigy if you aren't a child anymore. And I'm not. Pretty soon, I'm just going to be a regular adult who happens to be good at the cello." I wiggle my fingers in the bandages. "Or at least that's what was going to happen. Face it: I'm not that special anymore."

Mom makes a move to touch my shoulder but I shake her off, so she takes a step away from the bed. "You know you don't mean that," she says, struggling to keep her voice even. "I know how upsetting this is. We'll get the best therapist in the city and begin right away. If you want to be truly world-class, you can't afford to lose too much ground, or else—"

"You're not listening, Mom!" I shout. "You have to accept the reality that it might be over. I might never play again." Even as I say the words, I try not to concentrate on them, to fully comprehend that I might never pick up a bow again.

"You listen to me," she says. "You *are* special. You've always been special. Cello has been your destiny ever since you were a tiny child, and we've done everything we can to make that your reality."

"Well, it looks like destiny has other ideas now," I say.

Mom is just gearing up for a repeat performance about my wasted talents when there's another knock on the door.

"Can I come in?" Rayne asks from out in the hallway. I can't tell if she's overheard us or not.

"Please," I call out. Mom seems to deflate into the chair by the window, aware that our "discussion" is over, at least for the moment.

"How's it going?" Rayne asks, stepping further into the room, her eyes flickering momentarily to my bandaged hand and then to my face.

"It's okay," I say. "I get out of here today."

"Awesome," she says, bending down to give me an awkward hug. "What time?"

I glance at Mom. "Did he say what time?"

"No," she says. "Probably before dinner, I'd imagine." She stands up. "I'm going to get the nurse to start the paperwork so that it doesn't take all day."

I breathe a sigh of relief once she's gone and the door has thunked closed. "Mom wants me to stay home all week, but I can't wait for things to get back to normal," I say. "I'll probably miss school again tomorrow, but I might be able to go back on Wednesday."

"Good," Rayne says. She looks back at my arm again. "Is it going to be back to normal?"

"Sure," I say, sounding more confident than I feel. "It just might take a little while to get all of the feeling back in my fingers. It'll be fine."

"Will you be able to . . . play anymore?"

"I don't know," I say, trying to sound indifferent. "And if I can't, who cares? You're the one who's always saying there's more to life than practice. Maybe I need to take a break."

Rayne studies my face. "Yeah, but *forever*? You can't give up on your gift."

"So now you're on Mom's side too?"

Rayne sits down on the edge of the bed. "I'm not taking a side." She grins. "Especially your mom's. But there must be a reason that you're so good at cello. I'm not good at anything, but if I was, I'd make the most of it."

If she only knew how close she is to the truth. The reason I was so good at cello. I realize that I'm already thinking about it in the past tense. Something I *used* to do. Something that used to define who I was. And for the first time since I woke up and saw Griffon sitting by the bed, tears spill over my lids and down my face before I can do anything to stop them.

"Oh crappity crap crap," Rayne says, lunging for the tissue box and handing it to me. "I totally didn't mean to do that."

"It's not your fault," I say, losing myself completely into blubber mode now. "It's just something I have to deal with."

"But maybe it will be okay," she says eagerly. "They can do amazing things these days. Maybe it's just going to take a few weeks or a few months and everything will be just like it was."

"Nice try, Mary Poppins," I say to her. The tears that haven't made their way out of my body seem to be congealing into a tight, hard ball in my chest. "But you know and I know that it will never be the same."

"I refuse to know that right now. And so should you." Rayne

gets up and starts poking at the cards and flowers that are set around the room. "You sure got a lot of stuff," she says. "Too bad nobody likes you."

I laugh, because the biggest and craziest bouquet of wild-flowers is from Rayne and her mom. "Yeah. All of a sudden I'm the most popular person around. I guess almost bleeding to death has an upside."

"Must have been some mess," Rayne says, and makes a face. I've been trying not to think about that too much. By the time I'd woken up in my hospital room, my clothes were gone, and I've been wearing this hospital gown and my robe ever since. I realize now that they were so covered in blood Mom probably threw them away.

"Who sent you bamboo?" Rayne asks, looking at a small red pot with some green stalks in it.

"I don't know," I say. "I don't remember seeing that before. Is there a card?"

Rayne peeks among the leaves. "Nope. This pot has three stalks growing in it. That means long life for Chinese people."

"How do you know all this stuff anyway?"

Rayne shrugs. "You know cello. I know rocks and flowers." She rubs a silky green leaf with her fingers. "Weird. I wonder who it's from?"

Long life. And he'd said he'd been Chinese a few lifetimes ago. I smile, knowing exactly who the bamboo is from.

Seventeen

Gabi closes her locker with a bang and I jump. "Nervous?" she says, and laughs.

"No," I say. "I was just thinking about something else." All week, the smallest sound or movement out of the corner of my eye causes my heart to race, and I've been imagining I see Veronique everywhere.

"I think I know what that 'something else' is," Rayne says. "Or, rather, *who* that some*one* else is."

"Not true," I say, automatically feeling for the outline of my phone in my pocket.

"Going to see him today?"

"No," I said. "Probably not until tomorrow. I haven't seen him since I got out of the hospital."

"Well, it's too bad you didn't screw up your right hand," Gabi says, looking at the splint on my arm. "Then you wouldn't have to do Ms. Lipke's famous timed essay this afternoon."

"I'm seriously beginning to hate that woman," Rayne says. "Did she give you one first period?"

"Yup," Gabi says. "Sixty minutes of writing on one of the books we've read so far. We did *Their Eyes Were Watching God*, so at least you know it won't be that one."

"I'm so not in the mood," Rayne says. "It would almost be worth slitting my wrists to not have to do that today." She looks at me. "Crap. Sorry. I didn't mean for it to come out like that."

"It's okay."

"See you guys later," Gabi calls, rushing down the opposite hallway.

Just as the bell rings, I slip through the door of the orchestra room. I've felt so out of place here the past few days, just being able to watch and not join in. I start toward my usual chair on the end of the cello row, but then hesitate. I have no cello with me, and I can't play even if I did. At the last second, I head toward the back of the room and settle into one of the stools near the percussion section.

"Nicole?" Steinberg asks, looking out over everyone as they get out their instruments and start tuning up. In addition to teaching me privately, he's the orchestra director at school. I miss our afternoon sessions at the studio, but without being able to play, there's no point in showing up. "You don't have to sit back there, you know," he says. "You can stay in your usual position as long as you like. Did the doctors say when you might be able to play again?"

I shake my head. "Awhile." Despite the fact that the sounds of tuning echo through the room, I'm acutely aware that everyone in the orchestra is paying attention to our conversation. Claire White ducks her head, pretending to concentrate on her bow, but I know she's thinking the same thing that I am. "You should give my chair to Claire." She's sat next to me for the past three years, always ready for any challenge opportunity.

Steinberg glances back at my row. "You don't need to decide that now—"

"I already did," I say. "I'm no good to anybody at the moment. Claire deserves it. She'll be great."

"For now," he says.

"For now," I agree. "Then I'll come and challenge to see if I can win it back. Someday."

"Someday soon," Steinberg says. He gives me a barely perceptible wink before walking briskly back to Claire to whisper in her ear.

Claire looks back at me, and I give her a little wave of encouragement as she slowly gets up and shifts her music onto my empty stand, the red spots of embarrassment on her cheeks almost matching the red in her hair. I keep my head up and look straight ahead as the rest of the row realizes what's happened.

I sit motionless through warm-ups and Beethoven's *Coriolan Overture*, a piece that I've played a thousand times before. The fingers on my left hand twitch as they sit mostly unfeeling, weakly mimicking every single note of a piece that I know deep down I may never play again. As the music from the orchestra cascades over the small room, I start to feel the now-familiar break from reality as a memory begins.

Strong hands hold me up by my arms as my legs buckle. My

face is wet with tears as I struggle to get the image of a broken Alessandra out of my mind. Signore Barone speaks to the policemen who crowd the rooftop in a language I've come to recognize as English, his eyes shining with tears as he points his finger repeatedly in my direction. They begin to jerk me roughly toward the stairs, their faces masks of disapproval and contempt as I begin to comprehend what's happening.

"I did nothing wrong!" I cry, panic filling my body, but the men holding me up obviously do not understand my pleas. "It wasn't me! Please, won't somebody listen? Won't somebody listen to what really happened?"

"It can't be!" Paolo cries, rushing through the door and onto the roof, pushing past us as if we are invisible. "They say she has fallen! Where is Alessandra?" His face is filled with pain and disbelief as he rushes to the crowd surrounding the edge of the roof, below which she lies broken and bloodied. He peers over the side of the building, then falls to his knees, his hands over his face and a guttural, keening sound coming from his throat. "She is not gone! She can't be gone!" he cries over and over, rocking back and forth with the rhythm of his words as Signore Barone puts a protective hand on his shoulder.

"Somebody help me!" I cry, but my words are useless as I am dragged roughly to the doorway. Paolo glances up as the door closes, his eyes gleaming with hatred.

I look around the music room as the last notes from the Overture fade away, still filled with the panic I'd experienced that night on the roof. Alessandra died falling off the roof, and I was accused of doing it. My memories don't go further than the stairwell, but

I somehow know after that night in that lifetime, I never played the cello again.

∞

"It's just so incredible," Rayne says, taking a bite of the apple we swiped from the kitchen and pulling her books out of her backpack.

"Which part? The part where I lived in San Francisco over a hundred years ago? The part where I saw Alessandra dead? Or the part where I get hauled off by the police because they think I did it?"

I had to tell her. I know that Griffon said that we have to be careful, but this is Rayne we're talking about. And I'm not telling her about the Akhet or the Sekhem, just about Alessandra. I can't get the image of her lying on the ground out of my head. It took me a lifetime to remember it, and now I can't manage to forget.

"You aren't a murderer," she says. "That I know for sure. You can't be truly evil in one lifetime and then like you are now in this one."

"So now you're an expert?"

"Yes. I am. At least when it comes to this kind of thing." Rayne opens her calculus book, but stares off into the distance. "I wonder who I was in a past life. Maybe Cleopatra. Or Amelia Earhart. That would have been cool."

"Not everybody is a famous somebody," I say. "I think most of us were just ordinary people doing ordinary things."

"Well, somebody had to be famous in the past. Why not me?"

I manage a weak smile. "If anyone was famous in a past life, it would be you."

"Thank you." She gives a little bow. "If this all happened at some fancy house party, don't you think there would be a lot of publicity? An Italian musician falling off the roof of a famous mansion would probably make the papers. I know they had papers back then. Do you have a clue when it was?"

"All I've seen is a ferry dock and some horses and carriages," I say, starting to feel excited. "The late eighteen hundreds, maybe? Before the earthquake anyway, because everything still looked pretty good. There probably were a lot of papers back then." I look at her. "It might have been in one."

"Maybe we can look it up online," Rayne says.

"Not everything is online," I say. "There's no way anyone is going to scan hundreds of years of newspapers. But they must have old copies downtown at the big library. Anytime someone needs to find something like this in the movies they end up in the basement of a library, searching through old yellow newspapers." I look at her, hoping she'll come with me. "How much homework have you got?"

"Not so much that I don't want to go on a field trip right now."

We usually go to the library by my house, so the last time I was at the new one downtown was on a field trip for the big opening back in ninth grade. As we walk through the doors and into the main space, I look up at the ceiling looming several stories above us.

"Jeez," Rayne says. "I forgot how big this place is. It's like one of those inside-out hotels where all of the rooms look out over the lobby."

I stare at the flimsy-looking railings several stories up. "I sure hope they keep the newspapers in the basement."

"How can I help you?" the librarian at the main desk asks as we approach. She has short, dyed black hair and a nose ring. Trust us to get the only emo librarian in town.

"We need to see some old newspapers," Rayne tells her.

"How old?"

Rayne looks at me. "Um," I say, realizing I have no idea where to start. "Somewhere between 1870 and 1906."

Emo librarian raises a pierced eyebrow. "That's a pretty big time frame."

"You don't have any?" Rayne asks.

"No, we do," she says. "We have some in the history room on the sixth floor, and there's microfilm in the magazine and newspaper room on the fifth. It's just a lot to look through." She tilts her head. "Is there a reason you didn't want to look online?"

"They have newspapers online?" I ask. I can't look at Rayne because I know what she's going to say.

"Sure," she says. "At the CDNC website." She writes down the URL on a piece of scrap paper. "It's really cool. You can search the entire database using any terms you want, and they scan every page. It'll save you a ton of time." She points to a row of computers along one wall. "If you have a library card, you can use the computers here."

"Thanks," I say, taking the paper with me.

"Not like they're going to scan in hundreds of years of newspapers," Rayne says, mocking me.

"I know, I know," I say. "Don't push it."

I grab my library card out of my wallet and punch the number into a vacant computer. As soon as we get to the home page for the CDNC, I stare at the empty search box for the *San Francisco Herald.* I don't have a clue where to start.

"How about with the Pacific Coast Club?" Rayne suggests.

I slide over. "You type it in," I say, my right hand moving involuntarily to the splint on my left. Typing is another thing that isn't going very well at the moment.

Rayne looks at all of the links that come up on the site. "Everything here is after 1910. Didn't you say it was called something else back then? The door guy said it that day. The Something Mansion?"

"Right. It was." I search my memory, but as hard as I try I can't remember the name. I do the alphabet thing, picturing every letter in my head to see if that jars anything loose. When I get to *S*, I know I've got it. "The Sutter Mansion," I say.

"Here we go," Rayne says, as she clicks the links. Scans of old newspaper pages fill the screen. "Holy crap, there was some crazy stuff going on in San Francisco back then. Look at this one: 'Banker's Boy Returned for $5,000 Reward.'" She glances down the article. "They spelled clue 'clew.' Here's one where an army corporal was hanged. A rustler was shot out in Stockton, and there was a highbinder murder in Chinatown."

"Focus, Rayne," I say. I put my right hand on the mouse, moving the cursor to a tiny article that's highlighted. "Look at this! From July 20, 1895: 'Sutter Mansion Tragedy Trial.'" I read in a whisper. "'The jury in the case of Lucio Barone, on trial for the attempted murder of Clarissa Catalani and second-degree murder of Alessandra Barone last New Year's Eve, today returned a verdict of guilty on both counts.'"

"Oh my God!" Rayne says. "Is that it? Isn't Clarissa you? Who was Lucio Barone?"

I sit stunned in my seat. "Her father. Alessandra's." I think back to the chaotic scene on the rooftop where Signore Barone is pointing to me as the cops surround me. "I didn't do it. It was him all along. And he told the police that it was me." My heart races as I turn this information over in my head, and relief floods my body. "If Griffon's right, then Veronique must think it was me. That I was the one who killed her. But it wasn't. And now I can prove it."

"What's that about attempted murder?" Rayne says, reading the article over again. "It must mean that her dad tried to kill you too."

That stops me short. "I have no idea. I don't remember anything about that. All I know is that I was up on the roof looking down at Alessandra's body."

"Well, if there was a trial, there's got to be more information in here. Somewhere between January and July of that year." She reaches over and types something else in the search box.

"Who was Paolo Sartori?" she asks, looking back at me as the results come up.

"Paolo was Alessandra's boyfriend," I say. "I don't think I knew his last name."

"Well, apparently he didn't take her death well," she says. She tilts the screen so I can see the article.

January 7, 1895
SUTTER MANSION TRAGEDY CONTINUES—SARTORI KILLS SELF WHILE DESPONDENT

Paolo Sartori, a member of the Young Masters Orchestra involved in the Sutter Mansion Tragedy, committed suicide at 11:20 last night by shooting himself in the head with a small pistol. He died soon after firing the shot. Despondency is suspected as the cause of Sartori's self-destruction. After returning to the Black Swan Hotel last night, instead of going to his room, Sartori sat at the foot of the stairs, unfastened his coat and vest, placed the muzzle above his right eye, and pulled the trigger. Sartori was a native of Italy, 18 years of age. He was remaining in the City pending the outcome of the investigation into the death of a young woman at the Sutter Mansion some days past.

"Did you know him too?" Rayne asks as I finish reading.

"Yes," I say quietly. It feels like I just lost them both. I remember the handsome boy with the black hair and the kind eyes. "He was so in love that he couldn't live without her."

Eighteen

Mom pokes her head into the living room. "I'm going to take a shower," she says. "Veronique and Giacomo are due in about an hour." If keeping your enemies close means inviting them to dinner on a Saturday night, then we're all safe. Mom wants to thank Veronique for saving my life, and what better way to do it than with a giant pan of lasagna?

"Okay," I say, looking up from the book that I've been pretending to study. I haven't seen Veronique since the day of the accident—until my arm heals, not only cello practice, but all lessons are off. I have the pages from the newspaper printed and stuck in my desk drawer so that when the time comes, I can prove that I didn't do anything wrong. It's right there, in black and white.

Griffon glances up from his book and smiles at me. I feel a little bit guilty about not letting him in on all of my research, but

I want to talk to Veronique first—to prove to him that I really can take care of myself, that I'm smart enough to figure things out on my own. He's sprawled in the small chair by the fireplace, and all afternoon I've wanted to climb in there with him, but under Mom's watchful eye we've stayed on opposite sides of the coffee table.

"I've got a pan in the oven," she says. "Can you check on it in about ten minutes?"

"Sure," I say.

"If you need to take it out, have Griffon help you," she says, looking pointedly at the big black splint that covers most of my left arm. "It's too heavy to lift with one hand."

"Got it," I say, inwardly begging her to leave the room already.

The minute I hear her door shut, I bounce off the couch and walk over to him, taking the book out of his hands.

"Um, I'm reading that," he says, but the grin on his face says something different.

"*Things Fall Apart*," I say, reading the jacket. "That's a shame."

"He's a great Nigerian novelist," he says. "Don't mock."

I lower myself onto the arm of the chair and lean toward Griffon, dropping the book onto the floor. "I would never mock great literature," I say. "Plus, you're not really reading it. All you're doing is flipping pages every few seconds."

"That's how I read," he says. He lowers his eyebrows like he's hurt.

"Seriously?" I lean over and look at the book. The print is tiny. "Nobody can read that fast."

Griffon shrugs his shoulders but doesn't say anything, just touches my hand and laces my fingers carefully through his.

I pull my hand away, wincing a little with the pain the sudden movement causes. "Okay, smart boy," I say. I walk over to Mom's packed bookcase and run my finger over some of the titles. "Have you read this one?" I hold up *Death in Venice.*

Griffon nods. "Yep."

I put it back and look at another title. "How about *The Great Gatsby?*"

He laughs. "Everyone's read that."

I scowl and turn back to the bookcase. "'In the Penal Colony,' by Kafka?"

"Yes," he says. "Look, Cole, for a lot of the years I've been alive there wasn't much else to do for fun but read."

"I'll find something." I grab a thick, black book. "How about Poe?"

"Depends," he says. "Which story?"

I open up to the middle of the book. 'The Spectacles.'

"Ding! You win. I haven't read that one."

I look at him closely and can sense that he's telling the truth. "Great." I open the book wider to the second page of the story. "I'm going to give you ten seconds to look at this page, and then you have to tell me what's on it." I don't know why I'm pushing it— maybe I still want evidence. I want being Akhet to be something I can see and touch, something physical and knowable. Provable.

He reaches for my hand again. "Are you sure you want to start this now?"

"What? Are you scared you can't do it?"

He tilts his head in my direction. "Fine. Ten seconds."

I flip the book around so he can see it and count ten

Mississippis in my head before turning it back toward me. "Okay. What's on this page?"

Griffon groans. "I really hate doing stuff like this. Come on, Cole, I'm not some circus act. Let's just forget about it."

I smile at him. "So you can't do it. I knew it." Putting a chessboard back together is one thing, but I've caught him with the speed-reading.

He sighs. "Fourth paragraph, page 863. 'The magic of a lovely form in woman—the necromancy of female gracefulness—was always a power which I had found it impossible to resist, but here was grace personified, incarnate, the beau ideal of my wildest and most enthusiastic visions.' Griffon glances up at me. "Is that enough? 'Cause I can do the whole page, but it's probably going to get boring."

I stare at the words on the page, printed exactly as he'd said them, right there in black and white. Proof. It's what I'm after, but it gives me a shiver up my neck so violent I can't help but shake my head to try to get rid of it. "No. You don't have to finish."

"Well then, I guess you're going to have to trust me on the rest." He reaches up and pulls me into his lap, our teeth bumping as I laugh in the middle of the kiss. He's amazing, and here he is with me. Griffon brushes the hair away from my face and kisses me harder, pulling me into him so tightly it takes my breath away.

"You," he says, "are driving me crazy."

I toss my head and look at him out of the corner of my eye. "Good," I say, and lean in to kiss him again.

Griffon pulls away and watches the doorway. "Not good," he says. "Not with your mother in the next room."

"Relax," I say, trying to refocus his energy. "She can't hear anything."

"Wrong thing to say," he says, making a growling noise and nuzzling the back of my neck until I squeal.

"Okay, okay, I give up," I say. I twist in the chair to try to minimize the tingling sensation that's running through my body. "I'm totally ticklish."

"Ooh, duly noted," he says. "And filed for later." He picks me up around the waist and sets me back on the arm of the chair. "Much later."

He nods to the cello cases that are propped up in the corner of the room. They're just out of my range of vision, but are a large presence in the room anyway. They're a little dusty by now from being neglected for over a week. "Have you tried to play?"

I shake my head. "No." It seems like every time I pass this room, my eyes go automatically to the cellos. I don't want to admit that I'm afraid of what will happen. It's always been so easy. My fingers have always found the notes without my even having to think about it. The fear of not being able to play has taken over the idea that my gift is nothing but a lie. Part of me just doesn't want to know.

Griffon walks over to the cello case and holds it out to me. "Then would you show me?"

I raise my eyebrows. "How to play cello?"

He shrugs. "Sure. You promised to give me lessons back when we first met."

I walk over to the cello, almost afraid to touch it. Griffon lifts it out of the case and balances it gently against his shoulder. "Like this?"

"Yeah," I say. "That's right." I pick up the bow. "This goes in your right hand. Think of the bow as the breath of the cello. It's what draws the music out. Hold it like this." I show him the right way to hold a bow and hand it over. "Don't put your finger on any of the strings yet. Just let the bow glide over them."

Griffon has a light but firm touch, and only makes a few screeching noises when he gets too close to the bridge. "Show me a note."

I reach over and put his left hand in the correct position and his finger on the G string. "Now hold that down and use the bow to make the note." The bow bounces a little bit, but his fingering is strong. "See? That's an A."

"Great. Now only twenty-five more letters to go," he says, smiling.

"Ha-ha."

Griffon holds the cello away from his body. "You want to try?"

I stand looking at it, afraid to find out the answer to the question that has been hovering over everything for the past eight days. Because I took it almost everywhere and spent so many hours playing, the cello has always felt like a part of me, but lately it seems like a parasitic twin that's been removed. I'm not sure if either one of us can survive on our own.

"It's just us," he says quietly. "Not even your mom will hear it." He turns the cello in my direction, and I let it settle against me. The weight of the instrument against my body is so familiar, I haven't realized how much I missed it until now. I've always loved the curve of the wood and the delicate flashes of bronze in the sheen of the finish, and they seem even more beautiful to me now. I feel guilty for making it stay tucked away for so long.

I pick up the bow and hold it in my right hand, feeling like it's an extension of my fingers, of my thoughts, even. But my left arm begins to throb, and the tingling in my fingers feels more insistent. The splint covers the spidery black stitches, making that hand useless, and no amount of wanting or trying is going to change that right now. "It's too soon," I say, handing the bow back to Griffon. I shake my head, trying to push back the tears that are rising in my throat. "I can't."

Griffon reaches over and pulls the cello out of my hand, leaning over to kiss me gently. "I shouldn't have pushed you so quickly," he says. "It's not going anywhere. It'll be here when you're ready."

One lone tear courses down my cheek, and I angrily brush it away.

As he sets the cello back down in its case, Griffon's eyes flick to the doorway. I turn to see Mom pretending to walk into the room for the first time, although the shine in her eyes tells me that she's probably been standing there long enough. "I, um, was just coming in to tell you that the oven timer is going off." She hesitates, keeping her eyes deliberately off the big black case. She straightens her shoulders and regains her composure as she turns to walk back down the hallway. "I'll take care of it, though. You just keep studying."

∞

As the knives and forks clatter on the plates, I can't help but track Griffon with my eyes and try to keep the smile off my lips as he focuses his attention on Veronique. It only took a little begging to get Mom to invite him to stay too, and I've had her put them next to each other at the table. I watch as he sets his hand close to hers, and brushes her arm as he reaches for the butter on the table. If he's getting anything from her, it doesn't show on either of their faces.

The front door slams as Kat comes rushing in, her apologies reaching the table before she does. "I know, I know," she says, as she pulls back her chair. "I got hung up at work again. I'm sorry I'm late."

Mom forces a smile, while Dad has on one of his what-are-you-going-to-do looks. If you didn't know better, you could easily be fooled into thinking that they're still together instead of Dad only making appearances downstairs on special occasions. I wonder if they've ever been connected in a past life, and if there was something there that made things go so wrong in this one. Are they destined to keep coming together over and over until they either get it right or give up on the whole thing for good?

"Good thing we didn't wait for you," Mom says to Kat, her mouth set in a hard line. "Veronique, Giacomo—you know my oldest daughter, Katherine?"

"I don't think we've met," Veronique says, giving her a smile from across the table.

"I'm the one with no talent," Kat says, making Mom cringe in her seat. I can see her hands gripping the cushion of her chair as she tries to let Kat's words slide off of her.

"Kat," Dad warns from his place at the other end. Except he knows that none of us are buying his disciplinarian act, so he doesn't push it. Dad is always best in the role of Good Cop. Mom plays the Bad Cop without even breaking a sweat.

"Oh, come on," Kat says. "I'm only kidding." She points her

fork at Griffon. "Well hey, look at you there." Kat nudges me with her elbow. "Didn't think we'd be seeing him again." As she turns to me I catch a whiff of alcohol on her breath and wonder if Mom and Dad can tell that she's been drinking. "Owen's thinking about coming out here this summer. Do you talk to him much?"

Dad looks confused. "Do you and Griffon know each other?"

"Didn't Cole tell you? Griffon is the guy who helped her out when she fainted at the Tower of London that day." *Great.* Now I'm not only going to have to explain how we met, but also why I never mentioned it before now.

"Fainted?" Mom sits up straight. "You didn't say anything about fainting. Sam, did you know about this?"

Dad shrugs. "She said it was nothing. Jet lag. She's been fine ever since, haven't you, Cole?"

"Mom, please," I say, looking pointedly at Veronique and Giacomo. We're quickly becoming the world's best argument for not starting a family. Single and childless is probably starting to look pretty good about now. "It's nothing."

Veronique turns to Griffon. "So, let me get this straight. You were visiting London with Cole?" Dad glances at her and then over to Mom, and I know they're all waiting for an explanation.

"I live there part-time," he says. "That's where we met." He looks at me and I can tell he doesn't know how much to say.

"That's a funny story, actually," I say with a little laugh for emphasis. "Turns out that Griffon's dad is a Yeoman Warder at the Tower. I felt a little sick, and Griffon happened to be there, that's all. Kat found out through his friend that he lived around here and we got back in touch."

Kat spears a large forkful of salad. "Isn't that the cutest coincidence?" she says, jamming the salad into her mouth.

Veronique tilts her head toward me, her eyes locked on mine. "Totally," she agrees. "That's an amazing coincidence." Something about the way she says that word makes me uneasy, and out of the corner of my eye I can see Griffon sitting motionless next to her.

"A Warder?" Dad says. "That must be fascinating."

Griffon's focus shifts visibly as Dad speaks to him, and I wonder if anybody but me notices the effort. "It is," he agrees. "When I'm there I stay with him at the apartments inside the Tower."

Kat busies herself with the lasagna, and I can see Mom relax now that we're on to other, less volatile subjects. "I visited there years ago before the girls were born," she says. "What's it like after dark?"

"Haunted," Kat says, apparently listening to the conversation despite appearances. "Headless ghosts and chained prisoners roaming the grounds all night long."

Images from the vision at the Tower give me a sinking feeling in my stomach, but I press them down, determined not to let detached, fleeting memories overwhelm my evening. "Knock it off, Kat," I say. "There are no ghosts."

Giacomo smiles at me. "Ah, a skeptic," he says. "You do not believe in the supernatural?"

I can feel the smile on my face shift, and I will it back into place. "No. Not really." After all, people who can remember hundreds of years' worth of past lives, put overturned chess sets back together, and memorize a page of writing in ten seconds aren't exactly supernatural. Are they?

Mom jumps in. "Nicole has always been the practical one," she says. "She didn't even like fairy tales when she was little."

I can feel my face getting hot, and am grateful when Griffon takes over, steering the conversation in another direction. "There may not be ghosts at the Tower, but there have been a lot of famous people who came through over the years."

"Yeah," Kat says, "like who?"

Griffon starts naming all of the celebrities that he's seen at the Tower, starting off with a funny story about a famous heiress who insisted on trying to buy one of the pieces in the Crown Jewels collection and almost causing an international incident. Giacomo participates in the lively conversation in his halting English, but through it all Veronique remains unusually quiet, sitting across from me with her hands in her lap. Her eyes seem to focus on the conversation, but I can tell that her thoughts are elsewhere.

After dinner, Mom shoos us all into the living room for dessert. I sit next to Veronique on the wide couch, while Griffon takes his place in the chair by the fireplace. Although he looks relaxed, I can tell that he's watching us carefully. It's impossible to know if he's gotten any information from her, but he looks determined not to leave the two of us on our own.

"Has Veronique played the piano for you?" Giacomo leans over to ask me.

I look at Veronique, surprised. "No. I didn't know you played."

She shrugs. "I play a bit," she says. She looks over at Giacomo like she's going to kill him for bringing it up.

Giacomo snorts, either ignoring her or not seeing it at all. "More than, how do you say, 'a bit.' Go on," he encourages her.

"Oh, you must," Mom says, sticking her head in the room to get a coffee count. "Our piano is pretty lonely these days."

"If you insist," Veronique says, uncharacteristically shy. She perches on the piano bench and rubs her hands on her pants. As she exhales, she brings her hands down, and I recognize the opening bars of *Meditation*. My glance darts from her closed eyes to her hands as they flex and bend in a way that's natural and at the same time otherworldly. She plays the whole piece flawlessly, with more passion and emotion than even Julie did, her adagio section barely more than a fluttering whisper of the keys. As she finishes, she puts her hands back on her knees and looks embarrassed at our applause.

"You play a little," I repeat, amazed and a little irritated that she hasn't told me that she's some sort of piano genius before now. "And I play a little cello." Here I've been teaching her the basics like she didn't have a clue about music, and all along she could have been the one up on stage at the conservatory. "That's embarrassing."

"Oh, come on, it's not embarrassing," Veronique insists, coming back to sit next to me. "Okay, so I know how to play piano. I can't play the cello at all. At least I couldn't until I started taking lessons with you." She looks down at the black splint. "How's the arm? Did they say you can play again soon?"

"It's getting there," I say. Without thinking I rub my thumb against my tingling fingers, my mind flashing back to holding the cello earlier. "But they say that it might take a long time to get the feeling back in my fingers." *If it ever comes back,* I think, not able to say the words out loud. The black splint hides all but a few inches of the scar, and I see her eyes dart involuntarily to it as I speak. Is there a little bit of guilt in that glance?

"The important thing is that Cole came out of it in one piece," Dad says, standing behind me with his hand on my shoulder. "Thanks to you." He nods at Veronique. "If you hadn't been there to help, it could have ended very differently."

I can see a slight scowl on Griffon's face as Dad speaks, but I turn my full attention on Veronique. "He's right," I say.

"Well, it's not like I was going to let you bleed to death," Veronique says with a small smile. "I prepaid for this month's lessons, and I need to get my money's worth." She puts her arm around me and gives my shoulders a quick squeeze. I focus on where she's touching me and feel faint Akhet vibrations. As casually as I can, I look up at her face, scanning her eyes to try to see Alessandra in them, trying to see the essence of the girl I knew back then, but I get nothing. I suddenly want to tell her everything I know about Alessandra and what happened on the roof that night. That it wasn't me who pushed her off, that I would never do something like that. That I know we were friends and that I'd never try to take Paolo away from her. I want that connection again, to pick up the pieces of our old friendship that was cut short the last time. I feel like I'm surrounded by memories of Alessandra as the rest of the room grows distant.

The police wagon is waiting at the foot of the grand stone staircase as I'm pulled quickly through the front doors, the elegant guests quiet as they watch me struggle against the policemen's strong arms. The horses whinny and stamp at the ground, eager to be on their way.

"Wait! Please!" I cry. "This isn't right!" I feel like I'm in a nightmare and can't wake up.

There is a shout in Italian as I'm led down the stairs. "Stop!"

I turn, almost collapsing with relief. Someone heard me. Someone will understand. Paolo is rushing down the stairs after us, his gleaming dress shoes barely touching each step.

His eyes are wet with tears as he stops in front of me. "What happened?" he shouts, just inches from my face. "Were you so jealous of her perfection?"

My heart skips a beat. He doesn't believe me. I'm completely and totally alone. "I didn't do anything! I'd never hurt Alessandra."

Tears spill down his cheeks as he shakes his head in disbelief. "She loved you like a sister. Alessandra was the most perfect creature. And you destroyed her."

The policemen say something I don't understand and pull me toward the open back doors of the wagon. My legs refuse to carry me another step, so they lift me roughly and deposit me on one of the wooden benches lining the sides.

Paolo grips the edge of the open window and looks up at me with hatred in his eyes. "All I want to know is, why? Why would you do such a thing?"

I turn toward him, desperate for the words that will make him believe me. "I didn't. You have to believe me."

The wagon rocks as the policemen mount the front bench and the wheels jerk to life as the horses surge forward. Paolo stands at the bottom of the steps, hands at his sides, staring at me as the wagon races to our unknown destination, his figure getting smaller and smaller until we turn the corner and he's finally out of sight.

Giacomo leans over toward Veronique. "You should tell them that you trained to be a doctor before you went into research."

His words bring me back to the present, to the Veronique and Cole of the now instead of the Alessandra and Clarissa from before. I realize I have no idea what we're talking about. "I'm sorry, what was that?"

Giacomo looks shocked as I speak, but a small smile appears on Veronique's lips.

"I was just saying that Veronique studied to be a doctor. That's how she knew what to do with all of that blood," Giacomo repeats.

"I didn't know you were a doctor," I say, making a small attempt to pick up the conversation. I can still picture the hurt in Paolo's eyes.

"I didn't finish," she says slowly. "Not the medical part, any-way. I'm in research now."

"Still," I say, trying to shake off the memory. "The sight of blood would make most people run screaming out of the room instead of jumping in and doing what you did." I hesitate but lean toward her. "Listen, there are some things I want to talk to you about. Can you meet me tomorrow?"

"Nicole?" Dad is looking at me in alarm. "When did you learn Italian?"

I stare at him. What a random thing to say. "What are you talking about?"

"Italian," he says, his eyes concerned. "You're sitting there speaking flawless Italian with Veronique and Giacomo."

The room gets quiet as everyone seems to lean toward me. I search my brain for a rational-sounding answer, still not at all sure what happened. "We're learning it in school," I say quickly. "Enrichment classes."

Kat glances over at me. "I thought you were failing Spanish," she says. "Again."

"Well," I laugh, which sounds fake and forced even to me, "Spanish and Italian are really close—"

"And she's been studying with me," Griffon breaks in. "I'm planning on taking a year abroad in Italy, so Cole's been helping me work on my languages."

"Your accent is perfect," Veronique says. Her voice is steady, but she's looking at me intensely. "Almost as if you were born to it."

Mom bursts into the room carrying a tray of cookies, and everyone turns to help her clear a place at the coffee table. I smile gratefully at Griffon, while everyone else seems to forget about the fact that I can suddenly speak in tongues. Italian tongues, anyway.

Mom glances over at Kat, slumped in the chair by the window. "Honey, why don't you play something for us next?" She turns to Veronique. "Kat took piano lessons for years. She doesn't have the skill that you do, but she's quite the little musician in her own right."

I wince at her words, amazed as always that Mom apparently can't hear what comes out of her mouth. With the rest of her body totally still, Kat turns just her head in Mom's direction. "I don't think so."

Mom straightens up. "Oh, come on, Katherine," she says. "Give us a tune. You used to love playing Chopin. You and Nicole played the most marvelous duets together."

Kat stands up and runs her hands over her dress. In a voice

much quieter and steadier than I would have thought possible, she says, "We're not trained monkeys, you know. Just because Cole can't be your after-dinner entertainment anymore, it doesn't mean that I have to make a fool of myself." Nodding to Giacomo and Veronique, she crosses the room in four strides and heads down the hallway.

Mom smoothes her hair back and plasters a smile on her face as if nothing's happened. "Well, then," she says in a singsong voice. "Who wants coffee?"

Nineteen

As the door shuts behind Veronique, I can see Griffon relax for the first time this entire evening.

"That went well," Mom says, scurrying around the living room picking up cups and napkins.

"Thanks for inviting me, Mrs. Ryan," Griffon says, turning the full intensity of his smile on her.

She smiles back at him. "We're happy to have you," she says, glancing at me in a meaningful way that I pretend not to notice.

I can hear Dad washing dishes in the kitchen and figure it's best to ask when they aren't together. "Is it okay if we go out and meet Rayne?"

"I don't know, honey," Mom says. "You just got out of the hospital."

"The accident was more than a week ago," I say. Mom hesitates just a second, but I know she's lining up more excuses in her head. I jump in again. "I've barely gone anywhere since I've been home. Can't we just go out to get ice cream?" I ask quickly. "And maybe to the café. It *is* Friday night."

She glances at the clock. "Okay," she agrees. "Just be home before midnight. And take your phone."

"I will," I say from the hallway, already handing Griffon his jacket. We slip out the front door before she can change her mind.

As soon as we're down the steps and out of sight of the house, Griffon stops and kisses me, pulling me up to him so quickly that my feet actually leave the sidewalk. "I've been dying to do that for hours," he says, setting me back down on the ground.

I stand on tiptoe and pull his head down toward mine again. "Not as much as I have," I say, kissing him longer than he did me. I reach for his hand and he grabs mine, squeezing as if he'll never let go.

"Thanks for the save on the Italian thing," I say. "That was so weird. Was I really speaking Italian?"

"Flawlessly. Once you've opened your awareness of a past life, a lot of things come through easier," Griffon says in Italian, although I can understand him perfectly. He switches back to English. "Although it's happening really quickly for you. Did you see anything else?"

I hesitate. "Just a few things. I'm sure we were musicians together." Veronique agreed to meet me tomorrow so I can finally show her the truth. As soon as we clear it up, I'll let Griffon in on all of it.

Griffon slides his fingers through my hair, giving me a wicked

case of the shivers. "Despite the fact that we can't pinpoint anything in particular, I'm more convinced than ever that we need to
be careful."

"It'll be fine," I say. "Unless you want to meet me every single
day after school."

Griffon grins. "You say that like I haven't thought about it."

I look up the street, but I don't see his motorcycle anywhere.
"Did you drive?"

"It's around the corner. I figured it wouldn't help my case much
if your dad saw me parking the bike out front. Are we really going
to meet Rayne?" he asks.

"Yes," I answer. "But not up on Haight. She told me about a
bonfire out on the beach tonight—want to go?"

"Ooh, lying to your parents now?" Griffon smiles, raising his
eyebrows in surprise. "What happened to the straitlaced, cello-
playing girl I used to know?"

"She's decided that she needs to get out more," I answer. "Plus,
it's not a complete lie. We *are* meeting Rayne, and I do have my
phone. Maybe there will be ice cream—who knows?"

Watching the storefronts whizz by through what I'm quickly
thinking of as *my* helmet is such a different experience than riding the bus home from school every day. As we stop for a light in
front of Peet's Café, I feel like waving into the lit interior so that
everybody can see that I'm not just the schoolgirl on the city bus
anymore. So much has changed in such a short time.

As we get closer to the beach, the air becomes heavy with
moisture, and I can taste the salt on my lips as we drive. At the end
of the road, Griffon turns left, and the ocean stretches into the

horizon beside us as we ride down the hill, parallel to the water. Up ahead of us, shimmering spots of orange blaze as weekend bonfires light up the beach.

Coming out of a smooth turn at the bottom of the hill, Griffon suddenly hits the gas hard with his right hand. The bike jerks forward, and I press my body tight against his back. I can hear the motor strain as we pick up speed, the lines on the road turning into a continuous blur as we race along the asphalt.

For the first time riding with him, I'm afraid. Griffon takes his eyes off the road to glance over his shoulder for just a split second. Not wanting to turn my head, I peer around his arm until I can see headlights in the rearview mirror—headlights that are gaining on us so quickly it makes my breath catch in my throat. Whoever is behind us seems to be aiming right for the bike, and I will Griffon to go even faster.

As he lowers his head into the wind, Griffon lets go of the bike with his left hand to pull my arms together on his chest, and I know he means for me to hang on. With my right hand, I grab handfuls of his jacket and bury my face into his back, my heart beating fast and the plastic facemask of the helmet fogging up from my breath. The whine of the bike rushes through my ears, but not loudly enough to drown out the sound of the heavy car rumbling behind us. I don't dare lift my head to look, but I can tell by the sound and the way the headlights light up our silhouette that it is almost close enough to touch.

It seems as though the car's bumper is right at our back tire when Griffon eases up on the gas just the smallest bit and throws us into a left-hand turn so tight that we're horizontal to the cold black street as we swing away from the main road. The car races past us, unable to make the turn at the last minute. Hitting the throttle once again, we speed into the west end of Golden Gate Park, the bike easing upright as Griffon slows down and pulls over into the grass at the side of the road.

I sit frozen as he puts the kickstand down and turns the engine off. The sudden silence is deafening, and without the headlight, the darkness is only interrupted by the moon peeking through the trees.

Griffon puts his arms around me and I manage to get off the bike, my knees buckling as my feet touch the grass. "Are you okay?" he asks urgently. Gently, he unclips the strap and lifts my helmet off. I manage a brief nod before I start shaking.

"Son of a bitch!" Griffon yells into the darkness. He slams his helmet to the ground and paces a few short steps in front of the bike. The force of his anger is almost visible as my eyes adjust to the dim light, and I'm glad that it isn't directed at me. "I can't believe she'd pull something like this. What the hell is she thinking? Dammit!"

I stand motionless, willing my heart to stop pounding and brush away the wet spots on my cheeks. *We're fine. We didn't crash.* As long as I keep telling myself that, the panic will ebb to manageable levels. "What happened?"

His breath is coming quick and loud as he kicks at the wet grass. "Her car was behind us. It started coming up so fast, too fast to be an accident. She was trying to run us off the road."

I lean back so that I can see his face in the silver light. "You think it was Veronique?"

"I'm sure of it," he says quickly. "She must have waited for us outside of your house and followed us here. It would have been so easy to make it look like an accident—all she'd have to do is bump us from behind. If we'd gone down at that speed . . ." He shakes his head violently and shouts into the trees. "Stupid!"

After a few moments, Griffon calms down, the only visible remnant of his anger is the way his fists clench and unclench as he paces. "I'm so sorry," he says. He grabs my hand and presses it to his lips. "I totally let my guard down."

I close my eyes as I lean on him, feeling the strength of his energy as it flows between us. "It wasn't your fault," I say quietly. "You got us out of it."

"But I shouldn't have gotten us into it in the first place. I saw her headlights way back near your house, but I was enjoying the ride so much that I didn't pay enough attention."

"Stop." I reach up and run my fingers gently through his curls to try to calm him. "You did everything right. We're still here in one piece, aren't we?"

"For now," he says, his eyes shining with anger. "I won't let this happen again, I swear to you."

As comforting as it is to know that he'd do anything to protect me, the thought chills me to my core. Pulling Griffon to me, I wrap my arms around him and will him to let it go.

After a few seconds, he leans back. "Hang on," he says, looking into my eyes. "When you started speaking Italian with Veronique tonight . . . were you touching her?"

"I think so. She put her arm around me, just to give me a hug." I think about the look on her face when I started speaking Italian.

Giacomo's mouth was hanging open in shock, but she didn't seem surprised at all.

"Oh, God. That's why, then." Griffon looks back toward the main road. "When you touched her, Veronique must have been able to see that you were remembering—you don't have the skills to block out her senses yet. Now she knows that your awareness is returning."

I search his eyes in the dim light. "So what does that mean?"

His eyes narrow and he swallows hard. "It means she knows you're Akhet now. You remember your connection to her. And now there's no reason for her to hold back anymore."

Twenty

Do I even need to ask where the two of you have been?" Rayne squeals as we make our way slowly across the cold sand.

"Probably not." I glance at Griffon walking beside me, holding tight to my good hand. He wanted to go straight home, but I managed to convince him to keep going toward the beach. We lost the car, and they don't have any idea where we're going. A bonfire on the beach is probably the safest place in the city for us right now, and all I really want is to be with him, far from runaway cars and rogue Akhet. I'll tell Griffon everything I know about Veronique. Tomorrow.

"I'll bet. You should see how red your face is." She grins at me and gives me a quick hug. "I'm just glad you're here. Gabi's over there talking to some guy from Roosevelt." Rayne makes a face. She thinks all guys from Roosevelt are snobs.

There are probably twenty people scattered around the sand, some sitting on blankets in the shadows, others standing in knots close to the fire, the flickering flames casting a bright glow over their features.

"The coolers over there have drinks in them, but I'm not sure there's much beer left. I heard that someone's going on a run, but I don't know for sure."

Griffon looks down at where our hands join, and then at the cooler.

"Go," I say. "I'll be fine here."

"Okay. I'll check," Griffon says with a tight smile, giving my hand a last squeeze before he walks over toward the fire.

"I'm sooo glad you guys came," Rayne says, jumping up and down a little. "How was dinner?" I'd told her that Griffon was coming over, but didn't tell her why.

"The usual. Kat came home buzzed and totally pissed off my mom. She did kind of deserve it, though."

"Do they like Griffon?"

"Of course," I say. "He's polite to my dad and helped Mom clear the dishes. What's not to like?" I watch as Griffon pulls a can from the cooler and begins talking to a small group of people near the fire, glancing back my way every few seconds. In moments they're laughing in the easy way people do when they know each other well, and I wonder if they're from his school. A girl with short pink hair reaches up and puts her arms around his neck, pulling him down into a hug that looks uncomfortably friendly.

Rayne follows my glance. "Interesting," she says. "I heard that there are some kids from Marina here. I wouldn't worry about it, though. He came with you, didn't he?" She squints as she scans the group. "That guy in the black jacket is so yum. I've been watching him all night. Please, please, please let them be friends."

"Hmmm," I murmur as I try to tear my eyes away from Griffon and the strange girl. A sour taste rises in the back of my throat as I force myself to turn from them. *Griffon has a life completely separate from mine*, I remind myself. Different school. Different friends. As much as I'd like to pretend otherwise, it's not like he began to exist the minute I showed up.

"They had one beer left," Griffon says as he reappears beside me. "Hold the cup and I'll split it."

My emotions are so raw that I don't say anything as he pours the beer into the blue plastic cup. I hate beer, but after everything I've been through tonight I feel like I can drink a couple with no problem.

Never one to be shy about anything, Rayne pounces on him. "So what's the story with those guys over there?"

Griffon glances back at the group. "Just some guys from school," he says. He grins at her, relaxing a little. "Anyone you want to know about?"

"No," she says too quickly. Rayne glances back toward the group. "Although if I did want to know anything about anyone, it might be the tall blond guy in the black jacket over there."

"Peter," he says. "Good choice. Let's see—runs cross country, in my calculus class, no girlfriend at the moment. Want me to introduce you?"

"Definitely, please," Rayne says. "Let's go now."

They start walking toward the fire, but I hang back, not

wanting to share Griffon, even with people who knew him first. I like being able to make up my own image of him, and watching him with his friends makes me realize how much I don't know.

"Oh, for God's sake," Rayne says, stepping back to grab me by the arm. "Come on, already. Don't be drama."

I follow them to the fire, the heat immediately causing my cheeks to burn. Rayne's smile is wide as she easily joins the conversation already in progress, but I stand just a half step back from Griffon as he laughs with his friends.

Without breaking the conversation, Griffon leans back and puts one arm around my shoulders, drawing me forward into the circle. That one gesture alone is a statement to his friends, and they get quiet as they look at me expectantly.

"Guys," he says, "this is Cole. And that's Rayne."

They're nice enough as they say hello, mentally adjusting their view of Griffon as he stands with his arm around me. Griffon introduces the pink-haired girl as Alana, and while her smile is welcoming, her brown eyes are wary. She's pretty in an edgy way, with heavy eye makeup and a tiny nose ring that glitters in the firelight. The way her light hair contrasts with her dark skin makes her look otherworldly, and I immediately feel dull and boring—with hardly any makeup or extra piercings, I'm the picture of an aspiring cellist with no social life.

Alana holds her cup close to her chest and points one heavily ringed finger at me. "You go to Pacific, right?"

I nod slowly.

"So how did you meet our Griffon?" The "our" in front of his name is not lost on me.

"I picked her up in London," Griffon answers for me.

I laugh quickly while Alana raises her eyebrows. "London? Really."

"Yep. London." I smile at him and take a sip from the cup. *Our* cup. The one we're sharing. I hand it back to him just to make sure Alana notices that fact.

I spend the rest of the conversation trying to avoid Alana's eyes as she seems to track my every move. Rayne manages to find something in common with Peter, and the two of them step back from the fire to go sit on the concrete retaining wall at the end of the beach.

"Want to walk?" Griffon asks, gazing out at the shimmering ocean. He reaches back with his hand out and I take it, running a few steps to catch up with him. Away from the fire, the air is colder and the noise from the crashing waves is louder.

We walk down the beach just at the edge of the water, hearing scraps of conversation and shouts of laughter from the bonfires as they're carried by the breeze. Griffon bends down as a wave recedes and wipes the sand off something before handing it to me.

I look at the perfect sand dollar and run my hand over the smooth edges before putting it carefully into my pocket. The beach is littered with broken ones, but a whole one is always a treasure. "Thanks," I say, leaning into him as we walk.

There's a big log a few yards down the beach, and Griffon pulls me down onto it so that I'm sitting in front of him. I lean back, enjoying his warmth as we watch the surf pound the beach. I feel Griffon shift as he looks back toward the bonfire.

"Rayne seems to be pretty happy," he says.

I glance back to where I can see their silhouettes still sitting on the wall. "Thanks for introducing them," I say.

"Peter's a good guy."

We sit in silence for a few more moments, until I can't hold it in any longer. "Do you know Alana from school?"

"Mmm-hmmm," he says. I can feel his heart beating as I lean into him. His chest rises as he takes a deep breath. "Actually, I, um . . . used to know her sister."

"As in 'know,' know?" I get a sinking feeling, wondering if she's as pretty as Alana.

"I suppose. But it's not like she was my girlfriend," he adds quickly.

"You mean you slept with her?" I ask. I turn around to face him so that I can see his eyes as he answers.

He pauses, but won't meet my gaze. "She goes to college down in Santa Barbara and came home last summer for vacation." He suddenly seems older again, more mature than any guy of seventeen has a right to be. "Look, I didn't lie to you," he says. "I don't go out with girls my age. Nobody in high school, anyway." He lowers his eyes and bites his bottom lip. "At least, I didn't."

Despite the fact that this makes my heart race, I say nothing. Griffon leans in to kiss me, but I pull back just as his lips brush mine.

"Sometimes I think you just want to be the handsome prince," I say, studying the rough bark of the log. I haven't really thought any of this through, but I suddenly know that it's exactly how I feel.

"Um, thanks?" he says uncertainly.

"Not thanks," I say. "It's like I'm some kind of damsel in distress and you want to be the one to rescue me."

Griffon puts his hand over mine. "You're right. I do want to rescue you," he says. "But not because I think you can't handle things on your own. It's for my own selfish purposes." He leans in and kisses me again; the hunger he feels is almost visible in his touch. The vibrations that exist between us are like background noise now—so constant that they're just an extension of him.

I let myself melt into his body, my hands traveling up his thighs to pull his hips toward me, causing Griffon to inhale sharply. I wrap my legs around his waist and unzip his jacket, sliding my cold hands inside. I can feel the outline of the ankh pendant underneath his shirt as I explore his torso, my fingers tracing the muscles under his warm skin. We stay like that for what seems like hours, tasting and touching, and I'm grateful for the limitations imposed on us by being out on a wet, cold, public beach. If we'd been safe in his room on his big, wide bed, I'm not sure that I'd be able to say what I know I should to keep things from going too far.

As we sit listening to the waves, I feel peaceful inside, like I've finally found what I've spent years looking for. School doesn't matter. The cello doesn't matter. Even not playing the cello doesn't seem to matter.

"It makes a difference, doesn't it?" I say. "Knowing you're going to do it all again."

"In a way," Griffon says cautiously.

"I mean, what if something bad did happen? It would suck for the rest of this life, but we could find each other in the next life and start all over again. There's got to be a way to leave a marker to follow the next time around."

"It doesn't really work like that," Griffon says, a hint of sadness in his voice. "There's no guarantee that we'll even be back together in the same century—forget about the same continent."

"What about all those stories you hear about people who are destined to be together? Who find each other again because it's fate?"

"I wish it were that simple." Griffon leans over to kiss my neck. "There are no guarantees you'll find the people you were with before, even though technology does make it easier to find other Akhet."

The thought of coming back without him sends a stab of pain through my chest. "Does it ever end? Do people ever stop coming back?"

"Maybe," he says. "Some forms of Buddhism think that once you no longer need the earthly experiences anymore, you go permanently to a higher plane."

"Like heaven?"

"Probably where the idea of heaven came from," he says. "But I personally can't imagine no longer needing earthly experiences." He starts running his fingers through my hair, each contact with my scalp sending shivers straight down into my feet. I close my eyes, giving myself up to the sensation and the sound of the waves in the cold dark night.

The transition into the vision isn't as jarring as it has been before; the first thing I feel is the scratchy fabric at my throat, and the familiar rhythm of someone gently running a comb through my hair.

I sit at my dressing table, staring blankly out the small window to the courtyard down below. The grounds are unnaturally green, and contrasts with the dull brown cobblestones that run between the buildings. I can't see any workmen from here, but I've been listening all morning to the sound of nails being driven into lumber as they prepare the site.

Anna tries to hide her emotions as we complete our daily routine, but the occasional sniffle as she draws the silver comb down my back gives away her true state of mind.

"Anna, please," I say, turning toward my lady and taking her small hand in mine. "Do not waste your tears, all will be well."

"Yes, Lady Allison," she says, staring at the intricate comb in her hand. Two tears form parallel lines down her ruddy cheeks. "I know that you have done nothing to deserve this fate and that a just God will spare you. 'Tis only . . ." A sob rattles in her throat as she turns away from me.

"You musn't lose faith," I insist, my words bolstering my own failing conviction. "The good will triumph. It says so in the Book of Prayers." My eyes flick to the prayer book that lies on the trunk at the foot of the bed. We've been up all night, listening to the commotion in the yard down below and reading comforting passages from the only book I've been allowed these long months. I glance up, although I don't know what I expect to see except the heavy beams that cross the ceiling and stray cobwebs that adorn the corners of the room. So far, God has not come to intervene on my behalf, but I have no doubt that I will not be abandoned.

As Anna finishes tying the ribbon around my plait, we hear a shuffling outside the heavy door, followed by a gruff knock and a metallic sound as the lock is disengaged. Her pink cheeks fall instantly pale and her hand flies up to cover her mouth, for we both know these are no idle visitors. "It is time!" she says in a hoarse whisper.

Squaring my shoulders and drawing myself up to my full height, as Mam would have expected, I stand and smooth the heavy black skirt that falls nearly to the floor. I wrap my hand around the pendant as Anna reaches up and frees the clasp from around my neck. The metal is still warm as I drop the necklace into the small silk pouch, tears filling my eyes for the first time since this nightmare started. As we stand waiting for the door to swing open, I grab Anna's hand in a gesture of comfort. "Take heart, Anna, for we are well protected."

"Hey." Griffon's insistent tone brings me back to the present. "Everything okay?"

I nod slowly as the last traces of the image slip from my mind. "I'm fine."

"Where were you?" His voice is gentle now. "Did you see Veronique again?"

"It was different this time. I was at the Tower again," I say, trying to orient the image of the room with what I'd seen on my visit there. "Inside one of the buildings, looking out. I . . . I think it's just before the vision I saw at the scaffold." My heart starts racing as small pieces of the puzzle begin to fit together. "Oh my God, she called me Lady Allison!"

"Who did?" Griffon asked.

"The girl who was with me. She was brushing my hair, and

she called me Lady Allison! When I had the memory in the hospital, the woman at the cottage called me Allison."

Griffon pulls his fingers from my hair and wraps his arms around me. "It could mean anything," he says. "Maybe you're seeing a different life altogether."

"No," I insist, a little puzzled about why he isn't as excited as I am about the discoveries I'm making. "It's the same, I can feel it. The girl in the cottage on the cliff is the same person who was beheaded at the Tower."

"I don't think so," Griffon says. "I've been on my Dad's tour hundreds of times. There were only a few people who were actually beheaded inside the Tower walls, and none of them were named Allison."

My conviction is growing stronger as I turn the images over in my mind. The scratchy black dress, the little house on the cliff— the two things were parts of the same lifetime, I'm sure of it. My name was Allison, and I was executed at the Tower of London.

"Well," I say, "this time, history is wrong." I feel like a puzzle with gaping holes, as all of these separate lives are piecing themselves together. How many lives have there been so far? How many more are still to come?

Griffon pulls me closer to him and rubs my shoulders to warm me. "I'm sure you're right," he says. He looks out at the water. "I wish we could stay here forever. Away from Veronique. No school. No Sekhem. Maybe you should just move in," he says. "With me. Janine won't mind, and Veronique will never be able to find you."

"Right," I say, wishing it was only that easy. "Not like I don't have a real life or anything. I can totally picture that conversation with my parents. 'Um, I'm in danger from someone I may have done something bad to in a past life, so I'm just going to move in with my—'" The word "boyfriend" almost slips out, but I catch it in time. Or so I think.

"Your—?" Griffon says, leaving the next word hanging. He pinches my side lightly and laughs. "Your what?"

My mind is racing. I have no idea what we really are, and I'm terrified of saying the wrong thing. "Um, my semi-platonic friend who doesn't date high-school girls."

"Is that what this is?" Griffon teases.

I pull away from him, suddenly serious. "I don't know."

"I think you do," he says. A smile drifts across his lips, and he bends down to kiss me lightly. "Why are you afraid to say it?"

"I'm not afraid," I say, hoping he believes me. I don't want to come off like some lame teenager. I can feel my breath coming in short bursts, and I hope he doesn't notice.

Griffon kisses me behind the ear. "Two truths," he says quietly, his breath warm on my skin, "and a lie. My turn."

My mind is on overload, the sensations from his touch threatening to take over any remaining rational thought. "Okay," I manage.

"I once had a painting hanging in the Louvre. My cat's name is Stanley," he says, his lips tracing a route down my neck to my collarbone. "And my girlfriend has the most beautiful eyes in the world."

I swallow hard. "I've seen your art, so I think the painting one is true."

"One for one so far," Griffon says.

"And you already said you don't have any pets. So that's the lie."

"Good to see you were paying attention." Griffon sits back, his thumb tracing my cheekbone. "Which would make the girlfriend one...?"

I smile. "A truth?"

He looks at me and grins, his deep dimples flashing even in the dim light of the moon. "I told you that you were good at this. If you're my girlfriend, then what does that make me?"

"My boyfriend," I whisper. I watch his face, waiting for him to turn this moment into a joke, but his features have turned serious.

"That's the first time I've called anyone my girlfriend," he says quietly.

In this lifetime, I finish for him silently.

Without taking his eyes off my face, Griffon lifts my left hand and gently kisses the palm, his fingers brushing the edge of the splint that hides the angry scar on my wrist. He runs his lips across my fingers, and I think I see a tear shining on his lashes before he closes his eyes.

I reach under his shirt and run my right hand along his warm skin so that he shivers. "You're freezing," he says.

"Your hands must be cold too," I tease. I lead his hands tentatively under the layers I'm wearing. He looks at me questioningly as his fingers slide under my shirt, and it's my turn to gasp as he slowly begins to explore my bare skin. Shifting forward, I press myself against him, feeling the vibrations between our bodies growing stronger. What has been a distant, steady hum now becomes an insistent pulsing between us that matches the beating of my heart exactly.

Griffon's breath is heavy as I brush my palm against his chest, which tenses at my touch. I smile and look up into his face, pleased at the reaction I can get from just a small gesture. His eyes are closed, and he's biting his bottom lip as if he's struggling for control. He must feel my eyes on him, because his lids slowly open, revealing those golden amber eyes that are at once familiar and endless.

As my eyes lock on his, I feel a cold stab of fear flash through my body, a sensation so powerful it feels like a tremor.

I know those eyes.

They've been burned into my memory as one of the last things I saw before the metallic flash that brought total darkness. The same eyes that had shown no mercy, the only things visible beneath a hooded cloak on top of a wooden scaffold on a gray, foggy English morning. I've seen them in the vision—replayed that scene over and over in my head a hundred times—but failed to recognize them in real life. Everything else about him has changed, but the essence that's behind his eyes is the same.

I cannot save you, my lady. The words seem to echo around us as if they had been spoken out loud. I search Griffon's face, desperate to be wrong, but as I look into his eyes one more time, there is a recognition that can't be denied.

They are the eyes of my executioner.

Twenty-One

Oh my God!" I cry, scrambling backward and falling to the sand. "It was you!" I jump to my feet and take a step away from him. I stare at Griffon, but it's like I can't see him anymore. All I can see are the memories.

"Cole!" Griffon shouts, standing up quickly. There's confusion in his voice, and I can tell he doesn't think I know the truth, that I'm as clueless as I've been since the second we met. "What's wrong?"

I keep my eyes on him as I pull my jacket tighter around me. How can I have missed it all this time? Even now, as he stares at me, I recognize those eyes from that morning so long ago. "I can't believe you lied to me!" I say, glancing toward the bonfire. My heart is racing as I calculate how quickly I can reach Rayne.

Understanding flickers across Griffon's face, and he takes a step toward me. "It's not what you think! Cole, you've got to believe me." He reaches for my arm, but I push him away.

"Don't touch me," I say, trying to keep my voice even. I hold out my hands, ready to defend myself if he lunges toward me again. Instantly, I feel the difference in our sizes and know that if he wants to grab me, I'll have a hard time stopping him.

"Just hear me out," he pleads, taking a step back from me. "It's not what you think," he repeats, his voice attempting to calm me.

"It was you on the scaffold that day," I say. "You were the one who . . ." I can't even bring myself to say those words out loud. Sobs are hiding in the back of my throat as I realize that everything up to now has been a complete lie. His words. His touch. His concern. None of it is real.

Griffon seems to collapse from inside. "It was me," he says, not taking his eyes off mine. "I knew the second I touched you at the Tower who you were. And who I was to you. But I also knew you wouldn't understand—"

"Understand?" I shoot back. "You killed me! You raised an axe and cut my head off. What else is there to understand?" There it is, out in the open. As the words hang in the air, I have an over-whelming urge to get away from here, to put as much distance between us as possible.

There's a catch in his voice as he tries again. "It wasn't like that!"

But I can't get the image of his eyes, just barely visible above the black mask, out of my head. I'm through listening. I wish I could put back the years, the centuries between us. But right now all I have is a wide-open beach.

The sand is damp and I sink into it with every step as I run toward the orange glow of the bonfires. I can hear Griffon's foot-steps behind me, and he catches up with me just as I reach the edge of the scattered group, grabbing me by the shoulder and twist-ing me around to face him.

"You have to listen to me," he insists.

"I don't have to do anything," I say, trying to shake his hands off me. "I know everything I need to know. Let me go!"

"Not until you hear what I have to say!" he roars, and I notice the silence that descends around us as everyone turns to watch.

"What's going on?" His friend Peter pushes his way between us, and Griffon lets me go.

I look around frantically. "Where's Rayne?" I ask, my breath coming in bursts from running.

"She went to the store with her sister and some other people," Peter says. "They just left." He turns to face Griffon. "What hap-pened?"

"I've got this," Griffon says to him. "Just a misunderstanding." He looks steadily into my eyes, and I know he doesn't want to have this conversation in front of all these people. "Come on, I'll take you home."

I step closer to Peter. "I'm not going anywhere with you. I'll walk if I have to."

Peter looks down at me. "You don't have to do that. I'll take you."

"Don't do this, Cole," Griffon pleads. "You're making a mistake."

"Can we go now?" I ask Peter, turning my back to Griffon and walking away. All eyes around the bonfire are trained on the three of us.

Peter hesitates, but trots to catch up with me. "I'm parked in the lot over there," he says, pointing to the left.

We walk in silence toward his car, the only sound is that of his keys jangling as he takes them out of his pocket.

"Are you okay to drive?" I ask.

"I haven't been drinking," he says. He opens the door for me and walks around to the driver's side. "Are *you* okay?" he asks as we slide into the front seats.

I nod quickly, feeling the ache in my throat as I think about what just happened. For weeks, Griffon has pretended to be the perfect guy, the one with all the answers. Apparently I haven't been asking any of the right questions.

Peter puts the key in the ignition just as a motorcycle roars to life behind us. I barely have time to look out the window before Griffon speeds past us, my helmet still attached to the side of his bike, the back wheel fishtailing wildly as he accelerates onto the Great Highway.

"That idiot's going to get himself killed," Peter says quietly. He pulls out of the parking lot and drives in the direction of Griffon's quickly disappearing taillight. I watch the bonfires get smaller and smaller in the side mirror as we climb toward the Cliff House. My heart is still racing, and although I've recovered from the run, it feels like I can barely breathe. In the darkness of the car, all I can picture is Griffon's face. The curls that always beg to be touched. The curve of his lip as his face widens into a dimpled grin. The eyes that have betrayed me from the beginning. Everything has been a lie. From the moment we met, I've been part of some kind of sick joke. The tears spill from my eyes, hot rivers flowing down my face faster than I can wipe them away.

Peter reaches into the console and hands me a wad of fast-food napkins, but doesn't say a word, and I don't trust my voice enough to say thanks. We drive in silence for a few minutes as I stare out the side window and try to get a grip on myself. The least I can do is wait to lose it until I get home.

"Cole?" Peter finally asks quietly. I close my eyes and try to breathe deeply to stop the suffocating feeling that's settling into my chest. I can't handle any questions right now, and how will I answer them anyway? Griffon betrayed me five hundred years ago? He was my executioner in a past life? The secrets that come with being Akhet are starting to intrude into real life, and I can't guarantee I'll say the right thing.

"Cole?" Peter asks again. "I don't know where you live."

I sigh with relief. "Haight," I manage.

"Where on Haight?"

I press my head against the window, suddenly exhausted. "Anywhere. At Masonic is fine."

"I'll take you all the way home," he says, glancing over at me with concern.

I shake my head. "That's close enough." I need to walk a couple of blocks to clear my head before I show up at home looking like a wreck.

Almost too quickly, Peter is pulling up to the curb near Ben & Jerry's. My neighborhood is always busy, but Friday nights are crazy. The sidewalks are crowded with people spilling in and out of the bars, clubs, and cafés that line the few short blocks between here and my house. It's the perfect place to lose myself for a little while, and I'll be as safe here as I will anywhere.

Peter looks out the front windshield. "You sure this is okay?"

"It's great," I say, grabbing the door. "Thanks."

I step out and let the swarming crowd envelop me and pull

me along the sidewalk, not thinking, just moving my feet toward home. All I want is to crawl into my bed and forget everything that's happened over the past month. As I walk past my corner where the homeless people always camp out, the sound of bongo drums and the smell of pot smoke hanging in the air is oddly comforting. The quiet of my street after the chaos of Haight is like slipping into a tub of warm water. Here and there people walk up the sidewalk toward the lights of the clubs, but mostly I have several blocks all to myself.

As I approach my house, the door suddenly opens at the top of our steps, and the light from the hallway shows Griffon in perfect silhouette at my front door. He isn't carrying his helmet, but his hair is wild, as if he's just yanked it off in a hurry. I press myself against the shadows of our neighbor's front wall and watch as he talks to Mom. I can't hear what he's saying, but it must be convincing, because in a few seconds, she steps back from the door and ushers him into the house, closing the door behind them.

"Damn," I say under my breath. I have no idea what he's telling her, but I'm positive that it has nothing to do with the truth. For the first time, the anger coursing through my body is beginning to feel a lot like fear. Like he said about Veronique, now that I know the truth, there's no reason for him to hold back. He killed me once before. What's to stop him from trying again?

I start to walk quickly back up toward Haight. If Griffon is going to be in my house, then I need to find somewhere else to go. Somewhere he doesn't know about. Somewhere he can't find me. I pull my phone out of my pocket just as it starts ringing. Mom. I swallow hard, hit ignore and pull up Rayne's number.

"Where are you?" Rayne yells into the phone. "We just got

back to the beach and everyone is freaking out about the fight you had with Griffon."

"I'm at my house," I say. "Except he's here too. I . . . I can't face him right now. Can I come over to yours?"

"Of course. Sienna's driving, want us to pick you up?"

"Yeah," I say. "Can you meet me at the café?" It will be warm and busy enough there for the ten minutes it will take her sister to drive over this way.

"We're leaving right now," Rayne says.

I walk toward the café as my phone starts ringing again, and I don't even have to look at it to know it's Mom. I hit ignore again and then open a blank message. The cursor sits there blinking at me as I realize I have no idea what to say. I'm going to have to tell her something or she'll freak out for sure. Just a short note saying I'm staying at Rayne's and that I'm okay. It'll have to do for now. My eyes are on the screen as I bump right into a guy walking the other way.

"Cole!" There's no mistaking the Italian accent.

I look up in alarm to see Giacomo and Veronique standing in front of me along with another well-dressed couple. "Oh! I, uh . . ." I can feel my cheeks getting red as I try to figure out what to say.

Veronique's eyes brighten as she smiles. "Hey! Your timing's great. I was just telling my friends all about your recital." She glances down at the splint on my wrist and her smile fades.

All I can picture are the headlights speeding behind us as we raced against time on the motorcycle. Veronique isn't supposed to be here. She should be far away from here by now. This isn't making any sense. "Where did you come from?" I finally ask.

Veronique looks confused. "From the martini bar," she says, indicating a spot up the street. "We met Siobhan and Hamish there after we left your house."

Now it's my turn to look confused. "You mean you didn't drive anywhere after dinner?" I ask. My thoughts are racing. I study her face to find any sign that she's lying to me. "You weren't on the Great Highway earlier tonight?"

"No," she says slowly, her eyes steady on mine. "We've been in this neighborhood all night."

If that's true, then Griffon lied about the car chase, too. So far, everything I've known about him is a lie. But why? What does he want from me? I've never felt so alone in my life. I burst into panicky tears. "Excuse me," I say pushing past them. "I have to go."

I run toward the café, blinded by the hot tears that burn my eyes. I hear the click-clack of high heels on the sidewalk just as Veronique catches up with me. "Cole! Stop." She puts her hand over mine as I reach for the door handle. "I can't just leave you like this. What's wrong?"

Suddenly nowhere feels safe. "I can't . . . I have to go," I say again, pulling at the handle, but Veronique puts her arm around my shoulder and steers me toward the doorway of the building next door.

"At least stay here for a second and calm down," she says, opening her bag and taking out a crisp white handkerchief. "Take this."

After a few minutes I manage to catch my breath, certain now my face is bright red and blurry from crying. "I'm sorry," I say, trying not think about Griffon, knowing that will start the tears all over again. "This is so stupid." I turn away. I need time to sort this all out. To know if there is anything safe I can say to her. "You should go."

"You can't keep this all locked up inside," Veronique says. She tilts her head. "Obviously something's wrong." She pauses. "Is it Griffon?"

Is it Griffon? A simple question, with such a complicated answer. Even his name feels like a dagger. I look into her eyes, trying to see the danger that Griffon always insisted is there. All I see is concern, and I start to feel ridiculous for listening to him; he's lied about so much. He tried to convince me that she was trying to kill me, but so far Veronique is the only person in my life who has done anything to help me. God knows I need some help right about now.

I want so badly to confide in her, to tell her what's going on. To have her tell me what to do. "Yes. Sort of. We . . . had an argument."

"Oh, no! Everything looked fine at dinner. What happened?"

I hesitate. Each of us is holding tight to a piece of our past, not ready to let the other one see. Or am I? Besides Janine, Veronique is the only other Akhet on earth that I know. Now, she's the only one who might be able to help me, to give me some answers. To teach me how to live like this. I watch her face as I answer. One little flinch, one glance away and I'm out of here. "Griffon lied to me. He's been lying to me for a long time." I glance toward the street. Giacomo and their friends are talking animatedly to each other and not paying any attention to us.

"Must have been a big lie to get you so upset." Something shifts in her movements. A decision has been made. Veronique steps closer and speaks more softly. "Is there anything else going on?"

She holds my eyes steady with hers. "I have to say, I was really impressed with your Italian tonight. I had no idea you knew how to speak it. And you sounded like a native. Like you'd been speaking it all your life."

Veronique has opened the door. All I have to do is walk through it. "I think I was born speaking Italian," I say. I pause, knowing that once it's out there, I can't undo it.

"But not this time," she finishes for me, a glint of hope in her eyes.

I shake my head slowly. "Not this time."

Veronique's face shines with relief as the words come out of my mouth, as if something heavy has been lifted between us. "I knew it!" she says quietly. "You're starting to remember, aren't you?"

"Yes. Some." I look around again to make sure nobody is paying attention to us. It feels like everything I've kept from her the past several weeks is coming out in a rush. "I already know. About the Akhet. Griffon told me. He told me a lot of things, even though I'm not sure how much to believe."

Veronique puts one hand up to her mouth. "Wow. That's a lot to deal with. How long has it been?"

"Not that long. A couple of weeks, maybe." I feel like I'm on the edge of something big, of figuring out a way to start repairing what happened between us in the past.

Something shifts in her features as I speak. "Did he ever say anything about me?"

"When you guys met that night at the recital," I say. It all seems so ridiculous now that I can hardly tell her. "He told me that you were a rogue Akhet and that all of the bad stuff that's been happening to me is your fault. Falling down the stairs that day at the conservatory, an accident we almost had on his motorcycle tonight." I look at my arm. "He even said that you'd somehow caused the broken window."

Veronique looks hurt, and I immediately feel guilty for all of the bad stuff we'd said about her. "But you don't believe any of that, do you?" she asks.

"No." I shake my head. "Not anymore. He's been lying to me from the very beginning." I can feel my stomach flip as I think of him. I glance up the street, ready to see Griffon riding by any minute. I look in her eyes so that she'll get the importance of my words. "Apparently, he's been lying to me for centuries."

She looks surprised. "He's an old Akhet, then? Iawi?"

"Very," I say. It's so weird to hear those words coming from someone else. "We were together back in the fifteen hundreds." I stop talking, seeing once again the vision of the axe flashing on the scaffold. "He . . . he killed me in that lifetime."

Veronique looks thoughtful. "If he's an Iawi Akhet, then he has abilities to hide things, to manipulate things. I'm sure he's been telling lies for his own purposes."

"I can't believe I listened to him for so long."

"You need to be careful," she says slowly. Her eyes dart up and down the street, and I get the sense she's looking for him too. "Now that everything's out in the open and he knows that you've seen his true essence, Griffon doesn't need to pretend anymore. If he killed you in one lifetime, then you might be in danger in this one."

"That's what I'm afraid of."

"Is there somewhere safe you can go?"

"I'm going to stay at a friend's house tonight. I'm not sure what I'm going to do after that."

"I'll do whatever I can to help."

The way she says it reminds me of Alessandra and how kind she was to me. I want that back again. I want her back on my side. "I remember other things, too." I can't look at her right now. I don't want to see her reaction. "About us. At the Pacific Coast Club."

Veronique doesn't say anything. The silence is so intense that I have to look up at her.

"What do you remember?" she asks. I might be reading too much into it, but her voice sounds colder to me. More distant than just a few seconds ago.

"Just bits and pieces," I say in a rush. "I remember the party. And you being so nice to me—letting me use your cello when mine broke." I stop, picturing the last time I saw her. "And I remember the roof." Her eyes are kinder now, and I'm shooting for forgiveness. "I don't know what happened exactly, but I know that I wouldn't have done anything to hurt you. We were friends. Weren't we?"

Veronique puts her hand on my arm, and I realize that for the first time, I feel nothing from her touch. No vibrations. No wayward memories. "Of course we were," she says. "You were like the little sister I never had. It was all an accident—"

"But it wasn't an accident. I can prove it." A horn honks, and Rayne leans out the passenger side window of her sister's car at the curb. I look over and wave. "That's my ride."

There's so much else I want to tell her. About the newspapers. About Paolo. But Rayne honks again and there's no time. The moment's gone.

Veronique reads my mind. "Call me. Tomorrow, okay? Then we can talk more."

I feel a shudder as I swallow the last of my tears. "I will. Tomorrow. And thanks."

She squeezes my right hand, and I feel the Akhet vibrations again. But there's something else. An uncomfortable undercurrent. Something desperate and uneasy. "I'll talk to you soon," she says lightly.

"Okay."

Veronique waves as I climb into Sienna's backseat, and for a split second I wonder if I've done the right thing. Can I really trust her? Can I really trust anyone? I push the uneasy thoughts away. I want to believe her. More than anything, I want to believe that someone, somewhere, is telling me the truth.

Twenty-Two

"Can I stay here tonight?" I ask as we slip through Rayne's front door and pull it shut.

"Counting on it." One thing I love about Rayne is that she doesn't ask too many questions. At least, not at first. She didn't ask me anything in the car while Sienna was driving, just kept turning around to watch me from the front seat.

Rayne's books are spread across her bed, and I slide a few of them to the side so I can lie down and curl up into a ball. I think that if I can make myself as small as possible, the ache in my chest will somehow magically shrink too. I know Rayne is staring at me, but she's uncharacteristically quiet as I lie there, trying to come up with a rational explanation about why my world is ending.

"So, I have to ask. What the hell happened? I'm assuming Griffon did something," she finally says.

All I can do is shrug. Just the sound of his name makes fresh tears spring into my eyes.

"Bad kisser?"

I shake my head no.

"Girlfriend?"

"No." If only.

Rayne sighs. "Well, you're going to have to work with me a little here," she says. "I can't try to make you feel better if I have no idea what's going on."

I push myself into a semi-sitting position and lean against the wall. There's been so much craziness the past few weeks that I can barely keep track of what I've told her. "I remembered more. About Griffon."

"Wait a second. I thought we were talking about Veronique and what happened in San Francisco."

"Another lifetime. In England. I thought all of my memories were just random, but it turns out Griffon was there after all." I take a deep breath, pull a pillow into my lap, and hug it tight. "Let's just say he's not who I thought he was."

Rayne's eyes get wide. "You mean that you were together in a past life? Oh my God, that is so freakin' romantic." Out of everyone I know, Rayne is the only one who will take that kind of news as normal. And think it's romantic. "Now you have to tell me everything."

So I try. "We weren't 'together' together in the time before," I explain. "Not like that. I don't remember all that much about it. Just that I lived a long time ago in England." I suddenly remember the graffiti inside the tower. It had a date on it. "In 1538, I think."

"In 1538 you *think*?" Rayne asks.

"Yeah. There's some graffiti . . . oh, never mind." I have to try to focus my thoughts. "I was some sort of Lady at the Tower of London."

"Like a queen?" Rayne asks excitedly.

"I don't know. I don't *think* I was a queen, anyway. I keep having visions of parts of this one day. It was . . . the last day. I was led up to a platform while all of these people watched. There was a guy there with a hood on, and the only thing I could see were these intense eyes." I have to stop here, my voice wavering as I picture the cold resignation of those eyes. I swallow hard. "It was the guy with the axe." I close my eyes. "It was Griffon."

Rayne puts her hand over her mouth. "No way! Are you seriously saying that Griffon executed you in another life?"

I nod, biting the inside of my cheek to keep myself from crying. "And he's known all along."

"Wait a minute," Rayne says. "Didn't you meet him at the Tower of London?"

"Yes. Right on the spot where the execution happened. He's been lying to me the whole time. He admitted it when we were at the beach."

"So what did you do?"

"What do you think I did? I got the hell out of there."

Rayne thinks for a second. "I can't believe he'd really do that. He seems so into you."

"People like him are good at hiding things," I say. "He can do things that other people can't." I've been pushing that thought to the back of my mind. It's bad enough that Griffon has been lying to me. Thinking that he might actually want to hurt me, that part of his reason for being here is to repeat that time at the Tower, is overwhelming. "Think about it. He did just happen to be outside when the window broke."

"That's ridiculous. He wasn't anywhere near you when you had the accident."

"What if he doesn't have to be near me?" Griffon was right. Being able to remember the days of the week or memorize entire books are just simple tricks. What else can he do? What other abilities does he have that I don't know about? "Every time something bad happened, Griffon was somewhere nearby. When the glass broke, he was right outside. He was the one who dropped the cello when I almost fell down the conservatory steps. We almost had a motorcycle accident tonight on the way to the beach. He said someone was chasing us, but all I saw was a car behind us—I took his word for the rest of it. For all I know, he made the whole thing up just to scare me. Veronique is right. The pretense is over."

"Veronique?" she asks. "Is that what you were talking to her about?"

"I ran into her while I was waiting for you. I told her what happened." I see the look on Rayne's face. "I had to. She's the only other person on earth who might really understand."

"Thanks."

"Come on. You know what I mean. The only other person I know who remembers too."

"Still, blabbing to Veronique about everything might not be the best move," Rayne says, skepticism still edging her tone. "Did Griffon really try to hurt you tonight?"

"He might have, if Peter hadn't been there. You should have seen the look in his eyes when I figured it out."

"Well, no matter what, you were smart to come here." Rayne looks up at the ceiling. She tilts her head as she looks at me. "When you were the queen back in England, what was your name?"

I shift on her bed, hugging the pillow tighter. "I wasn't a queen. And I really don't want to talk about this any more right now." I just want it to all go away.

"Griffon knows what happened," Rayne says quietly. "You said yourself that he admitted being the one on the scaffold that day. If he was the executioner, then he knows all about it. Don't you deserve to know the truth too?"

I nod, my mind flashing back to the scene at the Tower and the ritual the two of us performed with the payment and the polite words just before he carried out somebody's order to have me killed.

"Okay, now, don't freak out on me," Rayne says. "But maybe you should talk to him. Just once. Get all the facts so that you don't have to try to guess at things on your own."

"No way," I say, my heart contracting at the thought of not seeing him again even as I stand my ground. "You didn't see the look in his eyes on the scaffold that day. He could have been the one to stop it. He could have not raised the axe, but he did. How can you possibly be a good person when your entire job is to chop the heads off of innocent people?"

"I agree," Rayne says. "And I think that you should be careful. But maybe he had no other choice. You're mad at him for something that happened between you five hundred years ago."

"No," I correct her, "I'm mad at him for lying to me an hour ago. I'm more convinced than ever that he's lying for a reason, and that his soul or his essence or whatever you want to call it is evil."

"You don't think that's a little dramatic?" she says, sitting down at her laptop. She types in some search words and clicks on a link. "There's a ton of stuff here on the executions at the Tower of London. It says here that they only executed those of high rank inside the Tower walls."

"That's what they said on the tour that day. The ones on the hill were mobbed with spectators, but the executions that took place on the Green were always private."

"Private as in not wanting to humiliate them," Rayne says, looking over her shoulder at me, "or private because the execution was a secret?"

All this talk about my own execution is making me feel sick. "Let's just drop it, okay?"

"Come on, Cole," she says. "Maybe if we do a little research, we can come up with some answers. Might make you feel better if you know some of the details."

"Knowing details from five hundred years ago isn't going to make me feel better now."

Rayne clicks the mouse a few more times. "How do you know? Maybe it will." Her fingers hover over the keyboard. "You said fifteen-what?"

"Fifteen thirty-eight."

"Okay. We have 1538. We have England—the Tower of London, specifically. Do you know what your name was?"

I swallow hard before answering. If Rayne does find something, some sort of record of a beheading, it will make it that much more real.

"Cole?" Rayne prods. "A name?"

"Allison. Lady Allison. But I don't know the last name."

Rayne types quickly with two fingers. "Hmm," she says, peering at the screen. "Ooh, there's a list of all the beheadings at the Tower of London." She clicks on the site. "There's a lot of them. Mostly men, though." She turns to me. "You're sure you weren't a guy?"

"Not that time," I say, watching the screen over her shoulder.

"Really?" Rayne glances at me and then turns back to the screen. "I don't see an Allison on this list anywhere. Maybe I should do a search of 'Lady Allison' in Tudor England and see what comes up."

"Tudor England?" I repeat.

"Forgive me for owning the entire boxed set of *The Tudors*," Rayne says.

I suddenly remember his name. "Try 'Connor,'" I say. "See if there was a Connor executed somewhere around that time."

"Connor?"

I hesitate. "Lady Allison's husband."

"Let me do a search for that name, then." We both say nothing as the search results come up. "There's not much here." She studies the screen. "No. Crap. No. Wait, here's something." She clicks through to another site. "Here's one that has hundreds of Tudor and Elizabethan portraits scanned in. The search results says that there is a Lord Connor Wyatt somewhere in here." She clicks on a few links. "Here it is. It says it's from 1536."

The image of the young man in the flowing black robe is so familiar I gasp out loud. He has green eyes, and I can see blond hair peeking out of the flat black hat he's wearing. Looking at his picture, I can almost hear his voice in my ear, and I'm surprised at the sense of loss that slams into my chest. "That's him."

Rayne glances at me. "Hang on, I saw that name somewhere else." She clicks the back button on the screen until she comes to the list we'd been looking at before. "Here it is, on the list of people who were executed on Tower Hill. Lord Wyatt, burned at the stake, 1538."

I close my eyes, trying to put the image of the man in the painting in a specific memory, but all I can see is the engraving in the tower. *For eternity.*

I take a deep breath, trying to calm myself as the answers fall into place. "So there are records of him being killed, but nothing on Allison," I say, scanning the list.

"Let me look for her full name." She scrolls down the list of portraits, my stomach churning as I look at the people dressed in their finest robes. It's like playing a game of hot and cold, and although I don't know why, it feels like we're getting hotter.

"Here it is." Rayne clicks on a tiny thumbnail, and the portrait fills the screen. The woman in the painting is young, with dark brown eyes and strawberry-blond hair in a braid over her shoulder. She's wearing a dark red velvet dress, with the square neckline that you see in pictures of Renaissance Faires, and folds of golden fabric wrap halfway down her arms.

"I've seen her before," I say, recognizing her eyes and dress from somewhere.

"It was painted by an unknown artist in 1536," she reads. "It says it's of Lady Allison Wyatt and that it's now hanging in the National Gallery in London."

Allison Wyatt. I roll that name over in my mind. It seems vaguely familiar, but there's no jolt of recognition like I felt looking at the picture of Connor. And then I know where I've seen her before.

"Oh my God," I say. "This is the same girl that was in Griffon's room that day."

"In Griffon's room?" Rayne looks at me like I'm crazy.

"In a notebook," I explain quickly. "He'd been drawing her in a notebook." I shift the computer to my lap and study every detail, from her gold and jeweled belt to her outstretched hand. Looking closer, I can see that the painter has been true to every last detail of Lady Allison, from her small mouth and delicate gold earrings to the scar on her forearm. The scar that she'd gotten as a little girl when boiling candle wax spilled on her arm and her mother wrapped it up with special salve and crisp white dressings.

As I scan the image on the screen, my eyes are drawn to her right hand. A silver chain dangles from her fingers, and cupped in her palm is a barely visible pendant. The artist has painted it in shadow, but I can still make out the cross with the loop on top and the dark red of the ruby set in the center. My heart skips a beat as I recognize it. It was in my hand as I climbed the scaffold steps that day. My ankh.

Twenty-Three

The next morning I walk toward my house, and all I can think of is going to bed, pulling my shades down and the covers up and letting go of all this craziness. I want my old life back—the one without Akhet, memories of other lifetimes, and not knowing who I can trust. The life without Griffon.

By the time I see him lounging by the planter in front of my house, it's too late to turn back.

"Cole! Wait!" He stands up, but doesn't move toward me.

My heart is racing and I know I should run in the other direction, but my feet stay firmly planted on the sidewalk.

"Two minutes," he pleads. "Just give me two minutes and I'll go."

"Two minutes," I agree. I study his face as I walk toward him, feeling slightly satisfied by the fact that he looks tired and miserable. I stop a few feet from him and fold my arms across my chest. He's even more handsome today, the stubble on his chin and shadows around his eyes adding a rugged touch. His bike is nowhere in sight, but his curls look like they've been recently crushed by the helmet, and I wonder if he's been home at all. I force myself to look straight at him, but I don't say a word.

Griffon attempts a small smile. "Two truths and a lie?"

I stare at him without changing my expression. "I'm through playing games. What do you want?"

"I've been trying to find you," he says, standing up and taking a step toward me.

I watch his lips as he speaks, remembering being free to run my finger along their curves. I force myself to take a step back. "I was out." I pace my breathing and congratulate myself on sounding disinterested. Aloof, even. I wait a few more seconds, gazing at the house behind him. "Is that what you came all this way for? To find out where I went?"

He closes his eyes and bites his bottom lip, as if trying to find the right words. "No. You left so quickly last night. And then you didn't go home. I was worried about you."

I stand up as tall as I can make myself. "Don't be."

"Has Veronique been around?" he asks, glancing down the street.

"Doesn't matter," I say. "Despite appearances, I can take care of myself. And besides, it's you I should be worried about."

"Is that what you think?" he asks, his voice louder than before. "That I'm going to hurt you? Cole, you have to know that I would never do anything to hurt you."

"Too late for that," I say quietly. My anger boils over and I push past him to go into the house. He has nothing new to say, nothing that can defend what he's done.

"I deserve that," he says. "But you have to hear my side." He grabs my left arm, his strong grip sending shooting pains up to my shoulder. Griffon sees my grimace and lets go quickly.

"Don't touch me!"

"I'm sorry. God, I'm sorry. Really. Give me another minute," he pleads. He holds his hands up. "I promise. Just one minute. I won't come near you again."

I glance down the empty sidewalk, the anger coursing through my veins. "One."

Griffon looks off into the distance. When he looks back, his eyes are wet and rimmed with red. "Look, I'm sorry I didn't tell you the truth sooner, but you'd never have listened to me if I did." He pauses, waiting for me to interrupt him, but I say nothing. "I'd been able to control my thoughts and feelings so well that I figured I'd be able to hold off telling you the whole story until later when you might understand, but last night at the beach . . . it was as if everything I'd hoped for was coming together in one amazing moment. I couldn't keep my hands off you, and when I touched you, my concentration was broken. Which is why you were able to see . . . what had been in the past."

My mind flashes to that gray English day and the panic and disbelief that had followed me onto the scaffold. "The day you swung the axe and killed an innocent person."

"I had no choice!" he yelled. "Don't you get it? If I hadn't, we'd have both been killed, and it would have been worse for you. I wish I could change things." Griffon shakes his head sadly. "I found out later that you had refused the King's advances after he executed your husband." He looks at me. "Back then, that was enough."

I feel my legs shaking beneath me, but I focus my energy on staying steady. "That only makes it worse," I say.

"I know. Believe me, I know. So when I saw you and Kat at the Tower, I knew I had a second chance."

"A second chance at what?"

"To find out why our paths crossed again," he says. "To be with you. To watch out for you. And when I met Veronique that night, I knew that she was dangerous to you in this life."

"As far as I can tell, you're the only one who's dangerous to me," I say as evenly as I can.

Griffon runs his fingers through his hair, making it stick up even worse than before. "That is not true," he says, a slight tone of panic in his voice. "Yes, I lied to you. But only because I was try-ing to help you." He pauses and takes a sharp breath. "And because I was falling in love with you."

I let the impact of what he's saying hit me full force, and I crumple slightly. Closing my eyes, I picture him standing over me that day on the platform again so that I can get my nerve back. "I can't believe anything you say." I turn to walk past him, praying that the tears will hold off, when he starts to follow me up the stairs.

"Wait," he pleads. Griffon fumbles in his jacket pocket and brings out a dark green silk pouch. "This is really why I came." He holds it out to me. "It belongs to you. It's always belonged to you. I promised myself I'd give it back if I ever got the chance."

I step back slightly. "What do you mean, it belongs to me?"

"It was given to me over five hundred years ago. As payment."

My mind is whirling, because I suddenly know what's inside. "But how did you . . . how did you keep it all this time?"

Griffon lifts his eyes to meet mine. "There are places to keep things safe and go back for them later. Places that stay the same through the ages." He pauses again. "It was the one thing I could do for you." Pressing the pouch into my hand, he holds my gaze for just a second, and then walks purposefully down the street.

I watch him turn the corner, then race up our front steps and into the house, wanting nothing more than the safety and quiet of my room. Griffon is in love with me. Now. When it's too late.

The green pouch is heavy for its size, and I can feel the outline of the chain through the fabric as I set it gently on my bed. I take a deep breath, wondering for a second if I should open it at all, but feeling a tug of curiosity that forces my hand. There's a small ribbon holding the ancient fabric closed, so I gently untie the knot and ease the opening wide enough so I can slip the contents out into my hand.

Despite its age, the pendant is bright silver—like someone has taken the time to carefully polish every crevice. There are symbols engraved on the front and a deep red ruby embedded in the center. I touch the curving top of the cross and feel the familiar dizziness take over as the pendant and the room become a blur.

The windows look over the vast, rolling gardens that stretch as far as the eye can see. Early spring sunlight sparkles through the tall windows, competing with the remnants of a fire in the great fireplace. Connor's clear green eyes shine with excitement as he holds the box out to me.

"Another present?" I tease. "You spoil me!"

"Nothing could ever spoil you," he says, kissing me lightly on the neck. *"This is special. I had it made just for you."*

Giggling, I tear off the ribbon and open the small package. Lifting the cross out of its cotton wool nest, I smile at the pendant that is unlike any of the other jewels he's given me in our short marriage.

Connor grins. *"See that? I had it set with the finest, brightest ruby in all of England. Your birthstone. Do you know what the pendant signifies?"*

"Signifies?" I ask, looking at the unusual shape and intricate design. *"No, what?"*

"Eternal life," he says. *"With this, we will be together forever."*

I smile and kiss him gently on the mouth. *"It's beautiful."*

As the vision ends, I'm overcome with the feelings of loss and sadness that are beginning to seem at home in my chest. The ankh seems to vibrate with energy of its own as I examine it, like a long-lost link to who I once was. It's heavy in my hand as I turn it over and see something written on the back. I look closer, but I already know what it says. *Ad vitam aeternam.* For eternity.

Kat pushes my door open so fast I don't have time to react. "Sienna called and told me what happened last night, but then Mom said Griffon was just out front."

I quickly drop the necklace back on the bed and try to cover it up with the silk pouch, but even as I'm going through the motions I know that I'm too late. Kat's eyes are already wide with amazement.

"What in the hell?" She grabs the chain from my bed and holds it up to the light. "Seriously? This is good quality silver, and this ruby is at least a carat." She looks from the necklace to me and back again. "Did Griffon give this to you?"

I shrug, not having a clue where to begin.

"Why aren't you wearing it? This thing is worth a fortune." She unhooks the clasp. "Turn around."

If I put it on, it will be like forgiving Griffon. Which I don't. "Kat, I don't—"

"Oh, for God's sake, just turn around and let me put this on you," she says. "Doesn't mean you have to marry him. You don't even have to keep it. Just enjoy it for a little while." She drapes the pendant around my neck and fastens the chain in the back.

I feel the heaviness of the pendant settle on my chest. I usually hate necklaces, but the weight is comforting and familiar. I try not to think about the circumstances the last time I wore it.

"It looks pretty on you," Kat says, standing back to admire her work.

"Thanks," I say, feeling the outline with my finger. So many strange things have happened the past few weeks that it's getting hard to keep track of them all.

"Grab your bag," she says.

"Why?"

"We need to show this to Drew at the shop. He'll be able to tell us more about it."

I already know more about the pendant than I ever wanted to. More than he'll ever be able to tell me. "No. I don't want to go out. I just got home, and it's been a really crappy twenty-four hours—"

"Bull," Kat says, pulling me to my feet. "The last thing you need is to stay in here moping all day. We'll just go to the shop for a few minutes, then you can come right back and curl up in bed for your own pity party. If you won't come, then let me take it." She holds her hand out and looks at me.

I put my hand on the pendant. It took so long to get back to me that there's no way I'm going to let it out of my sight.

Kat puts her hands on her hips. "Drew's going out of town tomorrow, so we don't have a lot of time."

"I'll go," I say finally. "But we have to come right back."

"Mom, we're going out for a little while," Kat calls as we walk down the hall.

"Not so fast," Mom says, walking out of the kitchen. "You've been gone all night, Griffon's been here looking for you."

"I know," I say, trying to look sorry. "We sort of had a fight."

Kat loops her arm through mine. "Come on, Mom. You remember how it is. I just want to take Cole up to the shop to get her mind off things. She's been through a lot this week."

Mom signs. "Take your phone," she says, looking at me. "I left at least five messages last night." "Nicole?" she says, her voice rising. "You do have your phone, don't you?"

I feel around in my pockets, but it's not there. "Yeah. Somewhere." I grab my bag and look through it, but I don't see it there either. "I had it last night," I say, as she stares at me. "I sent you a text, remember? I must have left it at Rayne's."

"Nicole Ryan, if you left your phone on the bus again, we're not replacing it."

"I didn't leave it on the bus," I say. "I told you, I had it last night."

"Well, use Kat's phone if you're going to be long." She walks back into the kitchen, mumbling to herself.

The sun is peeking out from behind the fog as we walk around the corner to where Kat parked her car. The unexpected warmth is nice and I lift my face to it, feeling a tiny bit better for the first time today.

"So what's going on with you and Griffon?" Kat asks as we approach the car. "Is it so bad?"

I hesitate. Telling Rayne what's going on is one thing. Telling Kat is something else. "Yeah," I say. "It actually is."

"Listen," she continues, unlocking the car doors. "I'm not going to tell you what to do, but maybe you should give him another chance." She plucks a parking ticket from under the wipers, reaches across my seat, and stuffs it into the glove compartment with over a dozen others.

I fasten my seat belt and stare through the windshield. "He basically lied to me from the minute we met."

"About what?" Kat says, starting the engine.

"It's complicated."

"Fine," Kat says with a sigh. "Don't tell me. All I know is, it seems like he really likes you. And I don't want you to screw up a good thing."

"I know," I say. I have to keep pulling my mind away from how rough and sad he looked just now. I run my finger over the silver chain. This necklace is a constant reminder of how he betrayed me in both lifetimes.

"I don't know," Kat says, merging into traffic. "I think a necklace like that would inspire a lot of forgiveness on my part."

After a few minutes of silence, we pull into the tiny employee lot in the back of the store. As I open the door, I tuck the pendant into my shirt, feeling more secure with it hidden from view.

We walk in through the back, past covered racks of clothes and boxes stacked to the ceiling.

Francesca smiles at us as she wraps up a purchase for a customer. As soon as the woman leaves, she walks over to us. "Katherine, so nice to see you on your day off," Francesca says. She smiles at me. "And you brought your sister back to see us."

They air kiss each other on both cheeks. "Is Drew around?" Kat asks. "I have something he's going to want to see."

"He's in the office," Francesca says, turning to watch another customer come in the front door. She waves her hand in our direction. "Go on up."

We walk upstairs to a loft area, and Kat knocks on a closed door. I can hear the low mumble of someone talking on the phone.

"Hey!" Drew says, pulling the door open. He motions us in the tiny room. "I've got to go," he says into the phone. "I'll ring you back later." He snaps the phone shut and smiles at us. It's hard not to miss Kat's reaction as he turns his attention to us. If she were any giddier she'd float up to the ceiling, and I wonder if this whole rushing-to-see-Drew thing is really about the pendant or just an excuse to see him again. "What can I do for you lovely ladies?"

"Listen," Kat says, laying a finger on Drew's forearm, a totally unnecessary gesture that I'm sure we all notice. "You need to see the pendant that Cole just got." She bumps me with her elbow. "From a guy."

Drew looks at me expectantly. "Oh? A guy?" He raises his eyebrows in a way that's both amused and vaguely condescending. He's probably a little older than Francesca—maybe twenty-two or twenty-three, and the fact that he sees me as just a kid is obvious from his tone.

I glance at Kat, hoping she'll drop it. "It's no big deal."

"No, but it's really cool," Kat says. "I think it's an antique, and we thought you might be able to tell us something about it. Maybe you could use it as a model for a new line. Something Egyptian and gothic." She turns to me. "Drew's stuff sells out almost the minute we get a new piece in."

Drew smiles at her, acknowledging the compliment. "I'd love to see it. I'm always looking for new inspiration."

They're both looking at me expectantly, so I sigh and reach for the chain, wishing she'd never seen it in the first place. As I pull the ankh out of my shirt, Drew gasps, and all the blood seems to drain from his face. He reaches for it, and as his fingers brush my skin, I feel the same unmistakable vibrations I'd learned to detect with the others, a flash of overwhelming emotions.

Drew is Akhet.

I search his face, trying to find a connection, but as he regains his composure, it's as if a heavy curtain comes down and the vibrations go from sharp and pronounced to dull and faint.

"Allison," he murmurs. Slowly he brings his eyes up to meet mine, their clear blue color marked with pain and questions, but somehow familiar. I hold his gaze as jolts of electricity race up my spine. Drew knew Allison. There's no question that somehow we were connected five hundred years ago.

"It's Cole," Kat says, looking from me to Drew, a questioning look on her face.

"I'm sorry?" Drew says, as if he's just remembering she's in the room.

"Her name is Cole. You called her Allison."

Drew clears his throat. "Yes. Sorry. Cole." He turns back to me. "This pendant. It's . . . it's fantastic," Drew says, running his fingers lightly over the ruby. "Where did you say you got this?" His voice is no more than a whisper.

"It was a gift," I say clearly, feeling more in control. I glance over at Kat, who's just staring at the two of us, her eyes wide and her mouth slightly open.

"I would love to see this again," Drew says, letting the cross drop back to my chest. "To do some sketches. Perhaps take some measurements."

"Maybe," I say, knowing I'm not going to just hand it over.

"That would be wonderful," Drew says. Briefly, he lets his hand drop to my arm, and I get a quick but immediate sense of loss and longing—emotions I'm sure he's letting me see. He seems to shudder, coming back to the present, pulling himself away from any memories he's experiencing. His phone vibrates on the desk, and he glances at it and then back to me.

"You should get that," Kat says, her voice cold and distant.

"Right," he says. "I, um, probably should."

Kat pulls me away from the office and down the hall. "What the hell was that all about?" she demands.

"What was what?" I ask as innocently as I can.

"That whole thing!" she says quietly. "The two of you were staring at each other like you were in a trance."

"I don't know what you're talking about. He just liked the necklace," I say, hoping that's enough to get her to drop the subject. "Why do you care so much?"

"Look," she says, glancing toward the office door and ignoring the question. "I know when something's going on. Drew and Francesca are practically engaged, and if you so much as think of coming between them, you're insane."

"I didn't do anything," I say, following her down the stairs. "You were the one who dragged me all the way over here."

"I'm not stupid," she whispers to me. "Bye, Francesca!" she calls as we walk through the shop, her voice light and happy. Kat glares at me as Francesca waves back. I'm *so* not looking forward to the ride home.

Drew catches up with us as we head out the back door. "Thanks again for showing me the pendant," he says. He reaches into his pocket and pulls out a business card for me. "Here's my number if you need to get hold of me. Call me anytime. That necklace is truly one of a kind. I haven't seen one like that in a long time." His eyes hold mine so steady that I can't look away. "A *very* long time."

Twenty-Four

Veronique stands at the bottom of the Pacific Coast Club steps, linking her arm through mine like we're old friends.

"Why here?" I ask, looking up at the dimly lit windows. When I called Veronique from home, she suggested we meet here, saying it wouldn't be very busy on a Sunday. Now I'm not sure it's such a great idea.

"Where better to put this whole episode behind us than the place where we last saw each other? What we need is a new start." Veronique looks at me with a smile so wide she seems almost uncharacteristically giddy. "Definitely, a new start."

The big brick building seems more menacing now that I know what happened here. My stomach is in knots, and I tie my jacket tighter against the cold spring wind. I put my right hand into the pocket to make sure the newspaper printouts are still there and feel something crumbly at the very bottom. I haven't worn this jacket since Friday on the beach with Griffon. A lump forms in my throat, and I know what the pieces are before I pull out the broken sand dollar. Like everything associated with him the past few days, this has been destroyed, too.

I start up the front steps, but Veronique stops me.

"Not that way," she says, walking quickly around the right side of the building. "We have to go in the back way. Last time, when it was someone's home, things were different, but women have to go through the back now. Sexist bastards."

I remember the "members only" greeting I got the last time I was there. "Are you a member?"

Veronique glances over her shoulder and laughs. "No." She slows so that I can catch up with her. "I can't be. Not being a man and all. But it does help to know people who are."

We reach the back door and ring the bell. After a few tense seconds, it's opened by a bored-looking man in a uniform. "Welcome," he says and stands back to let us through.

"Thank you," Veronique says briskly as she pushes past him into the back hallway.

I stand for a second, taking in the ornate ceiling and wood trim that seems to cover every surface. The place even smells old, and the combined scent of hair tonic and cigar smoke that has worked its way into the building over the past hundred years triggers a pang of familiarity in my chest. I haven't seen this part of the building in my memories, but part of me deep inside remembers being here.

"Come on, this way," Veronique says, and turns down a back hallway. For someone who isn't a member of the club, she sure seems to know her way around. Somewhere in the distance I can hear soft piano music and the disjointed mumble of several male voices deep in conversation.

"Is there a meeting room or something?" I glance down at the doors that line the hallway and wonder if one of them is where I'd overheard Signore Luisotti seal Alessandra's fate that long-ago night.

"There are, but that's so boring," Veronique says, pulling open a heavy wooden door and gesturing grandly. "We're going to the roof."

I stop at the entrance to the stairwell, thinking about what happened the last time I was on the roof of this building. "I don't think so," I say

Veronique stops and turns back to me. "Why not?"

"Heights aren't really my friend."

"All the more reason you should go. You can't let one incident rule all of your lifetimes."

I hesitate. "Can't I just show you the articles I found down here?"

Veronique's face droops, and if I didn't know better, I'd think she was pouting. "You said that you want to start our relationship over again. The roof is the perfect place to start over." Without waiting for a reply, Veronique disappears through the door, and facing the choice between being left out here alone and following, I take a deep breath and follow her. I want to get this settled once and for all. It's only three flights up, and we walk in silence; the only sounds are our footsteps on the old, wooden stair treads. I try to calm the fear that's rising in my heart by reminding myself that, amid all of the bad things that have happened lately, Veronique has been doing everything she can to help me. I have to believe that, because at this point, I have no other choice.

At the top of the last flight of stairs is another wooden door, much less fancy than the one at the bottom. Veronique twists the knob and pushes the heavy door with her shoulder until it gives, opening onto the gray, overcast sky.

I stand in the doorway, not needing to look over the edge to know how high up we are. My breath begins to come in short bursts as I look around. Where the inside of the building is full of heavy, ornate decorations, the roof is almost bare, with just a few chimneys and a couple of skylights dotting the huge, flat space. In the middle there's a big open square with light shining up from below and a waist-high stone railing surrounding the roof on all sides.

"Seriously," I say, "can't we do all of this on the ground floor?" I cling to the doorway with my right hand, not trusting myself to inch any farther onto the roof. "There's got to be an empty meeting room down there somewhere."

"Oh, come on. This is perfect," Veronique says, throwing her arms to the side as if embracing the San Francisco skyline. "It's private, so we can talk without thinking that someone's going to overhear us. You're not afraid, are you?" She turns back to me. "You don't trust me. You think I'm out to get you just like Griffon said." She pauses. "He really messed you up, didn't he?" I don't want Veronique to think that Griffon still has any power over me.

"It's not that. It's just the last time I was up here, things didn't go well."

Veronique drops her arms and looks over at me. "Exactly why

you should come away from the doorway and check it out. Only by facing what happened to us in the past can we participate in our future." She grins. "Okay, I read that in a fortune cookie, but still, it applies." She holds out her hand, and after a few seconds I take it, allowing her to pull me out of the doorway and onto the roof. I feel nothing from her touch. She seems almost hyper, but it's as if her essence has shut down. She tilts her head toward the railing on the other side of the roof. "Do you remember anything else about that night?"

"Not really. But I don't have to." I reach into my pocket and pull out the papers Rayne and I printed out at the library. "This is what I want to show you. I can prove that it wasn't an accident, and it wasn't me who killed you."

Veronique twirls away from the pages in my hand. "I don't want to read anything right now," she says.

I watch her sway to some private music only she can hear. None of this is going the way I planned. Veronique seems so different than the other night, and I feel a creeping fear about my choice to trust her. She spins back around quickly. "Read them to me."

"Um, okay," I say. I read the article about the trial slowly as Veronique sways from foot to foot, her back to me the entire time.

When I'm done, she turns to face me. "So you're trying to tell me that you didn't push Alessandra off the roof? That it was Signore Barone?"

"Exactly," I say, wondering why she's started referring to herself in the third person. "I didn't do it, and the courts of San Francisco agreed."

Veronique stares at me. "That's crazy," she says, a lock of

hair falling in her eyes. "Why would Signore Barone kill his own daughter?"

"I don't know," I say, turning back to the pages in my hand, panic starting to build. This is not the way it's supposed to go. Veronique was supposed to see the newspaper and realize it was all a big mistake and be grateful to me that I'd finally shown her the truth—that I didn't hurt her. I try again. "But it says second-degree murder, so that must mean that he didn't try to do it. That it was an accident."

For a second, I see understanding in her eyes and I think I've done it, but then she waves her hand dismissively in my direction. "Anyone can fake an old newspaper."

"But look at this one," I say, the desperation obvious in my voice. It feels like I'm losing control of the situation. "Here's an article about Paolo."

Veronique stops moving at the mention of his name. "What about Paolo?"

I hold it out to her. "About his suicide," I say. "How he killed himself because he couldn't stand being without you."

She takes the paper and quickly reads the article, her eyes twitching as she digests the information. "How did you get this?"

"It's from a newspaper, a few days after you died."

Tears shine in her eyes as the news that Paolo took his own life registers. She's about to say something else when the stairwell door opens and Griffon stumbles onto the roof, followed by Giacomo.

"Griffon!" I look from him to Veronique, who doesn't look surprised at all. Despite everything that's happened, despite the danger

I know he can cause, despite the lies I know he's told. I still find my heart pounding at the sight of him. But I force myself back to reality. "What are you doing here?"

Griffon pulls his arm free from Giacomo's grip. "You texted," he says, not looking directly at me. "You said to meet you in front of the building at five." He glares at Veronique.

"I didn't text you," I say, feelings of betrayal starting to overwhelm me. "I lost my phone on Friday."

"Well," Veronique says, waving a small, blue metallic object at me, "*lost* is a bit of an exaggeration. You really should keep better track of your things."

"*You* texted me?" Griffon looks at her questioningly. "On Cole's phone?"

"I didn't really think you'd agree to come if it was from me," she replies, walking to the edge of the roof and dropping my phone over the side, watching as it hits the ground after a few seconds' delay.

Griffon takes a few steps toward Veronique, but Giacomo blocks his way. He's got ten years and probably forty pounds on Griffon, so there's not much he can do. Griffon squares his shoulders and turns away from me. "So, what's this all about? Kind of dramatic dragging us all up here to the roof, don't you think?"

Veronique looks at the wide expanse of sky in front of her. "Maybe," she says. "But up here on the roof is the only place that will really work."

"Because this is where it all started," I say, realizing what she's up to, why we had to come back to this spot—so that she can reenact everything that happened that night and right the wrong that she thinks was done to her. She wants to see my broken body down on the sidewalk like hers was back then. I turn to her. "Why bring Griffon up here? So that he can be some kind of sick witness?"

"Witness?" Veronique smiles in a way that sends shivers down my spine. Her eyes look dead. Emotionless. Unforgiving. "No. If anyone's here to be the witness, it's you."

I look at her, confused. "But I'm the one you want," I say. "I'm the one you think caused your death back then."

Veronique starts pacing in front of me, the nervous energy almost visible. "I don't want you dead," she says. "Death is way too easy. Don't you see? After everything that's happened, do you still think you killed *me* that night? You *are* the one who took everything from me in a few brief seconds, and I couldn't do anything to stop it. Alessandra was everything to me." Veronique stops and walks over to the spot at the railing where she fell so long ago. Her voice is soft as she starts to speak. "Do you finally get it? You took something precious from me a century ago, and now I have to take something precious from you." She takes several steps toward me and glances at the splint on my arm.

"At first I thought taking your ability to play cello would be enough. But then I saw that there was something even more valuable for you to lose." She glances at Griffon. "Something that you could never recover from. Like what you took from me. I'll never recover from my loss. In *any* lifetime." Veronique stands right in front of me. I can see every individual lash as she stares into my eyes. "Look carefully. Who do you see?"

I shrink back from the force of her energy. As I look into her eyes, her features blur, and for just a second I see a bright white smile and shining dark hair. I look up at the tiny birthmark over her right eye. It's in the same place a distraught boy would have put a gun to his head centuries earlier—just before pulling the trigger. My heart races as I recognize the essence I knew so long ago. It can't be. "Paolo?"

"Ha ha!" Veronique claps her hands and steps back. "Now, that wasn't so hard, was it?"

I stare at her, trying to see the handsome boy she once was. I've thought of her as Alessandra for so long, it's impossible to think of her as anyone else. "But I thought you were her. Alessandra."

Veronique shrugs. "You obviously assumed wrong. When I was Paolo, you took away the most valuable thing in my life, and I've spent every moment since looking for Alessandra's essence. When I recognized you at the conservatory concert, I hoped that maybe her essence had been drawn to you in this lifetime." She looks down at the gravel rooftop. "But I didn't find her." She looks up again, a cheerful expression on her face. "But I did find the next-best thing. The essence that *you're* drawn to above every-one else."

I hear a metallic click as Veronique pulls a thick black gun out of her coat and aims it at Griffon's head.

"Veronique!" I yell. "This is crazy. We're friends. It's me, Cole. Whatever happened in the past doesn't matter now. Griffon has nothing to do with this."

"I love that you think that," she says, not taking her eyes, or the gun, off of Griffon. "Such wonderful naiveté. However, I totally disagree. What happened in the past matters a lot. It's the only thing that does matter." I don't even see her hand move as the gun explodes to life, my heart racing with the deafening sound, and I can't help but flinch.

The bullet kicks up tiny fragments as it ricochets off the railing behind Griffon, but he keeps staring at Veronique as if he's daring her to do it again. "You missed," he says calmly.

Veronique narrows her eyes at him, her teeth flashing in a half smile as she steadies the gun on him once again. "I never miss."

Giacomo grabs Griffon by the arms and shoves him roughly forward. "That isn't necessary," Griffon says, looking at Veronique with hatred in his eyes. His voice wavers only a little as he speaks. "I'm not going to fight you." He turns to look at me for the first time, and the total honesty in his eyes makes me catch my breath. Despite everything that's happened the past few days, the thought of living the rest of this life without him is unbearable.

"I'll do anything for you." Griffon is speaking only to me, as if there's nobody else on the roof with us. "If it means that I have to end this life to save yours, then it's fine."

Veronique laughs, and I see nothing but cruelty in her smile. "Brave words. Let's see if you can match them with even braver actions." She motions the gun toward the edge of the roof. "Whether you go over on your own or need a little 'encouragement' makes no difference to me."

Griffon stumbles on the gravel as Giacomo pushes him toward the edge where Alessandra fell so many years ago. It feels as if everything is happening in slow motion. This can't be real.

As they walk, Veronique follows them with her eyes, the gun firmly gripped in her outstretched hand. "I hope you really understand what you're about to lose," she says, not looking at me. "Any last words for Griffon? Everyone deserves the mercy of a proper good-bye. That's more mercy than you showed to me and Alessandra."

"You can't kill him!" I scream, watching Veronique aim the gun at Griffon's head again.

"Oh, but I can," Veronique says flatly. "I have to. It's the only way to even things up so that we can all move on. I think popular psychology would call it 'closure.'"

I'm even more unprepared this time as the sound of the gun echoes off the buildings around us. Griffon jerks back as the bullet hits him and he falls back over the waist-high railing. My screams rush through my ears as I lunge forward, knowing it's already too late. "No!"

Veronique grabs my left arm as I try to twist away from her toward the railing. The pain is blinding, and I can feel the newly attached nerves and tendons straining and tearing where her hands are holding tight. Just as I feel like I'm going to pass out, everything seems to move into slow motion. I feel energy flowing between us where our bodies are touching. I'm slipping into a memory, but this time, I'm not alone. Somehow Veronique is with me.

As Signore Barone leans over the edge of the roof to show me the lights of the city, his right arm tightens around my neck until breathing becomes uncomfortable. I reach up in shock when I see him looking down at me, hatred and disgust flashing in his dark

eyes. He turns so that his back is to the railing and all of my weight
is now supported on his arm. I can hear myself gasping for air,
and I claw at his hands, but it makes no difference.

"It's your fault they want to force Alessandra out of the troupe,"
he says, spittle flying from his mouth. "If you hadn't arrived, her
career would still be on the rise!" He turns around so that I am
now hanging half over the railing, and I can see the light-colored
cobblestones far below. There is a loud ringing in my ears and
my vision is fading when I hear a commotion behind him.

"Papa! What are you doing!" Alessandra cries, and I can feel
her weight on him as she tries to pry his arm from around my
neck.

"Get away!" he yells. "Go back downstairs. This has nothing to
do with you. I'm only acting for your own good." His grip loosens
just a little as he pushes her back onto the gravel roof, giving me
two or three desperate breaths of air. In seconds she is up again,
flying at the two of us.

"This is not the way!" she yells. As she fights with him, Signore
Barone brings his arm back to fling her off, but misjudges his
own strength. As he pushes her, she loses her balance, and in seconds she has disappeared over the railing, her screams echoing
back up to us as she falls.

"No!" he shouts, the noise a primitive, animal cry. I turn to look
down, and see that her arms and legs are bent at unnatural angles
and watch the dark pool spreading out underneath her across the
hard stone walkway.

Signore Barone reaches over the railing as if he can still catch
her falling figure. I scream her name, not believing what I'm seeing.

Before he can turn on me, I run for the stairwell door, in time to meet a crowd of men rushing up from below.

My memory clears, and I see Veronique on her hands and knees a few feet away, her back arching and falling as she struggles for breath, Giacomo standing over her, looking lost. As she sits back on her knees, I can see the gun is still gripped in her right hand. I sit up and look frantically around for Griffon, but he's nowhere on the roof.

Suddenly, I don't care about Veronique. I don't care about the gun. I'm only focused on one thing. I race to the edge where I saw him last, prepared to see a repeat of the same scene I saw so many decades ago, knowing that if he's gone, there's nothing left for me here.

I hear scraping noises even before I reach the edge and look over. Griffon is hanging from a ledge about three feet down from the railing, holding on with his upper body while his feet swing wildly underneath him as he tries to get a foothold to pull himself up. There's a gash on his cheek and blood is dripping down the side of his face, but I feel an enormous sense of relief. He's alive.

"Griffon!" I yell.

Griffon looks up at me. His shoes scrape the brick wall. "I can't get back up."

"Hang on," I say. He's only a few feet from me, but too far for me to reach from this side. I wrap my left arm around an opening and ease myself over the railing, the pain increasing as I put pressure on it, but there's no other way. Bracing my feet against the outside of the railing, I lean down, my right arm outstretched as far as possible. "Can you grab my hand?"

"No. I'll pull you over," he says, his words coming in short bursts from the effort of hanging on. "It's too dangerous."

I can see his fingers turning white where they're gripping the ledge. He can't keep this up much longer. "No, you won't," I say quickly. My breath is coming in gasps. "There's no other choice. Let go and grab my hand. I'll pull you up."

Griffon hesitates, and I see him look down at the ground far below.

"Do it," I say. "Grab my hand." I reach down another few inches, my fingers about two feet from his face. If he lets go and doesn't take my hand, he'll fall for sure. We only have one shot at this. "Just let go quickly. Don't look down."

Griffon looks into my eyes, and a sense of calm seems to come over him. I tighten my grip on the railing just as he lets go with his left hand and wraps his fingers around my wrist. The force of his weight pulls me off balance for a second, and I close my eyes as I pull with everything I've got, knowing that the next few seconds can change everything forever. The strain on my arm starts to ease as Griffon uses my leverage to swing his feet up onto the ledge, and he reaches over and grabs for the railing. In one motion, he pushes me back over the railing to the safety of the roof and then jumps over after me.

I grab at Griffon as we sprawl in the gravel, feeling his relief as he pulls me into him. I close my eyes and feel vibrations, his breathing in time with my own, the rightness of it all reaching down deep beyond logic and understanding. I've been listening to meaningless words when all along I should have been paying attention to the feelings inside of me that always speak the truth.

In an instant I know that Griffon isn't rogue, and he isn't lying. What he wants is to be with me.

I look up and see Veronique and Giacomo about six feet away. She looks dazed as she glances over at us as if she's just realized we're there, the gun hanging limply at her side. Griffon jumps up, pushing me behind him, and I can feel him ready to run at her.

"Wait," I say to him quietly, putting my hand on his arm. "Just wait."

"Veronique?" Giacomo calls to her, obviously unsure about what to do next. I see the devotion in his eyes and realize that he'll do anything for her. He'll obey every order. He'll stay with her even though she's spent her life looking for another love. And I have no doubt he'd kill for her, too.

She ignores him. "What was that?" Veronique turns to me, fear in her voice. Her face is drawn, and she looks suddenly older. "I was with you. I felt the breath being forced from your lungs. I saw Barone's anger. I saw . . . I saw Alessandra die." She licks her lips and stares at me. "But how? I wasn't there when it happened."

I look at the gun she's holding loosely in one hand. I might be able to grab it if she's distracted. "But *I* was," I say, breathing heavily, my left arm throbbing in pain. Griffon silently squeezes my right hand, a gesture of unspoken encouragement. "And what you saw was what really happened."

"And you were telling the truth? The newspapers didn't lie? It was Barone who . . ." She can't bring herself to finish the sentence.

"It was Barone who tried to kill me," I say. "But he killed Alessandra by mistake."

Veronique shakes her head as tears stream down her face. She raises her eyes to mine, and I can see the hatred replaced by the depths of the pain she feels from losing Alessandra. For her, it's as if it has just happened. "I don't deserve to finish this," she says, and turns the gun on herself, the barrel trembling where she holds it against her chest.

"Don't!" Giacomo yells, the anguish in his voice matching mine when I called for Griffon just minutes before.

I make a move toward her, but that just makes her hand shake more. She's fired it twice already, and this time I know she really won't miss. All of a sudden I want us all to get off this roof alive. I force my voice to sound calm and even. "This wasn't the solution last time. Killing yourself just made things worse."

"But it makes the pain stop," she says. "For a while, at least." She turns away from us, shaking her head again. "It's better this way."

My mind is racing. No more blood should be spilled over what Barone did so many years ago. "But what if Alessandra *is* back?" I ask quickly. I let go of Griffon's hand and walk slowly around to face her. "What if you were right, and her essence is in this city somewhere, looking for you?" I take a deep breath as I see the end of the gun move away from her chest just a tiny bit.

Behind her I see Griffon moving toward us, Giacomo doing nothing to stop him. His footsteps make faint crunching sounds on the gravel, so I keep talking. "Are you willing to give up this chance to find her? For what? It might be decades before you can come back and look for her again."

Just as she's about to answer, Giacomo lunges at her, grabbing for the gun, but Veronique isn't willing to let it go easily.

"Do you care nothing for me?" he shouts as he pulls the gun away from her body. "Is it so easy for you to take what *I* love?"

Veronique shrieks in frustration as Giacomo wrenches her hand back and the gun skitters across the gravel. His arms surround her as her struggles fade, and soon the only sound is her quiet sobbing.

Griffon reaches over and grabs the gun, putting it in his pocket before rushing to my side.

"Are you okay?"

I reach up to wipe some blood from his cheek. "Are you? This is all my fault. I should have listened to you. I should have trusted you. I'm so sorry."

"Let's get out of here," Griffon says, and without looking back at either of them, we head for the stairwell.

Griffon pulls me with him as we rush down several flights. We don't speak, although a thousand things come into my head that I want to say.

Griffon breaks the silence as we reach the ground floor. "I just need you to believe that I would never do anything to hurt you. I can't stand going through the rest of this life alone. Without you."

"I know," I say, tears starting to form in my eyes. "Oh God, I know. I'm so sorry."

Griffon takes my hand and grips it tightly. "But you do now? You believe me?" The desperation in his eyes makes me feel guilty and hopeful all at the same time. "I wasn't Akhet back then. I didn't know what else to do."

I shake my head. "I don't want to talk about *then*. It's over. We're not those people anymore. All I want is now. And tomorrow. And the tomorrow after that."

"There's just one thing." Griffon stops just before opening the door to the hallway. "I let you down again."

"What are you talking about?"

"I was supposed to save you, and instead you saved me."

"Maybe it was my turn this time," I say, pulling him down into a desperate kiss. "Next time it's yours."

Twenty-Five

I grab my bag off the hallway table. "I'm going now," I call to Mom, just as she hangs up the phone.

"Do you need a ride?" she asks, meeting me at the door.

"Yes. Thanks." I lean over and give her a quick kiss on the cheek. "Griffon's mom invited me to dinner too. Can I stay?"

Mom's lips flatten into a straight line, and I can tell she's trying to come up with a reason to say no. "Sure," she finally says. "But call me when you need a ride back."

"I'm heading that way. I'll take you," Kat says, walking down the hall. "I'm probably going to be hanging out with you guys a little more—Owen's coming out in June to stay with Griffon for a couple of weeks."

"That's great," I say, wondering how weird it will be to double-date with my own sister.

"Did you ever find your phone?" Mom asks.

"Um, no," I say, hoping she's not going to ask any more questions. Knowing that it's in a million pieces from being tossed off
a three-story building isn't exactly the same as finding it. The past
week has been a nightmare, trying to act normal at home and at
school with all that's happened. I keep worrying I'm going to slip
and give myself away.

She sighs. "We'll see about getting you another one," she says.
"Be careful."

I smile at that. If she ever had a clue what happened on the
roof, maybe she wouldn't worry so much about a simple trip to
Berkeley. Or maybe she'd worry more.

"I might be out later, though," she says, not quite as an after-
thought. "If I'm not here, just call me to tell me you got home okay."

I give Kat a look, but she just shrugs. Out? Mom never goes
out, especially on Saturday night. "Out as in, on a date?"

Mom's face gets surprisingly red in a very short time. "No. I'm
going out with your father. Just to dinner and a play at the Orpheum."

"Really?" I say. I've noticed that they've been spending more
time together since the window accident, but I didn't think it meant
anything. Maybe they really are working through something in
their distant past.

"It's just dinner, guys. I know that look. Don't get your hopes up."

I put my hands up. "No hopes. I promise. Just glad that you're
going to do something fun. Maybe you should call *me* and tell me
you got home okay."

∞

We're barely through the door before Janine surrounds me with a giant hug. "Girl! Just look at you!" She pulls back and holds me at arm's length. "Things could have turned out badly if it hadn't been for you."

I can feel my face flush. "If it hadn't been for me, it wouldn't have happened in the first place," I say, still not totally understanding everything that went on. "I'm sorry I got Griffon mixed up with Veronique," I add, not wanting to think about anything beyond today.

"I don't know what the two of you are on about. I had everything completely under control," Griffon says with a laugh. The black eye where the bullet grazed him is starting to fade, but he still has a bandage over the stitches on his cheek.

"Yeah," Janine says. She swats him with a kitchen towel. "That's exactly what it looks like."

"I did," he insists. "Veronique might be a good shot, but my reflexes are even better."

I remember what she said about never missing with the gun, and I breathe in sharply. I thought that she just meant to score him with the bullet. "So she meant to hit you?"

"I'm sure she did. Luckily I was able to get out of the way." Griffon puts a hand to his cheek. "Well, mostly."

Janine folds her arms in front of her chest. "And ending up dangling off the edge of a roof, three stories up?"

Griffon grins. "Yeah. That was a little miscalculation."

Janine reaches over and squeezes my hand. "All I'm saying is that things could have turned out much differently if Cole hadn't been there. As it is, you're going to have a nice scar on your cheek."

"Oh, I have something for you," I say, pulling a jar out of my bag and handing it to Griffon. I want to stop thinking about what might have happened if things *had* turned out differently. "It's from Rayne."

He opens it and sniffs the cream inside. "Smells good."

"It's some kind of honey-lavender thing that's supposedly good for scarring. She says you need to put it on your cheek twice a day. I swear, she must have been a healer in a past life, because she's always coming up with this stuff."

"Then I'd better do it," he says. "Tell her thanks."

It's nice to be somewhere that I can stop monitoring everything that comes out of my mouth. The past several days at home have been rough, with so much going on in my life that I'm required to keep from Mom and Dad.

"How's the arm?" Janine asks. "Any more damage?"

I look at the splint. "I don't think so," I say. "It doesn't hurt like it did. I have another appointment next week, so we'll see. Although I might have to come up with a different story about what happened."

Janine puts one arm around me. "Griffon tells me that my pathetic empathic skills have nothing on yours. Were you really able to transfer your images and emotions to Veronique?"

"I guess. I was just concentrating really hard on the truth and what I knew. When she grabbed me, there was a strange energy between us. For some reason, she was able to see my memories. I'm just glad that convinced her, because it didn't seem like anything else would."

Janine shakes her head in amazement. "Akhet have talked

about telempathy for generations, but as far as I know, nobody has ever seen it work. The Sekhem have been wanting to develop emotional intelligence for some time. A new Akhet who has natural abilities like yours will be a valuable addition."

"The Sekhem?" I ask. "Really? I thought that wouldn't happen for a long time."

"We don't discriminate against newbies." Janine smiles. "For right now, just learn to trust your abilities and nurture them. They are your true gift. There will be time for the rest later."

"What's going to happen to Veronique?"

"She's on the Sekhem's radar now," Griffon says. "They'll be able to keep more of an eye on her. She's so focused on finding Alessandra's essence that she can't see anything past that one goal. Everything she does in every lifetime is about finding her."

I think about how I felt when I thought Griffon might die. It's hard to believe, but I actually feel sorry for her. "I think I almost get that," I say, knowing they can see me tearing up.

"One great advantage to being Akhet is that we remember everything. Unfortunately, we are also unable to forget anything," Janine says. "Are you alright?" She gives me a quick hug.

"I'm fine," I say, feeling overwhelmed. "It's just . . . it's just been a really long week."

Janine laughs a short, staccato laugh. "Now *that* may be the biggest understatement I've heard all year."

"Do you need us to help you with anything?" Griffon's eyes shine with excitement, and he looks at Janine questioningly.

"No. I know you're dying to show Cole, so go on. I'll take care of this stuff."

"Show me what?"

"It's a surprise," Griffon says, leading me out of the kitchen and up the stairs. Instead of turning right into his room, we walk farther down the hall until we come to a closed door. Griffon cups my face in his hands "God, it's good to see you," he says, leaning in to give me a quick, intense kiss. "Feels like it's been forever."

I laugh. "It's only been a couple of days."

"Guess I'm trying to make up for lost time," he says. "And there's a lot of lost time to make up for." He runs his finger over the ankh that hangs around my neck.

I put my hand around it, the silver warm from my skin. As I touch it, I hear Drew's voice in my ear. *Allison.* Goose bumps form on my arms as I try to shake off a feeling of foreboding. "I never did say thanks," I say, shifting my focus to Griffon. To us. "For bringing this back."

"You don't have to," he says. "I'm just glad that it's finally where it belongs."

He opens the door to what looks like a small, sunny office. "Don't get mad, but I got you something." Leaning up against the desk is a big black cello case.

"A cello?" I look at him sideways. "I have a cello. Two, even. For all the good they do me now."

"Not just a cello," Griffon says. He unlatches the sides of the lid and lifts it out. "A right-handed cello."

"Right-handed?" I take a step closer. "What do you mean, right-handed? Cellos only come one-handed."

"Not this one," he says. "This one has been completely rebuilt to be played with right-handed fingering. Since you're having trouble using your left hand, I figured you could try this one and still keep playing."

"I've never heard of anything like it." I sit down in the office chair and examine it. The strings are backward, right to left, and the bridge is set at a slightly different angle than I'm used to. It's a beautiful instrument. I'm almost afraid to touch it.

"I did some research. Charlie Chaplin used to have one just like it," he says. "Try it."

Experimentally, I lean it against my right shoulder and put my right hand on the neck. "This is so weird," I say. I look up at him. "It's amazing, but . . . I don't know if I can do it. I've been playing one way all my life."

Griffon sits down across from me and lifts my left hand, kissing the fingers that no longer work as they should. "Veronique tried to take everything that's important to you. We can't let her win. The knowledge about how to play isn't in here," he says, tapping my ring finger. "It's in your head. And your heart. You just have to retrain the body in order to release that knowledge. A note is just a finger on a string. It doesn't matter which finger." He hands me the bow and a block of rosin.

I tighten the bow and put the rosin on it, my hands shaking just a little. I can't believe he's gone to so much trouble, and I can't spoil the look on his face by disappointing him. The balance on the bow is a little weird in my left hand, but I can put enough pressure on it to make it work.

"Here goes nothing," I say. Closing my eyes, I let my right hand find the notes to one of my own compositions as best they can. It isn't perfect by any stretch, but my reach is okay, and it's just a matter of rethinking where everything goes. Instead of worrying about hitting the right notes, I reach deep inside for the emotion that makes them sing. I pull up everything that has happened in the past several weeks—the fear, the trust, and mostly the desire—and let it all play across the strings. The music resonates in the room as I lift the bow and open my eyes to see Griffon grinning like a madman.

"That was amazing," he says quietly.

"Not amazing." I set the cello gently back in its case, surprised at the lump I feel in my throat, like I've just been given a gift that's bigger than strings and wood. "But maybe it will be someday." I lean over and kiss him intensely on the mouth. "It's the most beautiful thing anyone has ever given me. I can't accept it, though. It must have cost a fortune."

Griffon shakes his head. "It doesn't matter," he says. "Money isn't a problem. Trust me. You have to take it, because I can't return it."

"Still—"

Griffon blocks my objections by kissing me, one hand running fingers through my hair. He moves to the floor and pulls me down to him. "You have to. I owe it to you."

"You don't owe me anything."

"But I do," he says. "The minute I touched you on Tower Green, I knew that one of the things I had to do in this life is to look after you. And I didn't."

"You tried to warn me," I say. "It's not your fault that I didn't trust you." I lean in and kiss him, feeling his soft, full lips on mine and inhaling his warm, spicy scent.

"I meant what I said the other night," he whispers, his breath on the side of my neck sending shivers through my body. "When I said I love you. I've never meant anything more in any lifetime."

I study his face, but this time I don't see the eyes of my executioner. I see the eyes of the boy that I can't imagine living without. For once, I'm not wondering about how he really feels, about what he really means. I can feel the truth in his words—the truth that is in his heart.

"Two truths and a lie," I say. "My turn."

"Okay." He grins.

"Right now is the happiest I've ever been. Tomatoes are my favorite food." I pause for just a second. "And I love you."

Griffon studies my face. "I'm hoping that you still hate tomatoes."

"See, you're getting better at this."

Griffon laughs as he leans in to kiss me again. I feel his desire as I press myself into him, and I know that whatever happens in this lifetime or the next, I'll remember this moment, these emotions. From now on, good or bad, nothing is lost. Everything will be kept. Forever.

Robin Mellom, for long rambling phone calls, anguished e-mails, and propping me up. And for junk food.

Daisy Whitney, for regularly being available to text after midnight.

Gabrielle Charbonnet, for going there before me and giving great advice.

Ammi-Joan Paquette, Julie Phillips, and Kip Wilson, for being so enthusiastic about those first early chapters.

Portia Kunz, Liesl Kunz, and Devin McKeown, the most critical and intelligent teen readers around.

RJ, Linzey, Anna, Danielle, Dakota, Harper, Philip, Devon, and all of the other teens who hang around my house, eat my food, and always answer honestly when I shout out questions like: "How would you kill a person and make it look like an accident?"

Amy Lipke, Barbara Stewart, Jessica Romero, and Karen Ryan. I can't do anything without the support of my friends.

Jill Raimondi, for plastering a smile on her face and looking interested whenever I go on about revisions. And on. And on.

Mom, Joe, Dad, Sue, Jessica, and Wendy give me the courage to follow through.

Bayo, Jaron, and Taemon. My boys. I can't say enough.

Last but not least, I'm inspired by the people who loved Griffon the most: Denise, Ed, Ron, Kathy, Juliet, Lukas, Brittany, and Tyler. Thank you for sharing his memory.

Acknowledgments

The acknowledgments page is the hardest one to write because it takes so many people to create every book, and I'm terrified of leaving someone out. But I'll do my best. This story wouldn't exist without the following people:

Erin Murphy, who makes us lean in closely to hear her soft-spoken words of agent-y wisdom.

Mary Kate Castellani, the editor who never lets me get away with anything, and who transformed a manuscript I thought was pretty good into an extraordinary story.

Emily Easton and everyone at Walker, for their vision and support from the very first idea.

Jen Cervantes and Amy B. White, for reading the early draft when it really wasn't very good.

Natalie Lorenzi, for emergency Italian translations.

8/12, 10/13, 11/14, 9/15, 4/17, 12/17